Dear Reader,

It's amazing how characters become real when you write about them. When I first introduced Faith and Hope Butler, I never imagined that they were anything more than twins. But I was having dinner with a couple of Harlequin sales reps, when one of them quipped, "What about Charity?"

I suddenly realized, "Oh, my God. There *is* a Charity!" But why would one third of a set of triplets be separated from her siblings? Why would loving parents allow two sisters to grow up thinking they were twins when they had a sister who was lost out in the world somewhere? Answering those questions became the challenge when writing *Sisters Found*. I hope you'll enjoy reading the story of Faith, Hope and Charity as much as I enjoyed writing it.

I appreciate hearing your comments and suggestions. You can reach me through my Web site, www.joanjohnston.com. Be sure to sign up on the mailing list at my Web site if you'd like to receive an e-mail/postcard when the next Joan Johnston novel is in stores.

Take care, and happy reading!

Joan Johnston

JOAN JOHNSTON

Sisters Found

HQN™

ISBN-13: 978-0-373-77329-9
ISBN-10:   0-373-77329-3

SISTERS FOUND

Copyright © 2002 by Joan Mertens Johnston, Inc.

www.HQNBooks.com

Printed in U.S.A.

My deepest gratitude to my editors
Karen Taylor Richman
and
Dianne Moggy
for your unending patience and support.

Hawk's Way Family Tree

Key:

Hawk's Way
1. Honey and the Hired Hand
2. The Rancher and the Runaway Bride
3. The Cowboy and the Princess
4. The Wrangler and the Rich Girl
5. The Cowboy Takes a Wife
6. The Unforgiving Bride
7. The Headstrong Bride
8. The Disobedient Bride
9. The Temporary Groom
10. The Virgin Groom
11. Hawk's Way Christmas
12. The Substitute Groom
13. Sisters Found

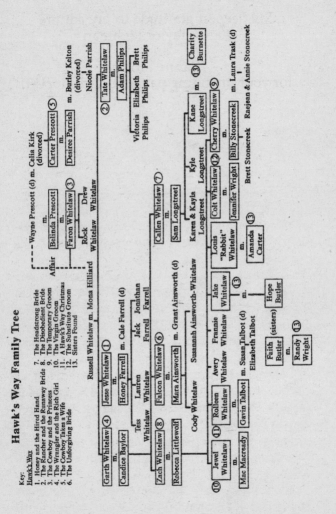

PROLOGUE

HOPE

HOPE BUTLER WAS DESPERATE. The man she loved was engaged to another woman, and he planned to marry her in two weeks. Hope had to do something. Jake Whitelaw didn't belong with that other woman. He should be spending the rest of his life with her.

Jake had fought his attraction to Hope from the very beginning. She could hardly blame him. She'd been only eighteen when she'd first realized she loved him. He'd been thirty-six. Perhaps her infatuation would have died a quick death if Jake hadn't returned her interest. But he had.

She hadn't known for sure until that fateful day more than three years ago, when she'd placed temptation in his path. She recalled their confrontation in her daddy's barn as though it had happened yesterday.

She'd been waiting a long time for the chance to get Jake alone, and it had come when he made a delivery of hay.

His shirt was dirty, the sleeves rolled up to reveal strong, sinewy forearms. His Stetson was sweaty around the brim, and shaggy black hair was crushed at his nape.

His cheeks were hollow, and he had a sharp nose and wide-set, ice-blue eyes. He was half a foot taller than she was, lean at the hip, but with broad, powerful shoulders. He made her body come alive just looking at him.

"How are you, Jake?" she said, walking with her shoulders back so her breasts jutted and her hips swayed.

He eyed her sideways. "Just dandy," he muttered.

"Daddy wants that hay in the barn," she said, hop-skipping to keep up with his long strides.

"Why didn't you just say so? You don't need to come with me, little girl. I know where it goes."

Little girl. Hope ground her teeth. She'd show him she was no *little girl!* "There's some stuff needs to be moved first," she hedged. "Machinery that's too heavy for me to pick up by myself."

"Why didn't your daddy move it?"

"I told him I could do it. That is, before I realized how heavy it was," she fibbed.

Jake didn't look suspicious, but it wasn't going to take long once they got inside the barn for him to realize she'd lied. The space where the hay was supposed to be stacked had been cleared out that morning. She opened the door and went inside first, then waited for him to enter before she closed the door behind him.

The barn smelled strongly of leather and manure. Sunlight streamed through the cracks between the planks of the wooden barn, leaving golden lines on the empty, straw-littered dirt floor.

He turned to confront her. "What the hell is going on, little girl?"

She was backed up against the door to keep Jake from leaving. She put her hand over the light switch when he reached for it, afraid of what she'd see in his eyes in the stark light of the naked overhead bulb. He didn't force the issue, merely stepped back and stood facing her, his legs widespread, his hands on his hips.

"What happens now?" he said. "You want sex? Take off your jeans and panties and lie down over there on that pile of straw on the floor."

Hope's eyes went wide when he started to unbuckle his belt. "Stop! Wait." She was shocked by his brutally frank speech, by the rough sound of his voice, by his plain intention of taking what she seemed to be offering without any pretense of romance. This wasn't how she'd imagined things happening between them.

He had his shirt unbuttoned and was ripping it out of his jeans when he paused and looked her right in the eye. "You chickening out, little girl?"

Maybe if he hadn't made it a dare, she would have run, which is what she realized he expected her to do. She stared right back at him and began untying the knot at her midriff.

"I'm not going anywhere."

She watched his eyes go wide, then narrow. A muscle jerked in his cheek. He no longer seemed interested in taking his clothes off. He was too busy watching her. Waiting, she suspected, to see how far she would go.

Her mouth was bone dry, but she wanted him to know why she was doing this. "I...I love you, Jake."

He snorted. "Get to it or get out."

Her cheeks pinkened in mortification, but she refused to run. It wasn't easy undressing in front of him. She kept her eyes lowered while she fumbled with the knot.

He stood watching, waiting like a lone wolf stalking an abandoned calf, certain of the kill.

When the knot came free, her shirt fell open. She let it slide off her shoulders and onto the floor, revealing the pure white demi-cup pushup bra she'd bought with her baby-sitting money, which revealed just about everything but her nipples.

When she lifted her gaze to his face, she was frightened by what she saw. His eyes had a dangerous, feral look, his jaw was clenched tight, and his hands had balled into fists. He looked intense, unapproachable, but she forced herself to walk up to him, to slide her hands around his neck, to lift up on tiptoe to press her lips against his.

A second later she was shoved up hard against the barn door with Jake's hips grinding against her own. His tongue was in her mouth taking what he wanted, and she was so full of sharp, exciting sensations that she couldn't breathe.

Just as suddenly he backed off, leaving her with Jell-O knees that wanted to buckle, a heart that was threatening to explode and her insides tied up tight, hurting and wanting. "Jake," she said. It was a cry of emotional pain. A plea for surcease from her unrequited need.

"I'm twice your age," he said flatly. "You're too damn young for me, Hope."

"You want me," she said boldly.

It would have been hard to deny. His jeans bulged with abundant evidence of his desire. "I'm a grown man. Old enough to know better," he said with a disgusted sigh. He unbuttoned and unzipped his jeans, but only so he could tuck his shirt back in. He buttoned his shirt, buckled his belt and adjusted his clothes, then leaned down and picked up her shirt. "Put this on," he said.

She did as she was told. She hadn't gotten what she'd expected when she'd come into the barn with Jake. But she'd gotten what she wanted. Proof that he desired her. Proof that if she pushed long enough and hard enough, she might convince him that she was what he needed.

Her hands were shaking too much for her to tie a knot in the shirttails.

"I'll do it," he said, pushing her hands out of the way.

Her stomach quivered as his knuckles brushed against her flesh. She glanced up and saw the feral look was back in his eyes. He yanked the knot tight and stepped back.

"Now get the hell out of here!" he snarled.

Hope yanked open the barn door and ran.

She'd kept running until she got to the house, unaware of the tears on her face until she slammed into the kitchen. Her twin sister Faith had lurched from the table where she was sitting with her boyfriend Randy and demanded, "What did he do to you?"

"Nothing," Hope sobbed. That was the problem. To Jake Whitelaw she was just a *little girl*. She'd run to her room and locked herself in and stayed there the rest of the day.

But the more she'd thought about what had happened, the more encouraged she'd been. Jake might not want to be attracted to her. But he was.

She'd been devastated when she'd discovered at dinner on the night of her high school graduation that he'd gotten himself engaged to the high school English teacher, Miss Carter. Hope was aptly named, because even then, she hadn't given up hope.

She'd seen Jake once more before the summer was over. And what she'd discovered in that meeting had directed the course of her life over the past three years.

Jake had offered Faith and Randy a ride into town and Hope had gone along. After Jake dropped them off, she was alone with him for the first time since the day she'd revealed her feelings to him in the barn.

Jake was angry. Hope recognized the signs. The vertical lines on either side of his mouth became more pronounced because his jaw was clamped, and his eyes narrowed to slits. There was an overall look of tautness to his body—shoulders, hands, hips—that suggested a tiger ready to leap.

She knew she shouldn't have invited herself along. She knew Jake didn't want her around. She also knew he didn't want her around because he was tempted by her presence, like a beast in rut responding to the relentless call of nature.

Hope let her gaze roam over Jake and saw his nostrils flare as her eyes touched what her hands could not. She wondered whether she ought to push him into something irrevocable. Like taking her virginity.

He would marry her then. She was sure of it. But would he love her? She didn't want him without his love. She knew that much. But she was running out of time. Why, oh why, had he gotten engaged to Miss Carter? She wouldn't feel this desperation if he hadn't forced her hand. She knew in her bones that they belonged together, and she didn't intend to lose him to another woman.

"You haven't asked where I want to be let off," she said when Jake had driven half the length of the main street in town without stopping.

He shot her a look filled with scorn. "Don't insult my intelligence. You haven't got any errands to run. But I do. So sit there like a good little girl and be still."

It was the *little girl* that did it. It was a flash point with her and always would be, because it diminished who she was, which was more than the sum of her age. She began to unbutton her blouse right there, driving down Main Street.

Jake glanced in her direction and nearly had an accident. "What do you think you're doing?"

"Taking my clothes off."

"Do you want me to get arrested?"

"I'm not a minor, Jake. We're two consenting adults."

"I'm engaged. I'm promised to another woman."

"Not once word of this gets around," she said, glancing at the passersby who gawked in through the window as she pulled her shirt off her shoulders, leaving her wearing only a peach-colored bra.

Jake swore under his breath and gunned the engine, heading for the old, abandoned railroad depot on the outskirts of town. He braked to a halt in front of the depot and turned to glare at her. She saw the flicker of heat as he glimpsed the fullness of her breasts above her bra.

"What the hell do you think you're doing?"

"I'm not a little girl anymore, Jake. I don't know what I have to do to prove it to you."

"I'm not going to marry you, Hope. You're not what

I want. I want someone who can share my memories of the world, someone who's lived a little."

"I can catch up," she said desperately.

He shook his head. "No, little girl. You can't."

Hope felt her chin quivering and gritted her teeth to try to keep it still. "So you're going to marry Miss Carter?"

"Yes, I'm going to marry her. Put your blouse back on, Hope."

She grabbed her shirt and tried to get it on, but the long sleeves were inside out, and her hands were shaking too badly to straighten it.

She heard Jake swear before he scooted across the bench seat, pulled the shirt from her hands and began to pull the sleeves right-side out. He held the shirt for her while she slipped her arms into it. Her cheek brushed against his as she was straightening. She turned her head and discovered his mouth only a breath from her own. Their eyes caught and held.

She wasn't sure who moved first, but an instant later their mouths were meshed, and his tongue was inside searching, teasing, tasting. He was rough and reckless, his hands cupping her breasts as a guttural groan was wrenched from his very marrow. His mouth ravaged hers as his hands demanded a response.

She couldn't catch up. He was moving too fast.

And then he was gone. Out the opposite door. She scrambled after him, pausing in the driver's seat when she spied him leaning against the van, his palms flat against the metal, his head down, his chest heaving.

He stood and faced her. "That was my fault," he said. "I…" His eyes were full of pain and regret. "You're formidable, Hope. I'll grant you that. Somewhere out there is a very lucky young man."

"I want *you*," she cried.

"I belong to someone else."

"You're only marrying Miss Carter because you don't think you can have me. But you can!" Hope insisted. "There's nothing stopping us from being together except your own stubborn bias against my age."

"Your youth," he corrected.

She snorted. "Eighteen years isn't that much. Lots of men marry younger women."

"You need to go to college. You need to find out what you want to do with your life. Maybe you'll decide you want more out of life than simply being some rancher's wife. If I were to marry you now, the day might come when you decided marriage to me wasn't fulfilling enough, that you needed to go find yourself."

"Is that what happened with your first wife?" Hope asked, her eyes wide.

"I've seen it happen," Jake said without answering her question directly. "You're too young to know what you'd be giving up, Hope. Go to school. Get an education. Find out what you want to do with your life."

"If I do that, if I go to college, will you wait for me?"

She saw the struggle before he answered, "In four years I'll be forty. I—"

"Wait for me," she said, stepping out of the van. "Don't marry Miss Carter. Promise you'll wait for me."

"I can't promise anything, Hope. There's another person in this equation you're not considering. I've proposed to another woman, and she's said yes. Unless

Amanda breaks the engagement, I'm honor-bound to marry her."

"Even if you don't love her?"

"Who says I don't?"

The shock of his words held Hope speechless. "How could you love her and want me like you do?"

He shoved a frustrated hand through his hair. "I respect and admire her. And she loves me. We can have a good life together."

"You *don't* love her," Hope accused.

"I don't know what I feel anymore," he retorted. "You've got me so damned confused—"

"Wait for me," Hope said. "There are such things as long engagements."

"That wouldn't be fair to Amanda," Jake said stubbornly.

"It is if you don't love her. Don't you think she'll notice? Don't you think she'll miss being loved?"

Jake stared at the ground, then back at her. "I'll go this far," he said. "I won't press her to get married. But I'm not going to walk away if she sets a date."

"Thank you, Jake," she said. "At least that gives me a chance."

Hope had finished college in three years, waiting with bated breath the entire time for news of Jake's wedding. But it had never come. She'd seen as much as she could of the world in her two summers off, traveling once to Australia and once to Europe. She'd kept her eyes wide open, absorbing as much of life as she could, trying hard to catch up to Jake.

She'd come home in September, still in love with him, still wanting to spend her life with him, only to discover that Amanda Carter had at long last set a date for their wedding—Christmas Eve.

Which gave Hope only two more weeks to find a way to stop it.

CHAPTER ONE

FAITH

FAITH BUTLER HADN'T SEEN HER twin sister Hope since shortly after they'd arrived at the party celebrating Jake Whitelaw's impending marriage to their former English teacher Miss Carter. Not that Hope's entrance hadn't been noted by one and all.

The afternoon gathering that was supposed to be held inside Miss Carter's two-story frame house had been moved into her backyard when a warm Chinook wind came through, making the mid-December afternoon feel like a summer day.

Hope had stepped out onto Miss Carter's back porch dressed in a tight black skirt barely long enough for decency and a form-fitting, V-necked black cashmere sweater cut low enough to raise a man's heart rate. Ruby-red lipstick emphasized her full lips, and she wore enough mascara and eye shadow to dramatize a dozen dark, smoldering eyes.

Faith knew her sister's outrageous behavior only stemmed from desperation and determination. Because the man Hope loved was about to marry someone else.

Nonetheless, Hope's get-up had done the trick. She'd

managed to attract the one pair of eyes she'd been hoping to snare. Jake Whitelaw hadn't been able to stop staring at her. Or maybe it was more honest to say *glaring* at her.

Faith sighed loud enough to catch her boyfriend's attention.

"What's wrong?" Randy asked.

Faith reached for Randy's hand without noticing that she did so with the prosthetic device on the end of her left arm, where a hand was supposed to be—but had never grown. Randy Wright's total devotion over the past three years had made it possible for Faith to forget sometimes that she wasn't perfect, like her twin.

"I wish Hope would give up and accept reality," Faith said. "Jake Whitelaw might be physically attracted to her, but—"

"Might be?" Randy said with a snort. "He practically paws the ground every time he lays eyes on her."

Faith lifted an expressive black brow. "All right, he's got the hots for Hope. But he's going to marry Miss Carter."

"It sure looks that way," Randy said, eyeing Jake, who stood with his arm around Miss Carter's slender waist. "Unless somebody does something fast."

"Hope has done everything she can to make herself into a potential wife for Jake. She raced through college in three years to get her degree in computer science from Baylor this past summer. And she's spent the past two summers traveling the world and experiencing as much of life as she can. But—"

"But she can never catch up to him, because he's lived too much longer than she has," Randy finished for her.

Faith sighed again. Jake Whitelaw might be only eighteen years older than Hope, but he was ages older in life experience. She didn't understand her sister's attraction to the older man, but Hope had fallen head-over-ears for Jake years ago, and was still tumbling even now.

"So what are you going to do to help her out?" Randy asked.

"What can I do?"

Randy grinned. "You might have acted like the shy sister growing up, but I know better. Whenever you want something and go after it, you get it. So, I ask again, how are you going to help Jake discover that he belongs with Hope?"

"Do they belong together?" Faith asked skeptically.

"Look at Jake," Randy said. "His gaze is constantly searching out Hope. And his behavior with Miss Carter is anything but loverlike."

"Oh," Faith said as she watched Jake's eyes scan Miss Carter's backyard, even though Hope was nowhere to be seen in the crowd. His arm was linked around Miss Carter's waist, but they stood a good six inches apart. And although they were physically together, Miss Carter seemed to be talking to everyone except Jake.

Faith watched as Hope appeared at one of the five entrances to the gazebo in the center of Miss Carter's backyard, laughing and flirting with one of Jake's hired hands. When Hope looked toward Jake to see if he'd noticed her, Jake quickly and carefully averted his eyes. Oh, Jake was attracted, all right. But it looked like he'd be damned before he'd let Hope know it.

"There's something else you may not have noticed," Randy said. "Check out Jake's younger brother Rabb. Look who has his eye."

Faith searched out Louis Whitelaw, who'd earned the nickname Rabbit as a kid, which had been shortened to Rabb as he'd grown older. Rabb was attractive, with chestnut-brown hair and hazel eyes, but nowhere near as good-looking as his brother Jake, who was easily four inches taller and broader in the shoulders, with chiseled features that demanded female attention.

It was amazing how they ended up being brothers. Zach and Rebecca Whitelaw had adopted eight kids in all. None of them looked much like the others, but they were as close-knit as any family tied together by blood. Maybe more so, precisely because there was no blood tie to bind them. Each kid had a different background, some more horrific than others, but once they'd been adopted into the Whitelaw clan, they'd cleaved to one another like ivy to oak.

Which made the situation Randy had pointed out to her all the more compelling.

Faith watched in fascination as Rabb Whitelaw stared with lovesick eyes at his older brother's fiancée. "Oh," she murmured. "Oh, my. That *is* interesting."

"Rabb has been eating Miss Carter with his eyes all afternoon," Randy said. "Surreptitiously, of course. He'd never poach on his brother's territory."

"So he'll let Jake marry Miss Carter, even though he loves her himself?" Faith asked.

"It looks that way," Randy said. "So you see, you'd be doing more than one person a favor if you helped break up this engagement."

"Believe me, I'm tempted," Faith said. "It's just too late. The wedding's in two weeks."

"Consider the fact that Jake and Miss Carter didn't set the date for their wedding until now, the exact time Hope finished school and has returned all grown up," Randy said. "What does that tell you?"

Faith pursed her lips and made a humming sound. "You think that Jake's only marrying Miss Carter to avoid his attraction to Hope? Is that possible?"

"Jake and Miss Carter have been engaged for three very long years. If they were in love, why didn't they get married a long time ago?" Randy asked.

Before Faith could speak, he answered his own question.

"Because Jake isn't in love with Miss Carter. Because being engaged to her has kept him 'safe' from acting on his attraction to your sister. You told me he believes he's too old for her. And he was married before to a younger woman, who left him when she got bored with ranch life."

"Hope loves living and working on a ranch," Faith said in defense of her sister. "She'd never get tired—"

"I didn't say she would," Randy interrupted. "But Jake got burned once. You can't blame him for wanting to avoid the fire."

Faith frowned. "I have to admit I thought Hope was too young for Jake when she first told me she'd fallen in love with him. But her teenage crush hasn't gone away. If anything, she seems more determined than ever to have him."

"If they're meant for each other, you'd be doing them a favor throwing them together," Randy said, "before

Jake marries the wrong woman. And if they're not destined to be together, it'll be better in the long run to help Jake get over this infatuation he has for Hope before he marries Miss Carter."

"But the wedding is in two weeks!"

"Then you'd better get started, sweetheart," Randy said, kissing her on the nose.

"Are you going to help me?" Faith asked.

Randy held up his hands. "Uh-uh. Not me. Matchmaking is for females."

"You just stood there and talked me into it!" Faith protested.

Randy grinned. "You were going to interfere anyway. I merely gave you the nudge you needed to get started."

Faith grimaced and then laughed. "All right. I admit it. I can't stand to see Hope so unhappy. Especially if there's something I can do about it."

"You go, girl," Randy said with a wink.

"I do love you," she said as she lifted herself on tiptoe and kissed him on the mouth. His arm slid around her waist and pulled her close, deepening the kiss as she leaned into his solid strength. When he let her go, she looked into his eyes, hoping he could read the gratitude she felt.

If she was no longer the shy person she'd been in the past, it was because she saw a beautiful woman reflected in Randy's eyes, not the imperfect person—the twin without a left hand—she'd been when they'd first met.

"I think I'll go get myself a drink," he said as he released her. "You have work to do."

He kissed her again, a quick, hard kiss that told her he wanted to take her somewhere and lay her down and

make mad, passionate love to her. Then he let her go and
headed for the open bar that had been set up in the
wooden gazebo in the center of Miss Carter's backyard.

Randy was right, Faith thought, as she watched him
saunter away. If someone didn't do something, the
wrong people were going to end up married to each
other.

She turned her attention back to the engaged couple.
Maybe she should start by seeing if she could get Miss
Carter interested in Rabb Whitelaw. Maybe if Miss
Carter met up with someone who really loved her, she
would be willing to give up Jake. The question was how
to accomplish this miracle in two weeks!

There was no time to waste. Faith contemplated her
surroundings and plotted the best way to create…a
ruckus.

RABB WHITELAW HAD FALLEN IN love with Amanda
Carter long before his brother had come along and
gotten engaged to her. Rabb had first noticed Amanda
when they were both in the ninth grade. All through high
school he'd admired her from afar, because he'd never
felt like he was anyone she'd be interested in. Amanda
was smart; he hadn't done well in school. And Amanda
was tall. He hadn't caught up to her in height until he
was a senior.

The long and the short of it was, he'd never been able
to work up enough courage to ask her out. He'd figured
she'd want to talk about Shakespeare and Molière and
Faulkner and Hemingway, and reading was difficult—
make that *excruciating*—for him, because he was
dyslexic. She'd dated lots of different boys, but he'd

always been grateful that she'd never settled on any one in particular.

When Amanda had pursued her teaching degree at the local university, Rabb had been in agony worrying that she would fall in love with someone else. But she'd finished her education unattached and gotten a job teaching English at the local high school.

During the years Amanda had been in college, Rabb had found his niche working with his hands. He'd started small, making kitchen cupboards for his mom and then graduated to a bedroom suite for his sister Jewel and her husband Mac. Most recently he'd made a baby crib for his brother Avery and his wife Karen.

He took pride in his work, and now made a very comfortable living creating unique pieces of wood furniture that were in demand across the country. About the time professional success had given him the self-confidence he needed to pursue a relationship with Amanda, her mother had been diagnosed with Alzheimer's, and Amanda had become her mother's nurse.

He'd asked her out anyway. She'd gone to the movies with him once, leaving her mother home alone, because at the time Mrs. Carter's disease wasn't very far advanced. But Amanda had come home to find her mother distraught and confused about where she was. Amanda had been so upset that she'd hurried inside. Rabb hadn't even gotten to kiss her good-night.

He'd asked her out a number of times after that, even offered to come over to her house with some popcorn and a rented video, but Amanda always refused.

But he hadn't stopped loving her. He'd figured that at some point Amanda would put her mother in a home where she could get round-the-clock care. But Amanda had never sent her mom away. She'd hired a nurse for the days when she was teaching high school. And spent her evenings at home.

Mrs. Carter had survived a long time. She'd died only three years ago. And Jake had swooped in at a vulnerable moment shortly after the funeral and asked Amanda to marry him.

She'd said yes.

Rabb had felt like punching his brother's lights out. Instead, he'd swallowed his anger and wished both of them well. He'd been miserable, wondering how soon he would have to sit in church and watch the brother he idolized marry the woman he loved.

But they'd never set a wedding date, and Rabb had begun to hope it would never happen.

Two years ago, he'd volunteered to build a gazebo for a charity raffle, and amazingly, Amanda had purchased the winning ticket. He'd spent far longer working on the gazebo he'd built in her backyard than was necessary. But it had given him the opportunity to get reacquainted with her.

He would never forget the hot summer day she'd come out back with a tray of lemonade and oatmeal-raisin cookies. She'd been wearing one of those summer dresses held up with a couple of skinny straps over the shoulders and sandals that showed off toenails she'd painted pink. Her brown hair was cut in a short bob that made her look more like a teenager than the nearly thirty-year-old woman he knew she was.

"Thought you could use something cold to drink," she'd said, setting the tray on the unpainted steps of the gazebo.

He'd started to reach for his shirt, but she'd said, "You don't have to cover up for me. I've lost my modesty where the human body is concerned."

It was a strange thing to say, but he knew that, at the end, she'd taken care of the most intimate duties for her mother. He sat down beside her on the steps, took the glass of lemonade she handed him and drank most of it down. When he lowered the glass, he caught her staring at him.

She blushed and said, "I'm sorry. It's just that…you look so…healthy."

"My job keeps me in shape," he said matter-of-factly.

To his amazement, she reached out a hand and traced the corded muscles from his shoulder, down across his biceps, all the way to his forearm. She seemed totally absorbed in what she was doing, unaware of the response it was eliciting in him.

He waited, keeping himself totally still, wondering when she would realize what she was doing, not wanting her to stop. When she traced a small scar at his wrist, his hand reflexively clenched into a fist.

"Oh," she said, looking up at him with startled eyes. "I'm sorry."

He caught her hand before she could flee. "No problem. I liked you touching me."

"You did?"

"It felt good."

"Oh," she said. "I wondered if… I mean as an experiment I wondered if you'd mind if I…"

"What?"

"I'm just curious, you understand."

"About what?" he asked, his voice harsh with unexpected desire.

"Nothing," she said, rising abruptly.

He still had hold of her hand and rose with her. "About what?" he persisted.

She looked almost frightened as she gazed into his eyes. "I wondered…" She laid a hand around his nape, drew his head down and kissed him. Her lips were soft and gentle, and he was so surprised that he didn't respond, although the kiss was electrifying.

She broke the kiss abruptly and stepped back, her blue eyes stark. "Excuse me. I have some papers to grade."

He'd wanted to hold on to her, and if she'd been engaged to anyone but his brother, he would have. But when she ran, he let her go.

Rabb had never mentioned the kiss. And neither had Amanda.

She'd brought him lemonade and cookies several more times over the summer as he built her gazebo. She even stayed to talk about her work and the books she was reading. She'd made sure their conversations stayed on a friendly footing. But she'd been careful never to touch him again.

Rabb had felt frustrated that he couldn't tell her how much he admired her. How much he loved her. But she was engaged to his eldest brother.

It seemed odd to him that Jake never seemed to come around much. He'd watched the engaged couple together and realized something shocking. His brother didn't seem to have an intimate relationship with Amanda. Rabb was grateful, but frustrated. Especially since Jake kept throwing him together with Amanda. Whenever Jake couldn't escort his fiancée to some event, he would deputize Rabb to take his place. And since Rabb was grateful for every moment he could spend with Amanda, he was happy to oblige.

Over the past two years, it had gotten harder and harder to be a good brother. Especially when he wanted his brother's woman for his own.

To make matters worse, he wasn't sure if Jake even loved Amanda. Even now, at a party to celebrate his impending marriage, Jake couldn't seem to keep his eyes off Hope Butler. That little sex kitten really had her claws into his brother.

Rabb took a breath and let it out. Amanda would never be happy married to a man who didn't love her. And Jake wouldn't be happy living with a miserable wife. He owed it to both of them to make his feelings known...before it was too late.

The first problem was how to separate Jake from Amanda so he could talk to his brother. In the end, he decided the direct approach was best. He walked up to the two of them and said, "I need to talk to you, Jake."

"Can it wait?" Jake said. He smiled at Amanda. "I'm a little busy right now."

"It's important," Rabb said.

Jake turned to Amanda and said, "I'll be right back," then released her and followed Rabb.

Rabb led his brother to a deserted corner of the backyard where forsythia bushes had grown out of control.

"What is it?" Jake said impatiently.

"I don't think you should marry Amanda Carter."

Jake frowned. It was a look that would've cowed Rabb a few years ago, but he couldn't afford to be daunted by his older brother's displeasure. This was too important.

"You don't love her," Rabb said bluntly.

"How I feel about Amanda is none of your business," Jake retorted.

"I'm making it my business."

Jake's blue eyes narrowed. "Did Amanda say something to you about us?"

"No, but—"

"Then how is my relationship with her any of your business?" Jake demanded.

"Do you love Amanda even a little?" Rabb asked. "Tell me you love her, and I'll back off."

Jake's eyes narrowed even more. "I already told you—"

"You don't love her," Rabb accused. "Do you? That Butler girl has her claws in you so tight, you can't see anything but those big brown eyes of hers and that knockout body."

"Keep Hope out of this. And keep your voice down," Jake said, shooting a glance at the gathered friends and family who were just out of earshot.

"Hope Butler is very much a part of this," Rabb said in a low, urgent voice. "Because I think you're in love with her."

"How I feel about Hope is none of your business, either," Jake said heatedly.

"You have to break off this engagement, Jake. You have to set Amanda free."

"You know I can't do that," Jake said. "I proposed to Amanda, and unless *she* calls it off, I intend to go through with the wedding. Because she'll make a damned fine wife!"

"You are the most stubborn, bullheaded—"

"If you're done—"

"I'm not done," Rabb said, grabbing at Jake's shoulder to keep him from walking away. "If that sexpot Hope Butler wasn't wagging her tail—"

Rabb never got to finish his sentence, because Jake swung a fist at his chin. He reacted quickly enough that the blow only grazed him, but even that was enough to knock him off his feet. Rabb lay on the ground staring up at his stunned brother.

"Damn it, Rabb. I'm sorry," Jake said. "I don't know—"

Rabb avoided the hand his brother offered and quickly got back on his feet. "I know exactly what's wrong with you. You're in love up to your eyeballs with Hope Butler, and you're marrying Amanda Carter out of some misplaced sense of honor. You're not doing either one of them any favors."

"Hope's too young for me," Jake said bleakly.

"Yeah, I know. And because Amanda's the right age you're going to marry her and live miserably ever after. I'm giving you fair warning that I intend to do everything in my power to stop this wedding."

"Amanda loves me, Rabb. I don't want to see her hurt."

Rabb was taken aback by Jake's statement, because it was something he feared might very well be true. "Maybe she does. And maybe she doesn't know her own mind."

They were both distracted by a commotion in the gazebo.

"What the hell?" Jake muttered.

Hope screamed.

Rabb was left standing by himself as Jake raced to the rescue.

Rabb quickly followed after him, but while Jake's attention was focused on Hope and the cowboy whose arms were wrapped tightly around her, Rabb had eyes only for Amanda.

She looked distressed as Jake marched up the steps of the gazebo and yanked Hope free of the cowboy's drunken embrace. When the man took a swing at him, Jake ducked, then planted his powerful fist in the cowboy's solar plexus.

The man stumbled backward, then went crashing through the delicate lattice that formed one of the five sides of the gazebo. That would have been bad enough, but as the drunken cowboy stumbled, he careened into another guest, who windmilled helplessly before smashing backward through another one of the fragile walls.

"Oh, no!" Amanda cried.

Rabb was beside her an instant later. "It's all right, Amanda," he said. "I can fix it."

"I don't care about the gazebo," she shot back. And then realizing who was standing beside her amended, "Well, of course I do, but…"

He followed her gaze to the gazebo and saw what was really troubling her. Jake was gripping Hope Butler tightly by the arm, dragging her out of the gazebo behind him and hauling her toward the house.

"That poor girl," Amanda said, staring after them. "I'd better go see what I can do to help."

For a moment Rabb was tempted to let her follow his brother, because he had a pretty good idea of what was going to happen when Jake got Hope alone. But he didn't want Amanda hurt any more than necessary. Which meant he had to distract her long enough for Jake to finish his "talk" with Hope.

"Wait," he said, setting a hand on her shoulder. "Jake can handle Hope." Which was probably the biggest lie he'd told in a good long while. "You'd better see to your guests," he said, pointing toward the disaster in and around the gazebo.

She glanced once more toward the house, where Jake and Hope had disappeared, then turned back to the gazebo. "You're right. I'd better see what I can do to smooth things over."

Rabb went with her, to make sure the drunken cowboy didn't repeat whatever insult had created havoc with Hope in the first place. He found Hope's twin Faith standing beside the fallen cowboy, her boyfriend Randy at her side.

"I'm so sorry," Faith was saying. "I swear I thought Hope said she liked you. But maybe it was some other cowboy," she was explaining.

"You'd better saddle up and move along," Rabb said as he approached the man.

"No argument from me," the cowboy muttered as Faith's boyfriend helped him to his feet.

The other guest who'd fallen turned out to be Amanda's principal, Mr. Denton. And his arm was broken.

"I'm so sorry," Amanda said as she stared helplessly at the older man.

"Aw, hell," Denton said as Rabb helped him to his feet. "I've been hurt worse. But this is going to make it a little harder to put together some of the Christmas presents I bought the kids—bicycles, baby carriages and the like."

"I can help you with that," Rabb volunteered.

"I'll help, too," Amanda said. "Just let us know when and where to show up."

"You got it," Denton said.

Rabb could see Amanda's hands were trembling as a couple of other teachers escorted Denton toward a car to take him to the hospital. "It wasn't your fault," he said. "It could have happened—"

"I should have been watching more carefully," she said. "I should have kept an eye on—"

"You can't watch everyone all of the time," Rabb interrupted.

"My beautiful gazebo," she said as she stared at the destruction. Her chin was wobbling and tears began to brim in her beautiful blue eyes.

Rabb put an arm around her waist, wanting to comfort. "I can fix it, Amanda. Really, I can."

She turned her face up to him and said, "Can you? Really?"

He wondered if she was talking about the gazebo…or her relationship with Jake. Amanda Carter was no dummy. She must have some inkling of what was going on between Jake and Hope. But if she did, why didn't she call off the wedding herself?

A moment later, Amanda had her face pressed against his shirtfront, sobbing.

"I'll start tomorrow," he promised her. And be at her back door every day for the next two weeks, he promised himself. He enfolded her in his arms, rocking her and murmuring soothing words, his eyes warning the guests not to make anything of it. He was merely deputizing for his brother.

But where the hell was Jake? Why hadn't he come back to comfort his fiancée?

CHAPTER TWO

HOPE

HOPE HAD BEEN TRYING ALL afternoon to get Jake's attention. Now she had it. But after knocking down the cowboy who'd been bothering her, Jake's blue eyes were cold, his granite features set in angry lines.

"I saw this coming from the moment you set foot in Amanda's backyard," he said as he grabbed her arm and hauled her out of Miss Carter's gazebo—or what was left of it. Two of the five sides were lying splintered on the ground, a result of the brief fracas between Jake and the young cowboy who'd gotten drunk enough to lay a hand on Hope in a place where it didn't belong.

Hope spared one glance for the cowboy, who lay groaning on the ground, before Jake's implacable grip propelled her toward Miss Carter's kitchen. This confrontation had been coming all afternoon, and she welcomed it. At least Jake would be forced to talk to her.

When they got to the kitchen, it was full of women, so Jake nodded curtly and kept moving. Down a narrow hallway. Through the parlor.

Up the creaking wooden stairs. Down another hallway. And into a bedroom that obviously belonged to Miss Carter.

The baby-pink bedspread was girlish, but that was the extent of the frivolity in the room. Miss Carter had always been a no-nonsense English teacher. Her bedroom gave proof that there hadn't been much fun in her life.

A shepherdess figurine with a broken arm sat on the dresser, along with what appeared to be a plain wooden jewelry box. An iron lamp and a paperback book—a horror novel by Stephen King—rested on the bedside table. A painted green kitchen chair occupied the corner. A worn pink bathroom rug was all that stood between Miss Carter and the wooden floor on a cold morning.

Hope felt her heart sinking. If Jake knew where Miss Carter's bedroom was, that probably meant he'd been here before. Which only made sense. After all, he and Miss Carter had been engaged for three years. It would have taken a miracle for Miss Carter to put Jake off that long. Hope hadn't been able to resist his charms for three seconds.

Jake thrust her inside the room and shut the door, then leaned back against it with his arms crossed, his eyes narrowed on her. "Well, young lady, what do you have to say for yourself?"

Hope firmly believed that you didn't get what you didn't ask for. She'd been the one to pursue Jake all along. Nothing had changed in three years, but her gut still clenched as she said, "I love you, Jake. And I think we belong together."

Jake sucked in a breath, and a muscle flexed in his jaw. She waited breathlessly for him to respond to her declaration, but his lips remained pressed flat in disapproval.

Which left her no choice but to act.

She closed the distance between them—two short steps—and stood with her breasts almost touching his crossed arms. He was a great deal taller than she was, but Hope refused to be intimidated by his size—or the forbidding look on his face. She glanced up at him from beneath dark, fringed lashes and said, "You love me, too, Jake. Admit it."

That statement demanded an answer, and Jake didn't disappoint her. "Damn you, Hope. Give it up."

"Never." Her chest felt like it was bound by an iron band, and she was having trouble breathing. She hadn't been this close to Jake since she'd gone away to college, but her feelings hadn't changed in the intervening years. She needed some proof that his hadn't either.

Three years ago, when she'd cornered him in her father's barn, the sexual sparks had flown. He'd gotten himself engaged to Miss Carter so quickly afterward, that she figured he must have done it to keep himself safe from temptation.

Her heart was pounding furiously with excitement— and with fear. What if he went through with the wedding? What if she couldn't make him see what she'd known since the first moment she'd laid eyes on him?

"It's destiny, Jake. We're two halves of one perfect whole. We're—"

"Cut the crap," he said harshly.

Hope heard the revealing gurgle as she swallowed back the threatening tears. She laid her hands flat on Jake's chest above his folded arms, undaunted by his rigid posture, and felt him inhale sharply. He wasn't as unaffected as he wanted her to think.

"All right, if you don't want romance, think of the practical ways I'd be a helpmate if you married me."

Jake snorted.

"I have a degree in computer science with a minor in business. For a start, I'd be able to do the bookkeeping on the ranch."

"I have an accountant who does that for me."

"But you wouldn't have to pay me," Hope said with a smile meant to charm. It didn't seem to be working, so she added, "And I'm very good with kids."

"That's because you're a kid yourself," he retorted.

"I've seen a great deal of the world," she continued doggedly, "and I can tell you, Jake, there's no place like home. I'd never leave you like…" Hope broke off as she saw the muscle flex again in his cheek. No sense bringing up memories of his previous failed marriage.

She knew Jake's experience with a wife who wasn't satisfied to live on an isolated northwest Texas ranch was part of the reason he didn't trust his feelings for her. Once before he'd succumbed to the charms of a younger woman, and she'd left him high and dry. "I'm not like her," Hope said softly.

"You're exactly like her," he accused. "Young and flighty and—"

"That's not fair," she said, her hands sliding down and clutching his folded arms. "There's nothing 'flighty' about me. I'm dependable and hardworking and loyal—"

"And too damned young for me."

She let the tips of her breasts graze his forearm and felt his whole body stiffen. "Maybe three years ago I was," she conceded. "Not anymore. I'm twenty-one, a college graduate, a world traveler, a—"

"Baby!" he spat. "You're a goddamn babe in the woods. How many men have you slept with, Hope?"

Hope blushed a rosy red, but she didn't retreat. "I don't want any man but you. I've never wanted any man but you. I'm a virgin, Jake, and I will be until you—"

"Shut up, Hope." The muscles in his forearms had turned to stone. "Shut the hell up." She could feel him withdrawing as her arms slid up his rock-hard chest toward his nape, but with his back to the door, there was nowhere for him to go. His eyes locked on hers, hot and hungry.

Suddenly, their positions were reversed. Jake had her by the shoulders, his body imprisoning hers against the door, and she could feel the hard male ridge against her abdomen that put a lie to all his protests. She saw the struggle in his eyes, felt the tautness in his body.

"I'm not going to do this," he said.

"Then I will," she said as she leaned forward and pressed her lips against his.

For a moment, he resisted her. For a fraction of a second, she thought all was lost. She softened her mouth against his, sliding the tip of her tongue along the crease of his lips.

His whole body quivered. He lifted his head and looked at her, his eyes heavy-lidded. "Aw, hell," he muttered. His mouth came down on hers, and he took her fast and deep.

She'd forgotten how it felt to be kissed by Jake, like sliding down a fast chute where there was no end in sight. She was on her toes, her body clasped hard against his, and she could feel his heart pounding in his chest.

She couldn't catch her breath, couldn't catch up, the feelings were so powerful, so overwhelming.

Suddenly, their positions were once more reversed, and she was standing the width of his outstretched arms away.

"You have to stay away from me, Hope." The anger was back again. And she heard desperation in his gravelly voice.

"I'm going to marry Amanda. And I intend to be a faithful husband. Don't do this again."

"What is it I did, Jake?" asked Hope, whose anger matched his. "If you were really in love with Amanda, you would've let someone else rush to the rescue when that cowboy got fresh with me. And you wouldn't have brought me here where we were sure to be alone. You wanted what just happened to happen. Because you I—"

"Don't say it, because it isn't true," he interrupted. "I brought you here because it's obvious to me—and it must be to anyone who cares to look—that you've got some kind of juvenile infatuation for me. It's embarrassing to be mooned over by someone half my age."

The insult hurt, as she was sure Jake intended it should. But she didn't let it discourage her. "You were jealous of that cowboy. Admit it. You don't want anyone touching me but you."

"Grow up, Hope," Jake said. "This childish behavior has to stop."

"You're the one who brought me up here, Jake," she retorted. "You kissed me back."

She saw the flush rise on his cheekbones. The admission that he wasn't blameless.

He let her go and leaned his head back against the door, rubbed a hand across his eyes and heaved a sigh. "I came up here hoping we could straighten out this...whatever this is between us. I was hoping you'd see reason."

"I'm fighting for my whole life, Jake. I'm trying to get you to see that you don't belong with Miss Carter. You belong with me."

"This isn't getting us anywhere." Jake reached for the doorknob, but Hope's hand covered his.

"Why can't you see what's staring you in the face?" she pleaded.

"I'm engaged to someone else," he said. "Even if I wanted to change my mind, I couldn't. I'd never do that to Amanda. She's waited three years—"

Hope's eyes had gotten round as she listened to Jake. She could see a tiny crack of light, where before there had been darkness. For the first time, he was talking in terms of changing his mind. "*You're* the one who's been putting off the wedding?" she asked. "Not Miss Carter?"

"It's been mutual," Jake said.

"Why has she been putting it off, if I may ask?"

"That's between her and me."

"Well, why have you been putting it off?" she persisted.

"That's none of your business."

"I think it is," Hope said. "I think you've been waiting for me to grow up," she said with the beginning of a smile. "I think you've been hoping I would come back from all my travels and convince you—"

"That's enough," Jake said. "The fact is, Amanda and I have set a wedding date. Nothing's going to change that now."

"Lots of people decide not to go through with their weddings," Hope argued.

"When I make a promise, I keep it," Jake said.

Hope cocked her head and frowned. "Even if it means being miserable for the rest of your life?"

"Amanda and I are well matched," he said. "We can be happy together."

"I notice you've never once said you love her," Hope pointed out.

"My feelings for my fiancée are my business."

"If you tell me you love her, I'll go away, Jake. I won't say another word. I'll accept the fact that I've lost your love to another woman, and I'll let you go." Hope's stomach was turning somersaults. What if he said he loved Miss Carter, just to get rid of her?

Luckily for her, Jake was too honest to lie. "I want you to leave me be, Hope. I want you to keep your distance from me between now and the wedding."

"Give me one good reason why I should," she said.

"Because if you love me, you'll understand how hard this is for me. My word is given. And I'm not going back on it."

Hope swallowed past the painful knot that had grown in her throat. "You don't play fair, Jake."

He didn't say anything, just looked down at her, a wall behind his blue eyes that shut her out.

"All right, Jake," she said at last. "I won't purposely tempt you again."

She felt some of the tension ease out of him.

"But I'm not going to leave town. I'm not going to hide myself from your sight. I'm going to be right here every day from now until you commit yourself to Miss

Carter. And I'm going to hope that between now and then you come to your senses."

She looked up at him and said, "Open the door, Jake. And let me out."

He seemed to realize suddenly that he was standing in her way, blocking the exit. He stepped aside, opened the door and held it while she walked from the room, shoulders back, chin up. She could feel the heat of him following her down the stairs. She was aware that he was no longer behind her when she headed into the kitchen. She greeted the women working there with a smile and said, "Need any help?"

"We're about done," one of the women said. "Things have pretty much wound down since that rumpus in the gazebo." The woman glanced over her shoulder narrow-eyed at Jake, who'd appeared in the doorway, and said, "You need a ride home, Hope?"

Hope smiled more brightly, aware of Jake's presence at her shoulder, and the worried, confused and distrustful looks on the faces of the other women. "I'm riding with Faith and Randy," she said. "I'll find them and be on my way."

She was out of the kitchen and into the backyard a moment later. The sun was setting, and the fenced backyard was nearly deserted. Faith sat on the steps of the wrecked gazebo with Randy beside her. She rose as Hope approached her.

"Are you all right?" Faith asked.

Hope kept the smile pasted on her face for Faith's sake. Her sister knew far too much about her feelings as it was. "Jake and I had a little talk and ironed things out."

"Oh?"

Faith had a way of getting her to spill the beans by looking sympathetic. "I agreed to keep my distance," Hope said.

"Did you, really?"

"Why do you sound so surprised?" Hope said irritably. "He's engaged to Miss Carter. The wedding is in two weeks."

"I thought you might have had some luck changing his mind," Faith said, sliding her prosthetic hand around Hope's waist. "You can be very convincing."

The knot was back in Hope's throat. "He doesn't love her," she said fiercely. "But he's going to marry her anyway."

"Well," Faith said. "Maybe he is. And maybe he isn't."

Hope frowned. "What is that supposed to mean?"

"There's many a slip twixt the cup and the lip," she said. And grinned at Randy.

"What's going on?" Hope said, glancing from Faith to Randy and back again.

"Faith doesn't want you to give up," Randy said. "Isn't that right, Faith?"

"Right," Faith said. "If you love Jake, you have to keep fighting for him. No matter what."

"I told him I'd keep my distance," Hope said.

"How much distance was it you promised him?" Faith asked.

Hope made a disgusted sound. "We didn't measure—"

"Do you love him, Hope?" Faith interrupted.

"That's a dumb question."

"Do you love him?" she asked again.

"Yes."

"Then keep fighting for him. Put yourself in his way. Keep your distance, but keep him thinking about you."

Hope hugged her sister. "Have I told you lately what a great sister you are?"

"Nope. But you can sing my praises while Randy drives us home."

Hope sat, crowded into the front seat of Randy's pickup, thinking and thinking and thinking all the way home. Jake needed to see how she could fit comfortably into his life. He needed to see what a good partner she would be. And there was only one way to prove herself to him. By being there. The only question was, how could she get herself invited to spend time at Jake's ranch?

AMANDA COULDN'T BELIEVE HER party had ended in such disaster. She'd watched Jake flatten the cowboy bothering Hope Butler, then stood mouth agape as he hauled Hope off into her house without a second thought for how it would look to their friends. It had been left to her to excuse Jake's behavior and say good-bye to their guests.

"Amanda, are you all right?"

She turned to find Rabb Whitelaw at her elbow. "I'm fine," she said, pasting a bright smile on her face.

Ever since Rabb had built the gazebo in her backyard she'd felt self-conscious around him. She didn't understand her attraction to him. She only knew it was there.

Maybe it was the fact he'd worked all those weeks with his shirt off. She'd wanted to touch his broad shoulders, his bronzed flesh. She'd attributed her attraction to the fact he was so obviously healthy, when she'd spent so many years nursing her mother's frail form.

She'd been drawn outside again and again to spend time with him, using the excuse of offering lemonade or iced tea on a hot day. And she'd stayed to talk, admiring his strong hands at work, creating something lasting and beautiful.

She realized she was staring at his hands and wondered now, as she had then, what they would feel like on her skin. She felt a frisson of excitement and flushed as she realized what she was doing. Flustered, she said, "Did you enjoy the party?"

She looked into his hazel eyes and was glad to see they revealed no awareness of her wayward thoughts. He was Jake's brother, for heaven's sake!

Rabb eyed the gazebo and said, "I'll be over tomorrow to start fixing that up for you."

Amanda felt the tears welling as she wandered into the ruined gazebo.

"Watch out!" Rabb caught her arm to hold her in place as he removed a jagged piece of lattice that had caught on her skirt.

He saw the tears and said, "Are you hurt?"

"No." But she was hurting.

A moment later he had her in his arms. "You're all right, Amanda. You're fine," he crooned.

Amanda sobbed against his shoulder. She hadn't even cried like this when she'd buried her mother. She had nothing to cry about. Her life was almost perfect. She'd loved her mother, but it had been a relief after eleven years of illness when she finally passed away quietly in the night. Amanda had been eighteen when her mother became ill. She was thirty-two and only now discovering the wonders of pursuing interests of her own.

Was it any wonder she hadn't wanted to rush into a marriage three years ago where she would have had all the responsibility of caring for a husband? She'd been flattered by Jake's attention, delighted by the prospect of having a boyfriend, looked forward to dating him and discovering the pleasures to be enjoyed by two consenting adults.

Only that hadn't turned out quite like she'd thought it would, either.

"Are you okay?" Rabb asked.

He was smoothing her short-cropped brown hair with his hand. It was a comforting gesture; there was nothing sexual about it. Nonetheless, it felt sensual.

Maybe that had something to do with the way her body was pressed against his from shoulders to thighs. She had no idea how her hands had ended up around his neck. Suddenly she disengaged herself and stood back.

"Thank you," she said. She felt awkward again, when there was no reason for it. Rabb was Jake's brother. And a friend.

"Jake doesn't suffer fools gladly," Rabb said.

"I know," Amanda said, managing a wobbling smile. "I don't know as much as I'd like to about him, but I do know that."

"And he has a soft spot for Hope Butler," Rabb said.

"It seems so." She was engaged to a man she admired, and soon they would be married. But there were issues they hadn't discussed.

One of them was Hope.

Even a blind man could see the girl was infatuated with Jake. Oh, he'd pointedly ignored her all afternoon. Until that cowboy had flirted a little too much and Jake had jumped in to save her. So maybe he hadn't been quite as unaware of Hope as he'd pretended. What did that mean? Anything?

Amanda felt tears stinging her nose again. If only Jake hadn't ruined her beautiful gazebo. She loved that silly, impractical structure. She'd planted morning glories all around, and they'd grown through the lattice, creating a cool, sweet-smelling haven when she'd wanted to be alone to think. Now lattice and greenery alike had been ravaged by the fight between her fiancé and one of his drunken hired hands over another woman.

Another woman. She found it hard to think of Hope Butler as a woman. She'd taught Hope in high school, and Amanda still remembered chastising the girl for being late to class, for popping bubble gum, for a dozen other infractions, none of which had kept Hope from getting an A in her class. Hope was smart and she did her work.

The Hope Butler who'd turned up today was trying to look and act like someone much older. And not doing it well.

Amanda surveyed her gazebo and sighed. "I think I'll take you up on that offer, Rabb. That is, if you let me pay you."

"There'll be no charge."

"I can't let you do that," she protested.

"Then I'll take it out in trade."

She raised an eyebrow and he continued. "I'll come by after church tomorrow, and you can make me lunch."

Amanda smiled. "Done. I'm a good cook. What would you like to have?"

"Meat loaf and mashed potatoes."

At that moment, Jake appeared at her shoulder, and she realized she was making plans to have a single man other than her fiancé over for supper. His brother, no less.

"Uh, Jake, would you like to join Rabb and me for supper tomorrow?"

"I promised my brother Colt and his wife that I'd take care of their two kids for the next two weeks, while they take a vacation. It's the last chance they'll have to be alone before their third child is born. You two want to come over and join me?" Jake asked.

"No," Amanda said quickly. She was afraid she'd said it too quickly. She didn't want Jake thinking she didn't enjoy his company. It was the kids she wanted to avoid. The same aversion to responsibility that had kept her from committing herself to a husband, had also made her leery of kids. She'd had enough of caretaking to last her a lifetime.

Maybe someday she would want children of her own, but she'd spent too many years changing diapers for her mother to want that kind of obligation again anytime soon. She'd loved her mother and, given the choice again, she would make the same sacrifice. But she wouldn't have been human if there hadn't been days when she resented the restrictions her mother's illness had placed on her life.

Now that she could make a choice, was it any wonder she wanted her life to stay as carefree as possible? Was it so wrong to want to make up for those long years when freedom had been impossible?

"If you don't mind," she said. "I'd really like to get my gazebo repaired as soon as possible."

"I'd offer to fix it for you," Jake said, "but I know Rabb's a better carpenter."

The two men exchanged a look that Amanda couldn't decipher.

"When will we see each other again?" Amanda asked Jake.

"As a matter of fact, I'd like some time alone with you now, if that's all right," Jake said.

The two men exchanged another look that Amanda found equally perplexing, before Rabb turned to her and said, "I'll see you tomorrow, Amanda."

"Thanks, Rabb. See you then."

A moment later he was gone, and she was alone with Jake.

It was ridiculous to feel awkward being alone with her fiancé. They were getting married in two weeks. Jake would be entitled to all sorts of intimacies then. As would she.

Amanda looked at Jake, wondering what it would feel like to have his hands on her naked flesh. It was as though her thoughts had conjured action. Because Jake took a step and drew her into his embrace.

She barely managed to keep herself from stiffening as she felt his hips pressing against hers. Even so, she pushed at his shoulders and leaned back enough to look into his eyes.

"What happened today?" she asked.

He averted his gaze. "He was my hired hand. It was my responsibility to keep him in line."

"Hmm." She raised a hand to brush at a lock of black hair that had fallen over his forehead. "What about that trip upstairs with Hope? Is it your job to keep her in line, too?"

He brought his gaze back to bear on her, and she felt her heart clench at the tortured look in his eyes.

"That girl gets under my skin," he admitted. "She's a nuisance. That's all. She's promised to keep her distance from now on."

"Until the wedding? Or afterward, too?"

He lifted a brow. "Are you jealous of her? You don't need to be. You're the one I'm marrying."

Amanda felt doubt niggling at her, but she wasn't sure how far she wanted to push Jake. He'd never said he loved her. But she'd never said the words to him, either. It had just been…understood.

"Kiss me, Jake," she said. *Make me feel loved. Reassure me that we're doing the right thing.*

His mouth came down on hers an instant later, hard and demanding. His hand rose to cup her breast, but she pressed herself harder against him, making it difficult for him to touch her. His hand slid down between them, across her abdomen, and her body tensed as she waited for his touch.

Before he reached his destination, she shoved hard at his chest and broke free. They were both breathing hard. His eyes glittered with…desperation.

Amanda shuddered. "Oh, God," she said. "What are we doing?"

She stared at Jake, waiting for an answer.

"I thought you wanted this. I thought you wanted us to make love. You've put it off all this time. I thought you were finally ready."

She shook her head. "No." Another breath shuddered out of her. "Not like this."

"Like what?" he said.

She searched his face, finding it devoid of any emotion. His eyes were shuttered, his features remote. "Do you love me, Jake?"

She was startled by the question. Strangely, she'd never asked it before. And she wasn't sure she wanted to hear the answer.

"I respect you. I admire you. I think you'll make a good wife."

She smiled sadly. "I see." She waited for him to inquire about her feelings for him. She wasn't sure what she would have said. But he never asked.

He was a very attractive man. He'd proved he could be faithful to a wife, even though his wife had left him in the end. He was a successful cattle rancher, well-respected in the community. He had a large and loving family. He was perfect husband material.

Amanda just couldn't seem to embrace the physical part of their relationship. She'd liked his kisses...at first. And aside from one disastrous incident a year ago, he'd never pressed her for more. But she couldn't seem to get past the barriers that had grown over the three years they'd been engaged.

"I wish I had more experience," she said lamely. She had slept with only one boy, although *slept* was the wrong word. Her one experience with sex had been quick and unsatisfying and she'd never wanted to repeat it. She wondered if Jake suspected how naive she was. She'd been putting off the moment when she shared her body with him, telling herself that it was better—for a lot of reasons—to save intimacy for marriage.

But what if she found out after they were married that Jake's kisses were just as threatening to her peace of mind as they were now?

"I want to have sex…make love…with you, Jake. I just…"

"You don't have to apologize. I was out of line."

"No," she said. "Your touches, your caresses, should be acceptable to—" She stopped herself, realizing that she was admitting that his touches, his caresses, were not in fact acceptable to her. She brushed her bangs out of her eyes and looked up at him unhappily. "Are we making a mistake, Jake?"

"I'm no less committed now than the day I asked you to marry me," he said.

Amanda made a face. "But are we right for each other? Will we be able to live happily ever after?"

Jake rubbed a hand across his nape. "I don't know," he said. "What makes a successful marriage? I married for love the first time around and look what happened. You have all the qualities I want in a wife. You must think I'd make a good husband, or you wouldn't have accepted my proposal. There's no reason why we shouldn't be happy together."

And yet, Amanda thought, she hadn't yet shared her body with him. Shouldn't there be some passion between a married couple? Wasn't that necessary for happiness?

She made herself close the distance between them and tugged on his shirt collar until he lowered his head for her kiss. She opened her mouth slightly, letting her lips rub damply across his, wanting gentleness, wanting...love.

The response she got was satisfyingly carnal. But there was no tenderness. No...love.

She broke the kiss quickly, before he could touch her again. "It's been a long day," she said. "I'm really tired."

"Can I come in with you?" Jake asked.

She knew what he was asking. Was she going to make him wait until their wedding night to consummate this relationship? Was she going to allow this awkwardness to continue between them until the moment she walked down the aisle? Was she ready for a physical relationship with the man who would be her husband in two weeks?

He smiled, his hand gently caressing her cheek and said, "You know, we're going to have to make it to bed together sometime if we want kids."

"I don't want children," Amanda blurted.

There was no mistaking the shocked look on Jake's face. His hand dropped away and he said, "Not ever?"

"Not for a while, anyway."

"How long is a while?" Jake said. "I'm thirty-nine, Amanda. I was hoping to have kids right away, so I'll be around to enjoy them when they're grown."

"I want to wait a few years," she said. "I want some time to enjoy being a wife before I have to become a mother." She wanted more freedom. There had been too little of it in her life.

"I can't believe we never discussed this," Jake said. "I just assumed…"

"I'm sorry if I've surprised you. Does it make a difference?"

"It does to me," Jake admitted. "Children were a big part of the reason I finally pushed for the wedding. I want to get started on a family."

Amanda felt a cold dread growing inside her. "I don't think—"

He pulled her into his arms and rocked her. "Let's not throw the baby out with the bathwater," he said. "We've got a lot of other things going for us. A year or two isn't going to make that much of a difference."

Amanda opened her mouth to say she was thinking more like five or six years, but clamped it shut again. Maybe she would change her mind once she was married. Maybe marriage to Jake wouldn't be the burden she'd been fearing the past few years. Maybe everything would be all right after all.

"Do you still want to get married?" she asked.

"Do you?" he replied.

"I do if you do," she said.

"Then in two weeks, we'll be husband and wife," Jake said as he dropped a kiss on her forehead.

Amanda shivered.

"The sun's gone," he said. "You're cold. You'd better get inside."

"All right," she said, stepping back from his embrace. But she wasn't cold. Except maybe deep inside, where she didn't think she would ever be warm. "Good night, Jake," she said.

"Get some rest," he urged. "I'll make some time to see you later this week."

Then he was gone. And she was alone in her backyard, wondering if she was about to make a terrible mistake.

CHAPTER THREE

FAITH

"Thank you, Faith," Amanda said as she finished washing the last of the potluck casserole dishes left over from the party and handed it to Faith to dry. "I really appreciate you coming by this morning to help me clean up after the party."

"It's my pleasure, Miss Carter. It's too bad your gazebo got smashed to smithereens," she said as she stared out the kitchen window. "Cleaning that up is going to take a saw and a wheelbarrow."

"Not to worry," Amanda said. "Rabb Whitelaw's coming over after church to put it back together. Which reminds me, I'd better get a start on his meat loaf and mashed potatoes."

Faith's dark eyes went wide. "*Rabb* Whitelaw's coming here for lunch?"

Amanda smiled. "It was the only payment he would accept for fixing my gazebo."

"He really is a nice man, isn't he, Miss Carter?" Faith said. "And handsome, too."

"Yes, he is nice," Amanda agreed. She smiled, remembering how sympathetic Rabb's hazel eyes had looked, how the last rays of sun had burnished his chestnut hair. How firm and muscular his chest had felt as he held her. "And, yes, I suppose he is handsome," she murmured.

She glanced at Faith speculatively. Was the young girl interested in Rabb? "I thought you and Randy were an item."

"We are," Faith said. "That doesn't mean I can't notice when a man is good-looking. Not that I'd do anything about it. No one could ever replace Randy. I guess you must feel the same way about Jake," she said. "Like he's the only man in the world you could ever imagine yourself spending the rest of your life with."

"Hmm," Amanda said. The problem was, she was having a difficult time imagining her life with Jake. Especially now that she knew for sure he wanted children right away. How were they going to resolve that dilemma?

"I'd be glad to help you peel potatoes," Faith said.

Amanda always marveled at how well Faith got by with a hand and a hook. "Thanks, Faith, but I can manage."

Faith folded the dish towel and hung it on the refrigerator door handle. "Well, if that's everything, I'll be on my way."

A moment later she was out the door. As Amanda watched her cross the backyard, she marveled at how different Faith was from Hope. It was difficult to believe the two were identical twins. Or almost identical. There was that missing hand that made them different.

When Amanda had first met the two girls, Faith had been a shadow of her sister, always walking behind her, her arm with the missing hand concealed behind her back. Amanda had soon realized that Hope's outrageous behavior was a decoy to keep people from noticing that other significant physical difference between the twins. She'd admired the fact that Hope was so fiercely protective of her quieter, shyer sister.

Amanda wasn't sure when she'd first noticed Hope's unfortunate attraction to Jake, but she'd been glad when Hope headed off to Baylor, and had been incredibly relieved when Hope had spent the past two summers traveling. Not that she'd ever considered Hope a serious rival for Jake's affections. Hope was simply too young for Jake.

Or she had been.

Amanda frowned. Hope was no longer a child, and there was nothing subtle about her current pursuit of Jake. The young woman had made it clear by word and deed that she was in love with Jake. Which was something Amanda had never done.

And Jake wasn't immune to Hope's adoration. She'd seen how his eyes followed the girl yesterday, though he'd done nothing to encourage her. What were Jake's feelings for Hope? Was he in love with her? Was she keeping two people apart who ought to be together?

But Amanda had given Jake a chance to back out of their engagement, and he hadn't taken it. She had to conclude that he didn't want out. Amanda found comfort in the fact that when push came to shove, he'd chosen her over Hope.

The knock on the back door startled her. She crossed and opened it to find Rabb. It was two weeks until Christmas, but Rabb was wearing clothes more suited to summer. She supposed the unseasonably warm weather justified his attire, but she nevertheless found it disconcerting.

His T-shirt had the sleeves torn out to reveal muscular arms and dark underarm hair, and his raggedy jeans gave taunting glimpses of the white briefs he was wearing. A leather tool belt hung heavy and substantial around his lean waist. She wasn't aware she was holding her breath until she tried to find the air to greet him and it wasn't there.

"Hi," he said with a smile that made her feel warm inside. "Thought I'd let you know I'm going to be making some noise out here."

She managed a smile, gasped for some air and said, "Let me get lunch on the stove, and I'll come out and join you."

He gave her a mock salute and said, "Yes, ma'am," then turned and headed back toward the gazebo.

She stood at the door, only belatedly realizing that she was ogling the fit of his jeans as he walked away. She quickly closed the door, but the damage was done.

What was this fascination she had with Jake's brother? She'd felt the same inclination to reach out and touch him when he'd built her gazebo two summers ago. She couldn't possibly really be interested in him. She had a recollection of Rabb not being a very good student when they'd been in school together. She wanted someone she could talk with, someone intelligent and perceptive. That wasn't the impression she had of Rabb Whitelaw. Good looks simply weren't enough.

Suddenly she realized that her hands were trembling. She shook them, made a *grrrr* sound in her throat and yanked open the drawer that contained the potato peeler. She was a woman engaged to be married—to Rabb's brother! The sooner she stopped letting her hormones control her head, the better.

Amanda took her time peeling potatoes and putting them on to boil and preparing the meat loaf. When she glanced out the kitchen window—she was just curious how repairs on her gazebo were coming along—she saw the flex and play of sinew and bone as Rabb physically manhandled the broken wood frame.

She forced her gaze from the window, got out a can of creamed corn and stuck it in a pot, then put some frozen string beans in a microwave dish. She pulled out some Jell-O salad left over from the party, then set the table for two.

By the time she'd finished, the potatoes were done. She mashed them with milk and butter, then set them on the stove where they'd stay warm. And realized there was nothing else to keep her from joining Rabb outside.

Had she been dawdling? Had she been delaying the moment? And if so, why? He was simply a nice guy doing her a favor. All right, an *attractive* nice guy doing her a favor.

Amanda paused on the back porch and stared at Rabb. He was intent on his work, completely unconscious of her, and she indulged her desire to look. His T-shirt was gone; bare to the waist, he was a delight for the eyes.

A fine sheen of sweat caused his tanned body to glisten in the sun, and it was hard to ignore the broad shoulders that tapered to a lean waist. She tried to remember if she'd ever seen Jake like this. If she had, it hadn't left a similar impression—of youth and strength and, well, the word that came to mind was *beauty*.

It was the wrong word for a man, but even with her vast vocabulary, she couldn't think of a better one.

Amanda backed away. She didn't want to be tempted physically by a man other than her fiancé. But Rabb turned and saw her and smiled, and the choice was taken out of her hands.

"Ready to go to work?" he said.

She walked toward him, aware she was smiling back at him and again feeling that warmth inside. "What do you want me to do?"

"I'm trying to save your morning glories," he said.

"Oh, thank you."

"Come here," he said, holding out a piece of lattice intertwined with greenery. "See if you can unwind some of these vines."

She was close enough to smell the scent of hardworking man. Surprisingly, it wasn't at all unpleasant. She was wearing a long-sleeved Oxford cloth shirt, and it wasn't long before she felt too warm.

"Just a minute," she said. She started to unbutton the sleeve of her white shirt and realized her hands were stained green. She considered wiping them on her khaki slacks, but the trousers were also clean, with a neat crease down the front. She made a face and reached for the button on her sleeve.

"Here, let me," Rabb volunteered. He dropped the

lattice, swiped his hands on his jeans and reached out to unbutton her right sleeve. He folded it up a couple of times and said, "How's that?"

"Fine," she murmured self-consciously. There was something intimate about having a man unbutton your clothes, even when it was something as innocent as a sleeve.

A moment later, he'd finished with the other sleeve. She took a deep breath of relief and looked up at him.

Amanda knew as soon as their eyes met that she'd made a mistake. Because he was looking back at her as though he had her in a bedroom alone, and he was just getting started. She'd never really looked closely at his eyes, but now she noticed they were golden with a dark edge surrounding the iris that made his gaze look intense, almost dangerous.

Leonine. Yes, that was the right word. *Like a lion.*

She was still staring up at him, breathless, a little frightened, when he smiled and said, "Here's the real problem."

Before she could protest, he'd reached for the buttons at her throat. He undid three of them and tugged the shirt wide. It fell open to reveal the edge of lace at the top of her bra.

She glanced down and flushed. And grabbed the edges of cloth and pulled them back together.

"Don't," he murmured. He freed her hands, which fell to her sides, and rearranged the cloth, opening it wide again.

Her eyes stayed on the toes of her sensible penny loafers.

He lifted her chin with a finger, forcing her gaze up

to his. "I've been wanting to do that ever since I showed up at your door. You shouldn't be all buttoned up, Mandy. You need to let go a little."

She hadn't heard that nickname since high school. It brought back memories of more carefree days that were long gone. She was a grown-up now. She was a responsible woman.

"It's hard to reverse the habits of a lifetime," she said, her fingers itching to rebutton her shirt. She reached up again, feeling much too exposed.

"Don't," he repeated quietly, taking her hands in his, tugging them away from the crumpled cloth.

His hands were warm and strong, and Amanda could feel the calluses on the pads of his fingers. Abruptly, he let her go and took a step back. "We'd better get back to work." He turned his back on her and picked up a piece of lattice and held it out to her.

Amanda resumed the chore he'd given her, wondering how she was going to make it through the rest of the afternoon. How awkward. How mortifying. How utterly—

"Penny for your thoughts," Rabb said.

She glanced up and saw he was grinning. "What's so funny?" she asked irritably.

"You are," he said. "You'd think I'd stripped you down to your bra and panties."

Her face caught fire. Because she had been imagining what that would be like.

"When was the last time you did something rash and impulsive?" he asked.

"I don't know what you mean," Amanda said stiffly.

Rabb dumped the broken piece of lattice in a nearby wheelbarrow and said, "I'm hungry. How about you?"

The sudden change of subject caught her off guard. "Hungry?"

"You promised me lunch. Let's go eat," Rabb said, grabbing her hand and heading for the kitchen door.

"What about the gazebo?" she said, glancing back at the carnage.

"It'll wait. We have more important things to do."

"Like what?" Amanda said.

"Eating first," Rabb said. "Then…I haven't made up my mind yet, but something…whimsical."

She glanced at him sideways. "You're making fun of me."

"Not at all," he countered as he opened the screen door and ushered her inside ahead of him.

She'd never realized how small her kitchen was, but there didn't seem to be room for the two of them. She was aware of Rabb's size, and the smell of raw male, and the fact that he was a very attractive man.

He caught her eyeing him and said, "I should get my shirt."

She was flustered and said, "Only if you're uncomfortable."

"I'm fine," he said. "But my mother wouldn't have let any of us boys come to the table like this. I'll be right back."

An instant later he was out the door again, and she took a deep breath trying to calm her nerves. What was wrong with her? This was Rabb. Jake's brother. Who couldn't read.

He was back a second later wearing the scrap of

T-shirt, but it wasn't much of an improvement. She could still see too much of him. And liked what she saw too much.

She'd had Jake over to dinner a number of times, but he'd always sat quietly and let her put food on the table. Rabb was into everything, leaning against her as he reached up for the glasses for tea and stretching around her as he got ice cubes from the freezer. He even held her chair for her, insisting that she sit before him.

Talk about siblings who were different from one another. Jake was the strong, silent type. Rabb never stopped talking.

"I've been working on some new designs for the furniture I'm building," he said. "More baroque."

"Baroque?" she blurted. She hadn't thought of Rabb as an artist, or as someone who understood artistic styles.

"Most of what I've done in the past has been plain and practical, simple lines. But I got started adding a little of this and a little of that and before I knew it, this particular bedroom suite started looking like something out of the seventeenth century."

"Hmm," she said, because she didn't know what to say.

"What's your preference, artistically speaking?" he said.

She took a bite of meat loaf and pointed, showing she couldn't speak because her mouth was full.

"I prefer the French modes to the Italian," he said. "The lines are—"

Amanda quickly swallowed and said, "Where did

you learn all this? I mean, this all sounds pretty complicated and…sophisticated."

Rabb shrugged. "I was never any good at reading." He paused and said, as though he were admitting to a sexually transmitted disease, "Dyslexic."

"Oh. I didn't know." Dyslexics weren't any good at reading because the letters and numbers appeared mixed up on the page, but that didn't keep them from being highly intelligent. Einstein had been dyslexic. She looked at Rabb with newly opened eyes.

"I always liked looking at the pictures, though," Rabb continued with a self-deprecating grin. "You can learn a lot about art and architecture from pictures."

"Hmm," Amanda said, because she was feeling foolish. As a teacher, she should know better than to jump to conclusions about people. It seemed she'd misjudged Rabb. "When did you find out you were dyslexic?"

"My mom and dad were pretty insistent that we get a good education. I spent a lot of time studying but never did well on tests. Turns out they were familiar with dyslexia because one of my uncles grew up with the same problem. It helped to know why I couldn't read well, but it was still hard not to fight back when someone called me a dummy."

Amanda's heart went out to Rabb. How awful for him. And she'd been as bad as everyone else. "I'm so sorry," she said.

"I got over it," Rabb said. He held out his hands and turned them over, as though marveling at them. "My hands have never failed me. I've found something I can do well, and I get a tremendous amount of satisfaction from creating unique, one-of-a-kind pieces."

"I've always loved my gazebo," she admitted in a soft voice.

"I'm glad," Rabb said.

"I'd love to see more of your work."

"You're welcome to come to my workshop."

"I'd like that," she said. "When?"

"When can you spare the time? With the wedding coming up, you must have a lot to do over the next couple of weeks."

Oh. The wedding. She'd completely forgotten. "I have so much to do I'm not sure how I'll finish it all," Amanda admitted.

"What about Jake? Is he helping?"

"He's busy with the ranch during the day, and he's agreed to keep your nephew and niece, which will keep him busy in the evenings."

"I'd be glad to help—although I'm not sure what I can do," Rabb said.

A furrow appeared in Amanda's brow. "I have to pick flowers for the church and a design for the cake and I have some final decisions to make on my wedding dress. I'm afraid I've left everything to the last minute. I was busy with school until a few days ago, and now everything has to be done at once. It would help to have another opinion."

"You've got it," Rabb said.

"I wouldn't want to take you away from your work."

"My hours are flexible, and I was planning to take a little time off for Christmas anyhow. Where do you want to start? Flowers? Cake? Or dress?"

Amanda laughed and realized how strange it felt. She couldn't remember the last time she'd laughed. She felt…carefree and happy. Suddenly, activities she'd been looking at as chores seemed like they might be fun. "I don't know. Can I call you later?"

"Sure," Rabb said. "Meanwhile, we have things to do."

Amanda sighed. Yes. There was always work to do. She stood and began collecting the dishes to carry to the sink.

"I'll help you with the dishes later," Rabb said. "I think the rest of the afternoon would be better spent taking a ride."

"What?"

Rabb took her by the hand and was tugging her toward the door. "Come on, Amanda. I know you ride. I've seen you with Jake."

"You mean go for a *horseback* ride? Now? This afternoon?"

"Sure. Why not?"

"What about the gazebo?" She looked around at the mess in the kitchen and said, "What about the dishes?"

"They can both wait. There's no telling how long this beautiful weather will last. Go put on your boots. Let's take a few hours and get away from it all."

That sounded so wonderful. It also sounded irresponsible. "I have so much to do," Amanda said, "I can't possibly—"

"I won't take no for an answer," Rabb said. "You have two seconds to go for your boots, or I'm going to throw you over my shoulder and haul you off like you are."

"You wouldn't dare," Amanda said, titillated by the threat, but not quite believing it, either.

"Oh, no?" Rabb said. He reached out and tickled her ribs.

Amanda scrunched her arms down tight and tried to wriggle away. His arms came around her as his hands insinuated themselves beneath her bent arms and wormed their way up to her underarms.

"Oh, God." She giggled. "Stop. I'm ticklish!"

"Gonna get your boots?"

"Yes!" she shrieked. "Yes."

"Then go," he said, freeing her abruptly.

Amanda took off at a run—she *never* ran in the house—giggling and laughing all the way.

"Hurry back," he shouted after her. "Or I'll come up and get you."

For one treacherous moment, Amanda considered letting him do just that. In her bedroom, she kicked off her loafers, shoved her feet into her black cowboy boots, and ran—good grief, she was running again—back down the stairs.

She was grinning when she stomped into the kitchen. "All right. I'm ready to go. Are you satisfied?"

"God, you're so beautiful."

Amanda's grin faded. What was she doing? What was she thinking? She had no business running off with Rabb Whitelaw for an afternoon of... merriment. She had dishes to wash. And plans to make. For her wedding. To his brother.

She gripped the back of a kitchen chair so hard her knuckles turned white. Because she had to hang on or go tearing out the door with him. "You'd better go," she said.

"Mandy—"

"Just go, Rabb. Now. Please." When he didn't move, she said, "Get out!"

A moment later he was gone. And she was alone. Again.

CHAPTER FOUR

AMANDA WAS STILL IN BED LONG past the time when she normally would have been up and busy. She'd tossed and turned all night, feeling guilty over her treatment of Rabb. She wouldn't blame him if he never came back to fix her gazebo. He probably thought she was crazy. She certainly had no rational explanation for her behavior.

She sat bolt upright at the first sound of hammering, then threw off the covers and scrambled out of bed, heading for the window. She turned and hopped right back into bed when her feet hit the frigid wooden floor. She reached down under the bed, found her bunny slippers and put them on, then trotted to the window. Well, the summer temperatures were gone.

She could see Rabb was putting up new lattice, but he was wearing a shearling coat and leather gloves. She shoved the window up and yelled down at him, "What are you doing?"

He smiled and waved and said, "Good morning, Mandy," as though the events of the previous afternoon had never happened.

Well, if he wanted to pretend things were fine, she was happy to forget the way she'd acted.

"I could use a cup of coffee," he said. "When you're up."

"I'm up now," she said, shivering as a blast of cold air hit her face.

"You're still in your pajamas," he countered. "But I like them. You look cute."

Amanda glanced down at the baby doll pajamas she'd slept in. They were impractical in a way none of her everyday clothes were. Skimpy and sexy and very… pink. No one had ever seen them but her. And no one was supposed to see them.

"I'll be down in a minute," she said, slamming the window and yanking down the shade.

He thought she looked *cute*. She ran and stared at herself in the bathroom mirror. *Cute* was a word for teenagers. Thirty-two-year-old women were never *cute*. She looked…ridiculous. She ought to be wearing something more appropriate for her age.

But she'd had to be up several times at night with her mother during those years when she could have worn silly, flighty, *fun* clothes to bed, so she'd made up for it once her mother passed away by buying things like the girlish baby doll pajamas she wore now.

She ruthlessly yanked them off, washed her face, brushed her teeth and put on the clothes she wore on cold days. Slacks, loafers with socks, an Oxford cloth shirt and a pullover crew-necked sweater. She shoved a brush through her short hair, slicked on some lipstick and headed downstairs.

No sense pretending she was anything she wasn't. Forget being cute. She kept her hair cut short because it was easy to take care of and, except for her pajamas, bought practical clothes that would last.

She boiled a cup of water in the microwave and added a teaspoon of instant coffee. No coffeemaker for her. Speed was of the essence. Time was something she never seemed to have enough of. Or at least, that was the way it had been for eleven years. It had been difficult to readjust her mindset in the years since her mother had passed away. All right, impossible. She had the feeling she could never catch up, never get back those years she'd lost.

She stuck her head out the screen door and said, "Cream and sugar?"

"Lots of both," he shouted back.

Jake liked his coffee black. Another little difference.

She preferred just about anything hot to drink *except* coffee, but she didn't feel like making either tea or cocoa right now. She wanted to get outside and apologize to Rabb.

She'd learned not to put off unpleasant business. Better to get it over with. She put on her goose-down vest and headed outside with Rabb's coffee.

He stuck the hammer in his tool belt when he saw her coming and turned to reach for the coffee mug. "Aren't you having any?"

"I don't drink coffee," she said. "I only came out here to say I'm sorry for yesterday." There, it was done.

He sipped at the coffee, winced, then blew on it. "Uh-huh," he said. He looked at her and waited.

She stuck her hands in her vest pockets, because it was colder outside than she'd expected it would be. Her breath plumed in the air. "Guess a norther came in overnight," she said.

"Uh-huh," he said. And nothing more.

"I'm sorry now I didn't take advantage of your offer

to go riding yesterday. That was probably the end of the warm weather."

"Uh-huh," he said and sipped again at his coffee.

"I know I was rude," she said, agitated at his lack of speech. "But I..." How was she supposed to explain how she'd felt? What she'd feared?

"But you're not used to having fun," he said.

She frowned. "That's not true."

"Prove it," he said. "Come riding with me today."

She shivered and scoffed, "It's freezing!"

"It's refreshingly cool," he countered with a smile.

She found herself smiling back at him. And sobered when she realized what she was doing. "I have things to do to get ready for the wedding."

"Oh, yeah. Let's see, the flowers. And the dress. And... What was the other thing?"

"The cake."

"Right. Which one needs doing today?"

"The fitting for the dress, I suppose."

"Okay. We'll do that and then go riding," he said.

She pursed her lips and wrinkled her forehead. "You don't want to watch me try on my wedding dress."

"Sure I do," he said. "So long as you agree to come riding with me afterward."

"How much more work had you planned to do on the gazebo?" she asked.

He looked at the gazebo, which had one of the two naked sides covered once more in lattice and said, "That's plenty for today. I'm ready when you are."

She shook her head and laughed again. It must be nice to be able to stop in the middle of a project, to simply walk away and come back later when you felt like it. Her life hadn't allowed her that sort of freedom. She felt a little reckless at the thought of taking off on horseback in weather cold enough to turn her nose red as a berry.

"All right," she said. "You asked for it. Let me get my boots and we'll go."

Rabb was standing in her kitchen when she came down, the coffee cup rinsed and sitting in the sink. She was thinking what a great husband he would make some woman when he said, "I don't see any breakfast dishes. Did you eat?"

"I usually skip breakfast. I'm in too much of a hurry," she admitted.

"You need to eat."

While she stood gawking, he opened a series of cupboards until he found some Cheerios, then a cereal bowl and finally a spoon. "This won't take long," he said, "and you'll need the energy when we go riding."

Before she quite knew what was happening, Amanda was sitting at the kitchen table, Rabb in a chair across from her.

"You need to take better care of yourself," he said.

She felt self-conscious eating with someone watching her, especially when he wasn't eating anything. When she tried to hurry he said, "Take your time. We've got all day."

She raised a brow and asked, "Don't you have to work?"

"I'm taking a holiday. Except for fixing your gazebo, I'm footloose for the next couple of weeks."

Amanda couldn't imagine Jake being able to take off like that. His ranch kept him busy from dawn to dusk, and it was a job that had to be done 365 days a year. He'd had little time off to spend with her, which had worked out well, because she'd been busy herself with all sorts of projects at school. However, during summers and spring vacation she'd wished he was around more. She'd felt…lonely.

She looked down at her empty bowl, gave a chagrined smile, and said, "I didn't realize I was that hungry."

Rabb was up and rinsing her bowl before she could stop him. "Ready to go?" he asked.

"We'll take my car, if that's all right," she said.

Jake always preferred driving. Rabb just said, "Let's do it."

She waited for Rabb to complain about her driving. It was as conservative as every other aspect of her life. She watched the speed limit and came to a full stop at every sign. But he said nothing.

"One of the teachers has an aunt who's a seamstress," Amanda said to fill the silence. "Mrs. Caruso is amazing. She's making my wedding gown from a picture I found in *Modern Brides* magazine."

"Sewing is a real talent," Rabb agreed.

Amanda resisted the urge to describe the dress. She'd fallen in love with it and couldn't wait to see Jake's face when he saw her walking down the aisle.

Because it was a winter wedding, she'd decided she needed long, fitted sleeves. The bodice was cut into a heart shape, then covered modestly with tulle, and the A-line skirt had a short train that began at her waist and flared four feet behind her.

As Amanda rang the doorbell at Mrs. Caruso's home,

she could feel Rabb breathing down her neck. Well, not literally. But she was aware of him standing in her space. His shoulder actually brushed hers. When she saw how close Rabb stayed, she suddenly realized that Jake always kept a few inches between their bodies.

"Hello, Amanda. I see you've brought your young man. What a lovely couple you make."

Amanda flushed at Mrs. Caruso's mistake and said, "This is my fiancé's brother, Rabb Whitelaw."

"Well, come in both of you," Mrs. Caruso said. "You go on back to the bedroom and slip into that dress, while I make Mr. Whitelaw comfortable. Then I'll come help you."

"Please call me Rabb," Rabb said.

Amanda hesitated a second, wondering if Rabb would be okay. Jake would already have been fidgeting in the confined space. Rabb simply smiled at Mrs. Caruso and said, "I hear you're a wonderful seamstress."

"Why, thank you, Rabb."

They were becoming fast friends as Amanda disappeared into the back bedroom. She had already stripped down to her undies when she heard a knock on the door.

"I'll be another minute, Mrs. Caruso," she said.

"It's Rabb."

Amanda felt a spurt of panic that he would walk in and catch her undressed and hurriedly pulled the gown over her head. But it had at least two dozen cloth buttons down the back, and there was no way she could do them up on her own.

"Mrs. Caruso got a long-distance call from her daughter," Rabb said through the door. "She suggested I come back here and help you button up."

Amanda gulped. Rabb seemed more the "help you to unbutton" type of guy. She wasn't wearing a bra, because Mrs. Caruso had sewn one into the dress, and her back was completely bare. And since the dress was open below her waist, Rabb was going to get a good look at the lacy—quite *un*Amandalike—panties she had on.

"Mandy? You okay in there? Can I come in?"

Amanda clutched the bodice against her chest and said, "All right. Come in."

He stopped in the open doorway and stared. "You're beautiful," he breathed. His golden eyes stayed focused on hers as he said, "I envy my brother."

Amanda felt the heat on her cheeks. To avoid his hungry gaze, she turned her back on him. Still, she heard his indrawn breath.

"Good God, woman."

She quickly turned back around and let go of the front of the gown to hold the back together. "I'm sorry. I should have waited for Mrs. Caruso."

He shook his head. "I wouldn't have missed this for…anything. Turn around. I'll do up those buttons."

She lowered her gaze and turned around, releasing the dress and letting her hands fall to her sides.

She heard the two steps he took on the hardwood floor to reach her. She felt a prickling along her back and knew he was devouring her with his eyes. She made herself stand still.

This was Jake's brother. He was going to be her brother-in-law. They were going to be seeing a great deal of each other. He was observing nothing that wouldn't have been exposed in a bathing suit at the river.

Except they were in a room alone with the door closed, and she was more than half undressed. And she knew he liked what he was seeing.

Maybe it was the novelty of being prized by a man for her looks. Jake had never told her she was beautiful. Had never admired her eyes or her figure. He had *liked* and *respected* her. Which was far more important. Wasn't it?

But she hugged to herself the notion of being beautiful enough to make a grown man gasp. It was hard not to be thrilled by Rabb's praise.

She could hear him wipe his hands on his jeans before reaching for the top button. His callused fingertips brushed her nape and she shivered.

"Sorry about that. My hands are still cold."

Her shiver had nothing to do with the cold. She'd liked the feel of Rabb's hands on her skin.

He blew on his fingers to warm them and started again. "These buttons are small," he said. "I'm afraid I'm not as good at this as Mrs. Caruso would be."

"Take your time," she said. And then realized what he might imply from that. "I mean, I know the button loops are difficult to manage. Mrs. Caruso said it would…"

She stopped herself, realizing what she'd been about to admit. Mrs. Caruso had chuckled and said it would prolong her new husband's—and her own—anticipation as he undid the buttons on her wedding night.

"I've got a pretty good idea what she said," Rabb finished for her. "It isn't hard to imagine the pleasure of undoing these buttons one by one—"

"Please don't say any more."

He didn't. Until at last he said, "I'm finished. Turn around and let me see."

She turned slowly, keeping her gaze focused on the ground, not wanting to see the look in his eyes.

"Damn it all to hell," he muttered.

She looked up, surprised by the profanity. She saw anger and envy and anguish in his eyes.

"My brother is a very lucky man."

"Thank you," Amanda said. "Then you like it?"

She was embarrassed by the question, because it suggested she was fishing for compliments.

"You must know you're stunning," he said. "I've always thought so, ever since high school."

She laughed at the absurdity of that. "I was flat-chested through most of high school."

He grinned and said, "I noticed the change. But that wasn't what I liked most about you."

She tipped her head and stared at him. Curiosity prompted her to ask, "What did you like most?"

"Your smile. It never stayed only on your lips. I could see it deep in your eyes. I missed your smile that last year of high school."

"I didn't have much to smile about," Amanda said softly.

"Your mother's been gone for three years, Mandy. And your smile hasn't come back."

"I smile plenty," she said.

"With your mouth," he said. "But your eyes...they don't smile or sparkle anymore. Why is that?"

A knock on the door interrupted them. "May I come in?"

Amanda hurried to the door and opened it for Mrs.

Caruso. "I'm all buttoned up," she said. She held her arms wide and turned in a circle for the seamstress. "What do you think?"

"I think there's nothing more for me to do," Mrs. Caruso said. The phone rang. "That's my daughter again," Mrs. Caruso said. "Would you mind helping Amanda get unbuttoned, Rabb?"

She didn't wait for an answer, merely turned and left, closing the door behind her.

Amanda stared at Rabb with wary eyes. It had been bad enough having him button the dress. It would be torture standing still while he unbuttoned it…as Jake would on their wedding night.

"Would you rather I left?" Rabb asked, apparently aware of her distress.

"I'm being silly," she mumbled. She turned her back to him and stood, her body taut, as Rabb began unbuttoning the gown.

She felt Rabb brush away the few curls at her nape so he could reach the topmost button. She could feel his knuckles brushing her bare flesh as he worked his way down her back.

He was halfway down her spine when he stopped. She angled her head around and said, "Is something wrong?"

"I can't do this," he muttered, taking a step back.

She turned and looked at his eyes. They were heavy-lidded with passion. She felt a stirring in her belly, a response to the avid look in his eyes.

"I wish… Jake is my brother," he said, his voice curt. "If things were different…"

Amanda was shocked at what she was hearing, and

it must have shown in her face because Rabb said,
"Look, Mandy, I can't control what I'm feeling. But I
can damn sure control what I do about it. Be sure that
Jake is the man you want. Because I don't want to see
either one of you hurt."

"I love—"

"Don't say anything," he interrupted. "Mrs. Caruso
can help you the rest of the way out of that dress." He
smiled crookedly at her. "I'm afraid I might not be able
to keep my hands off you."

Amanda stared at the empty doorway. She was
confused. And unhappy. If Rabb was truly interested in
her, why had he waited so long to say something? It was
only two weeks before her wedding. She couldn't
possibly back out now, even if she found herself discovering new feelings for him.

Not that she had such feelings. She was flattered by
Rabb's compliments and attention. That was all it was.

It wouldn't be fair to Jake to abandon him now, when
he'd been loyal enough to wait three years for her to be
ready for marriage. She'd been willing enough to get
engaged to him when she'd feared marriage had passed
her by and she was going to end up an old maid.

And Jake was especially vulnerable. She knew his
history. He'd already been dumped by one woman
who'd told him he wasn't what she wanted anymore.
She didn't think she could be that cruel.

But wouldn't it be dishonest to marry him if her
feelings had changed? Or rather, if she knew she had
growing feelings for some other man? Especially when
that other man was Jake's brother?

Amanda had answered the call to duty all her adult

life. It was very hard to turn her back on it now. She'd given up all hope of finding romantic love. She'd been ready to settle for *liking* and *respect*.

Rabb had changed all that.

She couldn't understand how he'd slipped past all the roadblocks she'd set up against her feelings. She'd put love aside for duty years ago and had been content. But Rabb had robbed her of contentment. Now she wanted more. Now she yearned for…love.

Oh, God. What was she going to do? How could she turn her back on Jake and marry his brother? It couldn't be done. Guilt and shame would kill love and prevent any chance of living happily ever after.

She had no choice. She had to crush the budding feelings she felt for Rabb. And follow through with her marriage to his brother.

She said nothing to Rabb until they were back in her car, the wedding gown wrapped in plastic and lying across the back seat. She reached for the key but didn't start the engine.

"I can't," she murmured.

"Can't what?" he asked.

She kept her eyes on her lap as she said, "I don't think it's a good idea for us to spend any more time together."

"Because I have feelings for you?"

She turned to him, her eyes stark and said, "No. Because I have feelings for you."

She saw his eyes flare with joy and rushed to cut it off. "They're feelings I will never, ever act upon."

"Why not?" he demanded.

"I'm going to marry your brother."

Rabb frowned. "You're not doing him any favors if you're not in love with him."

"I care for him. I respect him. I'll make him a good wife."

Rabb snorted. "That's hardly the same thing."

"I've committed myself to him. I owe him my fidelity. Unless he changes his mind—"

"You know he's not going to do that," Rabb shot back. "He's as foolishly honorable as you are."

"There's nothing I can do," she said. "I think it would be better if we don't see each other again before the wedding."

"Because you're tempted? Because you might find yourself preferring me to my brother?" he said in a harsh voice.

She flushed. But didn't answer him.

"All right, Mandy. I'll keep my distance. But I want to give you something to think about."

He caught her nape in his hand and held her captive as his mouth plundered hers. She was caught off guard by the sharp, exciting feelings that assaulted her. Feelings that had been absent when Jake kissed her. Rabb's mouth lingered, inciting an ache deep inside. She wanted the kiss to go on and on, yet knew she had to end it.

She felt the tears brim in her eyes, felt the sudden knot in her throat. Felt the sting in her nose and fought against the sob that escaped anyway.

"Oh, my God, Mandy," Rabb said, pulling her across the seat and into his lap, holding her tight. "I'm sorry. I'm so sorry."

She sobbed against his shoulder, unsure what it was

she grieved so bitterly. The lost years. Or the lost hope of love.

He caught a fistful of her hair in his hands and pulled her head back, his gaze tormented. "Promise me you'll think between now and the wedding. Promise me you'll give us a chance."

"I can't," she sobbed. "I'm sorry, Rabb. I can't!"

He set her back on the seat and smoothed her hair back from her face. She could tell he didn't want to let her go. But in the end, he did.

"It's not more than a mile back to your place," he said. "I'll walk."

"At least let me—"

"I'll walk," he said, gripping her hands, which she only then realized had been laid on his chest. "Goodbye, Mandy."

"Rabb—"

But he was already out of the car and headed down the street, the shearling coat pulled up around his ears, his body hunched against the cold, his hands thrust into his jeans pockets.

She wanted to call him back. Duty kept her silent and still. She would learn to love Jake. She owed him that.

CHAPTER FIVE

HOPE

HOPE HADN'T SEEN HIDE NOR HAIR of Jake in a week. He'd been hiding out at his ranch. She could feel the clock ticking. In eight days he would say his vows to Miss Carter and be lost to her forever. She couldn't let that happen. She had to find some way to convince him to marry her instead.

Friday night supper was over, and Hope was lying on her bed, hands behind her head, jean-clad legs crossed at the ankle, thinking. Desperate circumstances called for desperate measures. Hope knew what she had to do. She just wasn't sure she could go through with it.

She was going to seduce Jake Whitelaw.

Hope was certain that if Jake took her virginity, he would do the honorable thing and marry her. Unfortunately, seducing Jake meant acting dishonorably herself.

Jake treated his engagement seriously, and she knew he wouldn't touch her without some significant provocation. She was equally sure, because sparks flew—hell, a bonfire raged—whenever they were together, that he could be incited to have sex with her. She wasn't so sure he would be willing to forgive her afterward.

What if all he'd ever wanted was her body? What would happen when he'd slaked his appetite for her? What if she forced him into a marriage that would make both of them miserable?

She couldn't afford to think about the consequences of what she was doing. She couldn't afford to have second thoughts. She couldn't afford to listen to her nagging conscience, which warned her she might be sorry later.

Her bedroom door opened, and Faith leaned in and said, "May I come in?"

"When did you ever have to ask?" Hope replied.

Faith crossed and sat on the bed beside her. "I've been worried about you."

"Oh? Why is that?"

"You haven't been your usual happy-go-lucky self lately."

"I only have eight days left, Faith."

"Then what are you doing here? Why don't you go see Jake?"

"He's staying at his ranch. And his housekeeper is living in because he's got his niece and nephew with him. Frankly, it's not a situation conducive to seduction."

"Isn't Mrs. Hernandez Jake's housekeeper?" Faith asked.

"Uh-huh."

"I don't see how she could be at Jake's house. I just talked to her daughter, Stephanie, on the phone. You remember, she was a good friend of mine through high school? Stephanie told me her mother is on her way to Eagle Pass."

Hope sat bolt upright. "What?"

"It seems Mrs. Hernandez's granddaughter has a bad cold and Stephanie is pregnant again and needs her mother's help. So she begged her to come. And Mrs. Hernandez went."

"Oh, my God," Hope said. "That means Jake's alone with those two babies."

"Yep," Faith said. "I wonder how he's doing."

"He's probably going crazy. He probably—"

"Needs help?" Faith suggested.

"Of course he needs help," Hope said, sliding off the bed and hunting for her boots. She tugged one on and then the other. "I've got to get over there."

"Maybe you should call Miss Carter to go help him," Faith said.

"Miss Carter's busy getting ready for her wedding. I saw her car parked outside the florist shop this week. And at the bakery. And at the drugstore."

"Was Rabb Whitelaw with her?" Faith asked.

"Rabb? Why would he be with her?"

"He's been fixing her gazebo. I thought... Never mind," Faith said. "So you're going to offer to help baby-sit?"

"It's the neighborly thing to do," Hope said, rushing to her dresser and shoving a brush through her hair.

"Are you going to stay the night?" Faith asked.

Hope paused in midstroke and turned to face her sister. "Do you think I should?"

"I was going to suggest you stay the rest of the week, until Jake's brother Colt and his wife Jenny return."

Hope bit her lip. "You mean, offer to baby-sit for the whole week?"

Faith nodded. "Jake's going to need help from

someone. It might as well be you. And it'll give you a chance to spend some time together, really get to know one another."

Hope's mind was racing. She thought of cowhide rugs and flickering fireplaces. It would be much easier to seduce Jake if she was spending the night. Seven nights.

"Maybe you should pack a few things before you go," Faith said. "Just in case."

Hope shook her head. "I couldn't do that. It would look too much like I planned to come and stay. I wouldn't want Jake to think—"

"It was only a thought," Faith said.

Hope imagined not having a toothbrush. Or a comb. Or clean underwear for a week. And she did have that sexy black negligee she'd bought from Victoria's Secret when she'd graduated from Baylor and knew she was coming home to Jake.

"All right," she said. "Just a few things. But I'll leave the bag outside until I'm sure he really wants my help."

"Oh, he's going to want it," Faith said certainly. "With a rowdy two-year-old boy and a nine-month-old baby girl on his hands, he's going to welcome you like a gift from heaven."

"Oh, do you think so?" Hope couldn't keep the wistfulness from her voice. Jake seemed completely self-reliant. It would be wonderful if he really needed her.

"In fact, I'll drop you off," Faith said. "That way I can use the car while you're gone."

Hope grinned. "Sure. Why not?" She crossed to give Faith a hard hug. "God, I'm so glad you're my sister."

She felt Faith returning the hug, and when Faith let

go, they looked at each other and grinned. "Now go get him," Faith said.

Hope laughed and started packing. In fifteen minutes she was ready. She hurried downstairs and encountered resistance she hadn't expected.

Her parents were sitting at the kitchen table, where they usually remained having a cup of coffee and talking after the dishes were done. She'd always been amazed at how much they enjoyed each other's company. She longed for a husband who would still cherish her company after so many years together. She believed Jake was that man.

"See you later," Hope said as she breezed past them. She figured she would call them later and tell them where she was.

She only got halfway across the kitchen before her father said, "Hold up a minute."

Hope saw Faith standing in the corner by the door, her coat on, the car keys clutched in her hand. Her sister's lower lip was caught in her teeth and a frown furrowed her brow.

Hope turned to face her parents, who were looking at her expectantly.

"What's the bag for?" her father asked.

"I might be out overnight," Hope said.

"Where?" her father asked.

"Jake Whitelaw has his niece and nephew for the week, and his baby-sitter just took off. I'm going over there to help out."

Her parents exchanged a look, and Hope braced herself for the argument she saw coming.

Hope had always believed she'd been lucky in her

choice of parents. Not that babies had a choice, of course. But her mom and dad had always made her believe she could be and do and have anything she wanted, if she was willing to work hard enough for it. And they'd always been supportive of her decisions.

Except, of course, where Jake Whitelaw was concerned.

Her father believed Jake was too old and set in his ways for a young girl like herself to mold into a good husband. Her mother believed Jake was too taciturn and forbidding to be a good helpmate through life.

Faith said, "Mom, Dad, for what it's worth, I think Hope should go."

Hope shot her sister a look of thanks for the support. But it didn't silence her parents.

"Are you sure this is what you want to do?" her mother said.

"Do you even know if he'll welcome your help?" her father said. "Why don't you call him first?"

"Mom, Dad, I know you have my best interests at heart, but this is something I have to do." And she wasn't about to call Jake, because she was pretty sure he would rather rope a buffalo on foot than invite her to spend a week under his roof.

Her parents exchanged another look. Troubled. Worried.

Hope crossed and hugged her mother. "Please trust me to know what I'm doing."

"We don't want to see you hurt," her mother said.

She could see her father feared the same thing, though he would never say it. She leaned over and kissed his cheek. "Please, Daddy. I have to do this."

"You've been making your own decisions for a while," he said gruffly. "And you've done fine. Just be careful. You know we love you."

"I know, Daddy." She gave him another hug, aware of the scent of tobacco on his clothes, feeling the love he never failed to put into words.

She turned and followed Faith out the kitchen door.

Hope was silent during the drive to Jake's ranch, and she felt Faith's eyes on her, as concerned as her parents had been.

"I can wait while you check with Jake before I drive away," Faith said as they pulled up to Jake's kitchen door.

Hope hesitated. It would make a hasty retreat less embarrassing if Faith waited. But it would also make it easier for Jake to send her away. "No," Hope said. "Jake is too reasonable to turn down the help. Even if it means he has to cope with having me around."

"Are you sure you love him?" Faith asked. "Are you sure you aren't persisting because once you've made up your mind, you're too stubborn to change it?"

Hope was silent for a long time. "I've asked myself a million times why I haven't walked away. I know he's only one man and there are so many others out there." She turned and looked at Faith, seeing her own face looking back at her, except it wore a kinder, gentler expression than she'd ever seen in her own mirror.

"I don't understand why I love him," Hope said. "I only know that without Jake, a part of me is missing." She pressed a fist against her heart. "It hurts to imagine him with some other woman. It's agony to imagine spending my life without him."

Faith smiled. "Then go get him."

Hope managed to smile back, but her heart was beating hard with anxiety, and there was an ache in her throat as she watched her sister drive away. There was a mud porch in back, and she set her bag on the other side of a pair of boots that had been left at the kitchen door, then knocked loudly. She wished the weather had stayed warm, because then the back door would have been open and she could have yelled out and invited herself inside.

But the weather was frigid, so she stood there and waited for what seemed a very long time.

Jake opened the door holding a howling baby in his arms. A two-year-old boy, thumb in his mouth, had an arm wrapped around Jake's leg.

"Oh, my goodness," Hope said as she stepped hurriedly inside and closed the door behind her. "What's wrong with that baby?"

"How the hell—" He glanced down at the two-year-old, who clung to him as he backed away from the door, and amended, "How the heck do I know? I thought she was hungry, but she won't eat. I can't figure out what's wrong with her."

"Give her to me," Hope said. She put the wailing baby up over her shoulder, and she immediately stopped crying.

"I guess she wanted to be upright," Hope said.

"I already tried that once. It didn't work for me."

Hope didn't know what to say. She shrugged and smiled and said, "Maybe she wanted some female company."

Jake leaned down and picked up the little boy, who'd

been tugging hard on his jeans, before his narrowed eyes focused back on Hope. "What are you doing here anyway?" he demanded.

"I…" Should she admit she knew his housekeeper was gone? But what other reason could she have had for coming? "My sister is friends with Mrs. Hernandez's daughter. She heard you were here without any help. So, I thought—"

"No," Jake said.

Hope made a face. "You don't even know what I was going to say."

"I don't need your help. I'm managing fine."

Hope felt unaccountably hurt. "Fine. Here. Take the baby." She would walk home if she had to, even if she froze on the way.

Jake had the boy in one arm and had to put him down to take the baby. When he did, the boy began to cry, and when she placed the little girl in his arms, she started howling as well.

Hope heard him mutter something under his breath as she turned for the door.

"Wait," he said. "Come get this baby."

Hoped turned but stayed where she was. "If you want my help, you're going to have to ask for it. Nicely."

"Damn it—darn it, Hope," he snarled.

She stayed where she was, her arms crossed over her chest.

"Please, Hope, I need your help. Come get this baby," he muttered.

She quickly crossed to him and took the crying baby. She laid the little girl over her shoulder again and patted her back. Jake picked up the little boy, who stuck his thumb in his mouth and turned to stare at Hope with wide, tear-washed blue eyes.

"What are their names?" Hope asked, as she brushed at the little girl's soft baby curls.

"You're holding Becky. This young man is Huck," he said, wrapping his arms around the little boy.

The baby suddenly gave an enormous burp.

"My goodness gracious," Hope said, patting the baby's back. "I'll bet that feels better." Hope saw that the baby's cheek was smeared with what looked like strained peas, then noticed that Jake had a dollop of the same green goo on his temple.

"Did you by any chance feed her a bottle of milk?" Hope asked. "And then not burp her?"

"I gave her the bottle in between trying to get some green stuff in a jar down her throat," Jake said. "What's wrong with that?"

"Her stomach filled up with air. You have to throw her over your shoulder every once in a while and burp her."

"How was I supposed to know that?"

"You grew up in a big family. Didn't you ever have to take care of a baby?" Hope asked as she headed for the sink to find something with which to wash the baby's face.

"Colt was the only one of us who was adopted as an infant," Jake said. "And I had three sisters who fought over the chance to take care of him."

Hope found a roll of paper towels, dampened one and used it to clean Becky's face. She met Jake's gaze and said, "How old were you when you were adopted?"

Jake hesitated, then said, "Nine."

"What happened to your parents?"

He glanced down at Huck, who was staring up at him wide-eyed, and said, "This isn't the time for that."

"You're right," Hope said. "It's time to get these little ones to bed. Where are these two bunking down?"

"Upstairs," Jake said.

"Lead the way." Hope followed Jake, trying not to visibly stare at everything. But she was anxious to know more about him, and this was the first time she'd been past his kitchen door.

Jake strode ahead of her, turning on lights as he went. It was definitely a man's house, the furnishings spare but made of warm wood and leather. There were no curtains on the front windows, but what appeared to be his library had lacquered shutters blocking out the night. There was one bedroom downstairs with a sleigh bed, which she assumed had been occupied by Mrs. Hernandez. And which she hoped to occupy herself.

Jake led her upstairs and she followed, feeling the tension rise as they headed down the upstairs hallway.

"That's my bedroom," he said, gesturing with his chin at an open doorway at the top of the stairs.

Hope got a glimpse of a standard bed with an eight-foot Victorian headboard and a dark blue bedspread as she hurried to keep up with Jake.

He stopped at the end of the hall, shoved open a door and flipped on a light switch. "This is where the kids are staying. It's not as convenient for the housekeeper, but I can hear them if they wake up during the night."

The room was decorated as a nursery. Before Hope could ask, Jake volunteered the information, "My wife decorated it when we first got married...but the kids didn't come. Before long I had nieces and nephews, so I left it this way."

Hope looked at the charming room done in white and yellow and imagined how hard it must have been for Jake to come in here with his brothers' and sisters' children—but not his own. She wondered why he and his wife hadn't had children. She wanted to ask but glanced at Huck and realized this wasn't the time for that, either.

"Have Huck and Becky had a bath today?" Hope asked.

"Surely they can manage without a bath for one day," Jake said, setting Huck on the youth bed. He opened the top drawer of a nearby chest and started tossing clothes around.

"When did Mrs. Hernandez say she'd be back?" Hope asked.

Jake stopped what he was doing and stared at her. "She didn't say."

"How long did you plan for Huck and Becky to go without a bath?"

Jake pulled out a Batman sleeper and shoved the drawer closed. "They can manage without one tonight," he said. "I'll worry about tomorrow come daybreak."

"Are Becky's clothes in the same chest?" Hope asked.

"Second drawer," Jake said as he began stripping off Huck's coveralls and shirt.

"How did you end up with this baby-sitting job?" Hope asked. "I mean, if you have all these sisters who have so much more experience with babies?"

"I volunteered," Jake said.

When Hope raised an inquiring brow he said, "I figured it would be good practice."

Hope flushed when she realized he meant for the children he planned to have with Miss Carter. "Oh. I didn't realize you were planning a family so soon."

"I am. I mean I was," Jake muttered.

Hope smiled. "I suppose you changed your mind when you found out how much work a couple of kids can be."

"Nope. I've always wanted a big family. I'm not too experienced yet, but all it takes is practice," he said as he snapped Huck into his pajamas.

"I have a suggestion, before you get Huck all snapped into that thing," Hope said.

Jake looked at her. "I'm listening."

"You might want to make a visit to the bathroom before Huck goes down for the night. He can brush his teeth and...take care of business."

"Oh, yeah. Right. Come on, pal. Let's go." He set Huck on his feet and the little boy padded into the adjoining bathroom. It was dark enough that Jake needed to turn on the light.

"What happened to change your mind about having a large family?" Hope called out to him. "Did you decide you were too old?"

Jake leaned out the bathroom doorway and said through gritted teeth, "I am not too old."

"Then why—"

"Amanda told me last week she doesn't want kids right away." He disappeared back into the bathroom, but she heard him mutter, "But by the time she's ready, I may very well be an old man."

"I love kids," Hope said. "Considering the fact that twins run in my family, once I marry, I should have a large family in no time."

Jake leaned back out the doorway, a child's toothbrush in his hand and said, "I suppose you're going to say I should have married you if I wanted a family right away."

She grinned and shrugged. "It's a thought." A delicious, delightful thought. She wondered if Jake was considering it.

He disappeared into the bathroom again. She heard the water running in the sink, then heard the toilet flush. A moment later, Jake came out with Huck. The little boy had his arms around Jake's neck and was leaning his head on his shoulder. Jake's large hand was cupped around the child's head.

Hope couldn't help imagining it was their child who was being held so carefully, so protectively. It would be a shame if Jake never had children to fill this nursery. She wondered why Amanda didn't want children right away. As far as Hope was concerned, if she were married to the man she loved, the sooner she got pregnant, the better.

"I think this one's ready to hit the sack," Jake said. "How's Becky doing?"

"I found another reason why she might have been crying downstairs. This diaper is soaking wet."

"There's a box of disposables on that layette beside the crib," Jake said. He pulled down the covers and laid Huck in the youth bed, then pulled the covers up under his arms.

"Uncle Jake, read *Are You My Mother?*" Huck said.

"I can't even skip pages," Jake said to Hope as Huck scooted over to make room for him on the bed. "He has it memorized. Colt warned me the kid is insatiable when it comes to books."

"Children learn faster when you read to them," Hope said.

"I thought your degree was in business," Jake said.

"I've done a lot of baby-sitting," Hope replied. "The kids whose parents read to them learn to read themselves at a younger age. I certainly plan to read to my kids…when I have some…which I hope will be soon." Maybe that was laying it on a little too thick.

Jake ignored her and began reading aloud. Huck followed along, often saying the lines together with Jake and turning the pages.

Meanwhile, Hope changed the baby's diaper, washing Becky clean with a Wet-Wipe and generously powdering her before she taped on another diaper. She'd read once that blindfolded mothers could tell their own babies by their smell. She couldn't wait to test the theory on her own babies.

She found a green-and-yellow flowered flannel sack that tied at the bottom in the second drawer and changed Becky out of the cute corduroy overdress and trousers she was wearing into the warm nightgown. She sat in the rocker in the corner and held the baby snuggled against her, the rocker creaking, as she listened to the end of Huck's story.

"The end," Jake read at last.

"Read it again," Huck urged.

"Not tonight," Jake said. "Time for bed."

Huck started to whine, and Jake said, "You know the

drill. Brush teeth. Story. Bedtime. You need to get your sleep if you're going riding with me tomorrow."

"Okay, Uncle Jake," Huck said, quickly turning over. "Night night."

"Don't let the bedbugs bite," Jake replied, tucking the child in one last time. All of that was done with the sort of vigor she'd expected from a man dealing with a child.

Hope watched, her heart in her throat, as Jake gently tousled the boy's hair and then placed a tender kiss against his forehead. Her mother would never have called Jake forbidding if she'd seen what Hope had just seen.

Jake turned out the small light over the bed, which left only the lamp by the crib. He turned and saw her in the rocker with Becky. And stopped. And stared.

Hope wasn't sure what it was she saw in his eyes. It felt like hunger, but there was nothing sexual about it. Yearning, maybe. For his own child?

"She's asleep," he said quietly.

Hope glanced sideways and saw that Becky's eyes were indeed closed, the lashes a dark crescent against her perfect skin. Hope rose and laid the sleeping child carefully into the crib, covering her with a patchwork quilt.

She felt Jake's arm slide around her waist, and she leaned against him as they watched the shallow breaths in and out of the sleeping baby. Hope felt Jake's hand tighten at her waist and pull her close.

"Children are such a miracle," he said softly.

"Yes, they are."

Hope felt Jake's eyes on her and turned to meet his gaze. He was looking at her in a way he never had before. As an equal. As a prospective parent. She felt a swell of emotion as she realized he liked what he was seeing.

She felt his hand caress her cheek, a tender gesture of thanks. But the mere brush of his hand had caused her body to tense and coil in expectation. The sexual tension was there, as it always was between them. A palpable thing.

She felt Jake's hand grip her waist more tightly, felt him fighting the urge to respond to the heightened physical awareness she felt in his body. She was aware of the losing battle he waged with himself as his head slowly lowered toward hers.

She kept expecting him to find the control that was always there, the control that kept him from touching her the way she yearned to be touched. But whatever tether kept his emotions contained had broken at last, and she saw in his eyes what she'd never hoped to see. Love.

He gave in to his need as his lips caressed hers. A bare touch. A fleeting taste. A kiss of wonder and discovery. A kiss that dared to offer gentleness, while tightly leashed passion waited, barely restrained.

Hope's heart swelled with feeling, as she gave herself up to Jake's tenderness. She turned and felt his arms surround her like steel bands, holding her tight, as though he never wanted to let her go.

He deepened the kiss, and she felt herself going under, drowning in emotions that were too powerful to be controlled.

She could feel his need. Feel his vulnerability. He wanted more than sex. He wanted someone to share his joys and sorrows. He wanted a mother for his children. He wanted a life partner.

She felt his hands on her breasts, both reverent and needy. Heard his breathing change, felt his pulse leap as his hands lowered to her hips and pulled them close. She could feel his physical need, the urgent desire to join their bodies that had been there from the first and would never, ever die.

Hope suddenly realized the power she held. The power to hurt Jake, and to hurt him badly. She had never loved him more than she did at this moment. It filled her heart to overflowing. And gave her the strength to stop him before they went too far.

"Jake, no," she said against his lips. "Not this way."

She felt his muscles become rigid as he fought for control. He released her abruptly and took a step back. And stared down into her eyes, confused. He'd given himself up to passion. Given himself over to her as she'd always hoped he would. And she had stopped him.

A painful knot in her throat made explanation impossible. She looked up at him with all the love she felt, hoping he would understand why she'd backed away. She barely understood herself.

She only knew she couldn't seduce Jake. Not like this. She couldn't rob him of his freedom by letting him take her virginity. She wanted him to marry her because he loved her. Not because he had no other choice.

Hope stepped back and looked first at the sleeping baby, then toward the youth bed where Huck was fast asleep. "I guess you don't need me anymore tonight."

She was going to leave. She was going home, and she wasn't coming back.

She'd already turned away when Jake caught her wrist. "Wait. Don't leave."

She met his gaze and said, "This is dangerous, Jake. I need to go."

"I want you to stay."

She shook her head. "That isn't a good idea."

"Please. I need help with these two." He smiled and glanced from Becky to Huck.

"You've got sisters—"

"I want you to stay," he repeated. "We'll be fine, Hope. This won't happen again."

She knew that he meant his words. That the leash was strongly knotted again and there was no chance he would lose control a second time. He wouldn't let her see again that he loved her. And he wouldn't touch her.

It would be torture to stay here under those circumstances. But he'd asked for her help. And it was the least she could do.

"All right," she said. "I'll stay. When are Colt and Jenny returning?"

"Friday," Jake said. "The day before the wedding."

Hope swallowed past the painful knot that refused to go away. "Till Friday, then."

"Thanks. You can have the downstairs bedroom."

"Fine."

"Do you need a toothbrush or some pajamas?" he asked.

She was ashamed to admit that she had an overnight bag on the porch, that she'd planned to spend the week with him. So she said, "Yes, if you have extra."

He turned out the light over Becky's crib and said, "Let's go."

She felt his hand on the small of her back, urging her from the bedroom, and did a little hop-step to move ahead of him. She didn't want him touching her. Not ever again.

CHAPTER SIX

AN HOUR AFTER HE'D SAID GOOD-NIGHT to Hope, Jake pulled some jeans over his long underwear and crept down the stairs, avoiding the spots he knew were sure to creak. He crept into the living room, which was lit only by the banked coals in the fireplace. He quietly stirred the ashes and added a log, watching the fire come to life.

Then he slouched in one of the big leather chairs in front of the fireplace, laid his head back and crossed his ankle over his knee. He wanted a drink, but he wasn't about to turn on a light. Hope was sleeping down the hall.

He wasn't sure what madness had caused him to ask Hope to stay the week. He'd come close to doing something irrevocable tonight. He'd surrendered, given in to the urge to touch, to taste, to hold her in his arms. He had no idea why Hope had put on the brakes. But he was grateful she had. God help him, he was getting married in a week to another woman.

But his troubling thoughts were all about Hope.

He'd spent long hours over the past three years wondering if he ever could have made a marriage to Hope work. Wondering what would have happened if he hadn't gotten himself engaged so quickly to Amanda. He'd convinced himself his fascination with Hope Butler would eventually fade. He'd often reminded himself of the pain he'd endured when his first wife had run off, remembering the note she'd left him telling how unhappy she'd become.

He couldn't bear to go through anything like that again.

So he'd told himself he would get over Hope. And just as important, that Hope would get over him. But the truth was, the attraction was still there on his side, stronger than ever. And if last night was any indication, Hope still wanted him. So why had she pulled away?

He heard the floor moan and realized Hope must be up. He remained still, knowing that he wouldn't be visible if she was only on her way to the kitchen or the bathroom. A moment later she stood beside the empty leather chair across from him.

"Oh," she said, her eyes wide. "I didn't know you were here."

He sat up straight. "Couldn't sleep," he said brusquely.

"Me, neither," she said.

She was wearing the long johns he'd loaned her. They should have made her look shapeless, but she'd left the buttons at the neck undone, and he could see a hint of cleavage. And because they were white, he could see the shadow of her areolas. His body was responding to her even as his mind fought temptation.

"Mind if I join you?" she said.

He could send her back to bed, but he doubted either

one of them would sleep. Why not sit and talk? "Have a seat," he said, gesturing to the chair beside him.

She grabbed the fringed green wool blanket that lay over the back of the chair and wrapped herself in it as she sat cross-legged. He didn't know whether to feel grateful or regretful that she was so completely covered.

He slouched down in his chair and put his ankle back up on his knee and listened to the fire crackle, waiting for her to speak. To his surprise, she didn't fill the silence. He heard her shifting in the chair, seeking a more cozy position. When he glanced at her, she was staring into the fire, the blanket pulled up to cover half her face.

He wasn't sure how long they sat together in silence. He only knew it felt comfortable to be with her. Which was surprising, since he was completely aware of her physically. That is, aware of desiring her. Of wanting to pick her up in his arms and hold her. Of wanting to lay her down in front of the fireplace and put himself inside her.

"What was it like, being adopted?" she asked.

The question surprised him into answering more frankly than he might have wished. "Terrifying."

The blanket dropped from her face and she turned in the chair so she was facing him. "How so?"

He realized he couldn't leave that single word hanging, so he said, "I was in a lot of foster homes before the Whitelaws found me."

"Were your foster parents mean to you?"

He snorted. "Mean? That word's too simple to describe— You don't really want to hear this," he said.

"So you thought the Whitelaws might be mean, too," she said, ignoring his attempt to end the discussion.

"I counted on it," he shot back. "So I was as nasty to them as I expected them to be in return."

"But the Whitelaws weren't like all the others," she concluded.

"No," he said softly. "They weren't."

He thought of how he'd mistrusted their kindness, fought their attempts at affection, broken their rules, defied them at every turn. And how Zach and Rebecca Whitelaw had remained committed to loving him. He'd flinched every time one of them came near him, expecting a blow that never came. He'd stared at them from narrowed eyes when they offered love instead of contempt or condemnation.

He was the fifth child they'd adopted, and he didn't understand why Zach and Rebecca wanted him when they already had Jewel and Rolleen and Avery and Frannie. He'd expected the other four kids to resent him, to want him gone. It had happened before, in foster homes where the children of his foster parents had made it clear he was there on sufferance, and that he didn't belong and never would.

It hadn't been that way in the Whitelaw household. Zach and Rebecca had treated him like all the others. And the others had treated him like a real brother.

It had taken a year for him to feel like he was one of them, a year before he had finally wanted to call Zach "Dad" and Rebecca "Mom." He could remember how hard it had been the first time to get the words out. The lump in his throat had hurt, and he'd swallowed to try to get rid of it, before he'd said the words on Christmas morning. His gift to them.

"Merry Christmas, Mom," he'd said to Rebecca. And then to Zach, "Merry Christmas, Dad."

Rebecca had teared up right away, and she'd hugged him hard. He'd blinked a couple thousand times to keep his own tears at bay, and gritted his teeth to keep his chin from wobbling. He hadn't wanted them to see what a mess he was.

At last he'd had to face Zach. His own eyes had rounded in wonder, because Zach's eyes were also brimmed with tears. Zach had held out his arms and Jake had slammed into him, holding him tight around the waist, as though this strong but gentle man was his only anchor in a raging storm.

"What happened to your biological parents?" Hope asked.

The question jolted Jake from his reverie, and he realized his chest felt tight and his throat was raw with emotion. "They died," he said curtly.

"How?"

He should have known Hope wouldn't leave it alone. He never talked about what had happened. He wasn't sure why he was tempted to tell her. Suddenly, the bitter words started coming, and he couldn't seem to stop them. "My father shot my mother and then killed himself. She was getting a divorce, and he didn't want her to leave him. I was six. I found them when I came home from school."

"Oh, my God," she said. "How awful!" An instant later she was on her knees in front of him, the blanket abandoned. She shoved his ankle off his knee and crouched between his legs, her hands on his thighs, her eyes on his, full of horror and sympathy.

Her look of pain brought back the horrendous memories, and he reached out to her, seeking the compassion she offered.

He set his hands under her arms and drew her up and into his lap. She curled up against him, her cheek against his chest, his chin atop her head, her softness and warmth a much-needed balm for the cold inside him. He held her tight, not wanting to let her go, not wanting to let go of the comfort she offered.

For a long time, comfort was all he felt. Inevitably, he became aware of her soft, rounded breasts against his chest. The feel of her curved fanny cupped in his palm. The silky softness and the flowery smell of her hair. And her moist, warm breath against his throat. His arousal grew, and he knew she must be aware of it, sitting on his lap like she was.

He knew for sure when she tipped her head up and her eyes sought his in the light from the fire. Her pupils were dilated, her mouth was open slightly and she was breathing in short pants. Her lips seemed swollen, even though he hadn't kissed her yet.

That was easy to remedy. He lowered his mouth and pressed his lips gently against hers, feeling the softness, the willingness to give, the yearning. He kissed the sides of her mouth, her cheeks, her temple, and finally her closed eyelids. Then he captured her mouth with his. And found the solace it seemed he'd been seeking all his life.

He kissed her lingeringly, letting his tongue dip into the sweetness of her mouth, savoring the taste of her, enjoying the textures, feeling the tumult within him build. His hand cupped her breast, and he felt the nipple peak beneath his palm. He slid his hand down under her shirt, seeking the warm flesh at her waist, then slid it up to cup her naked breast.

He lifted his head when he heard her gasp and stared into her stunned eyes. "Are you all right?"

"Nobody's ever touched me like that," she said. "I never knew—"

"Sonofabitch," he muttered under his breath.

He shoved her off his lap, holding on to her as he rose himself, so she wouldn't tumble onto the floor. He could clearly see her peaked nipples through the soft cotton and felt his body harden, when he'd thought he was already as hard as he could get. Her eyes looked dazed and confused.

He gripped her hands tightly and said, "We can't do this, Hope. I'm sorry."

Her feelings were transparent, but she said the words anyway. "I love you, Jake."

"That's the hell of it," he said. His throat felt raw again. "I don't want to hurt you, Hope. I think maybe you should go home. We can call your dad—"

"No," she said, shaking her head. She pulled her hands free and took a step back. "I was offering comfort, Jake. Things just got—" She shoved a hand through her tousled hair. "Got a little out of control."

Jake snorted. "Any more out of control and you'd be lying on the floor and I'd be inside you."

He saw the flush rise on her cheeks, and she lowered her eyes. "I wouldn't have minded…or blamed you."

"That's precisely the point," Jake said irritably. "I'm

more attracted to you than I want to be, Hope. It isn't safe for you here."

She looked up at him, her heart in her eyes. "I know I can trust you not to do anything I wouldn't want."

His lips twisted ruefully. "That's precisely the problem. I can't trust you to stop me. And left to my own inclination, I wouldn't stop."

"It's not too late for us," Hope said. "You could talk to Miss Carter—"

"Don't even think about it," Jake snapped. "It isn't going to happen." He rubbed his eyes with his palms. "God, Hope. Why don't you just give up and go home?"

Her shoulders slumped and her chin dropped to her chest. When she looked up at him, the light was gone from her eyes. He thought she was going to leave, and he felt an ache inside. He steeled himself for what she had to say. But she surprised him.

"I think I should stay and help with Huck and Becky," she said. "Otherwise, you're not going to be able to get everything done that needs to get done…before the wedding. I promise I won't allow myself—or you—to be tempted into anything like what just happened."

He frowned. He ought to call her father and have him come right over and take Hope home, where she was safe from him. It wasn't like he couldn't get help with Colt's kids from one of his siblings.

But Hope was already here. And willing. And she'd promised to help him keep his distance.

On the other hand, it would only take one lapse for something irrevocable to happen.

"I'm not so sure this is a good idea," he said.

"We'll be fine, Jake," she said.

"I'm going out with Amanda tomorrow night." Hope might as well know that up front. "Are you sure you still want to stay and baby-sit?"

She swallowed hard. "You have a date? With your fiancée?"

"I've been busy the past couple of weeks. We haven't had much time alone, so we made plans to get together this weekend."

"Would you rather be here by yourselves?" Hope asked.

Jake chuckled. "With Huck and Becky around, we'd hardly be alone. And we need time to talk. What do you say?"

"No problem," Hope said as she backed away. "I'd better get to bed. Tomorrow's bound to be a busy day."

Once she was gone, Jake slumped back into the leather chair and stared at the last embers of the fire. He felt sick at heart. He tried to remember whether there had ever been a time when Amanda had made him feel like he'd felt tonight with Hope.

The truth was, Amanda had kept him at arm's length physically. The rest of the truth was, he hadn't minded.

He tried to imagine how he would have felt if Hope had rejected his overtures or been indifferent to his kisses.

Devastated. Crushed. Miserably unhappy.

He was a fool, that's all there was to it. Why was he marrying Amanda Carter when he felt what he felt—and he still wasn't putting a name to it—for Hope Butler?

Another worrisome thought occurred to him. Something he'd shoved out of his mind ever since his conversation with Amanda.

I don't want kids right away.

He was thirty-nine. He would be forty before his first child was born even if his wife conceived on their wedding night. And Amanda wanted to wait "a few years." Till he was forty-four? Forty-five? What if, when they finally started trying for a child, she didn't get pregnant right away? He might be fifty before his first child was born.

The thought made him unutterably sad. He was jealous of his brothers and sisters who had children to raise and love. He didn't even have to have children of his own blood. He would be willing to adopt. But Amanda didn't want the immediate responsibility of children.

He thought of what Hope had said. She loved children, and she would be happy to have one right away. She'd been surprisingly good with Huck and Becky and seemed not at all daunted by the prospect of having a bunch of kids around.

Jake pressed his hands together and pursed his lips. What should he do? The answer to his dilemma seemed so simple. He should break off his engagement to Amanda and marry Hope.

But he knew what it felt like to be thrown aside when you were no longer useful. He couldn't do that to Amanda and live with himself afterward. The guilt and shame would taint any future relationship with Hope.

Jake dragged himself out of the chair and headed for the stairs. He was going to have to get his head on straight before the next week was over. He was going to have to dedicate himself to making a happy life for himself and for Amanda. Maybe once she saw he was

willing to help with any children they had, she would
be more willing to bear them sooner. Maybe once they
were living together as husband and wife, she would be
more comfortable with the sexual aspect of their relationship.

Jake firmly believed that life was what you made of
it. He'd created the situation he was in. He had no choice
now except to make the best of it.

HOPE TRIED NOT TO CRY, BUT THE TEARS came anyway.
What a fool she was! She should have been more careful
around Jake. She'd only wanted to offer comfort, and
look what had happened. The kissing had been wonderful. The touching…had been exquisite. But she was so
inexperienced, she'd uttered that gasp of pleasure.

Jake had realized what he was doing. And he'd
stopped.

She couldn't honestly say she'd wanted to lose her
virginity on a cowhide in front of the fire. But she
wouldn't have been sorry if she had. That damned honor
of his. It wasn't fair to tease her with the possibility of
loving her and then back off when things got too hot.

Tears of frustration gave way to tears of anger. Damn
Jake Whitelaw! He should have known better. He
shouldn't have given in to temptation, especially when
he didn't intend to follow through to the finish.

Hope should have accepted his offer to call her father
to come pick her up. She should have left Jake high and
dry with Huck and Becky. Let him have his date with
Miss Carter and take the two kids along. At least then
Hope would know he wouldn't be doing with Miss
Carter what he'd done with her.

The thought was too painful to contemplate.

Hope didn't sleep well, and she awoke at the crack of dawn feeling cranky and out of sorts. She headed for the kitchen to make herself a cup of coffee, figuring it might put her in a better mood before she showered and dressed.

She found Jake there ahead of her.

His hair was still wet from the shower and a single dark curl fell over his forehead. He was leaning back against the sink, a cup of coffee in hand, wearing a crisply ironed shirt and worn Levi's. He looked like an ad for the Marlboro Man.

Hope felt like a frump. Her hair was a rat's nest, her mascara was clumped around her eyes, and she was barefoot and still wearing Jake's oversize long johns.

"Oh, God," she said. "I just wanted a cup of coffee before I started the day."

"I wouldn't be here, except I didn't think it was fair to take off without giving you another chance to leave."

She shook her head. "Give me some coffee and I'll be fine."

Jake set down his cup and poured her a cup of coffee from the coffeemaker. "Cream or sugar?"

"Both," she said.

He complied and held the cup out to her. "Here you go."

She had to take four steps to get close enough to take it from him. She flinched when their fingers touched and some of the coffee sloshed onto his hand. "I'm so sorry."

He grabbed a dish towel to wipe his hand and said, "It's nothing."

But she could see from the tightness around his

mouth that she'd burned him. She set her cup down and reached for his hand, where a red blotch had appeared. "You need to put ice on that."

"It's nothing," he said again.

She'd already gone to the freezer and retrieved some ice. She returned and gently laid a cube on his hand. "I know it's cold," she said, "but it'll stop the burn." She moved the cube over the burn while the ice melted, dripping over both their hands. At last, she threw the remaining ice in the sink and reached for the dish towel to dab his hand dry.

She'd been so focused on his hand that she hadn't once looked up at Jake. When she did, she found his eyes focused on her, his mouth grim. She wondered what she'd done wrong, and was preparing to defend her behavior, when he bent and kissed her softly on the mouth.

He stood again before she could react or respond. She touched her lips and stared at him, waiting for some sort of explanation.

"Thanks," he said.

A moment later he was out the door.

Hope stared after him, confused by his behavior, until she realized it had probably been a very long time since anyone had ministered to Jake Whitelaw.

She wasn't left with much time to ruminate, because she heard the baby crying upstairs and Huck's yell to announce that Becky was awake.

Hope hurried upstairs. She had no time to pause and think, but she'd long ago planned what she would do if she ever had the chance to impress Jake with her abilities as a housewife.

She was feeding the kids breakfast when the phone rang. She was almost certain it was Faith, checking to see how she'd fared. She answered the phone with, "Better than you'd imagine."

"What?"

Hope realized immediately the female voice wasn't Faith's. "Excuse me. Whitelaw residence, may I help you?"

"Who is this?"

"Hope Butler. Who is this?"

The silence lasted so long, Hope wondered if the other party had hung up, but there was no dial tone, so she hung on. At last the female voice said, "This is Amanda Carter. I was hoping to catch Jake before he took off for the day."

"I'm sorry, Miss Carter, he's already left."

There was another hesitation before Miss Carter said, "May I ask what you're doing there, Hope?"

"Jake's housekeeper had an emergency. I'm baby-sitting Huck and Becky."

"Oh. Well. Would you tell Jake he can pick me up at seven?"

"Certainly."

"Thanks." Another hesitation, then, "Have a nice day."

"You, too, Miss Carter."

Hope set the phone gently in the cradle. She hoped she hadn't sounded as jealous on the phone as she'd felt. She'd barely set the phone down when it rang again.

"Whitelaw residence, Hope speaking."

"That sounds formal," Faith said.

"Oh, thank God it's you. I thought it was you when

I answered the first call, but it was Miss Carter. I don't know what she must have thought."

"How's it going?" Faith asked.

"I'm glad I came," Hope said. "Although I'm not sure it's going to do much good."

"Hang in there. You've got a week to go."

"He's going out tonight with Miss Carter."

"Really? Do you know where they're planning to go?"

"I have no idea."

"Hmm," Faith said.

At that moment Becky flicked a spoonful of baby cereal at Huck, who yelled and swiped at his face.

"I've got to go," Hope said. "I'll talk to you when the kids are down for their afternoon nap."

Long before it was time to put Becky down for her nap, it was apparent she was sick. The baby had developed a fever of 102 degrees, and she kept grabbing at her right ear. "Poor baby," Hope crooned, as she paced with the baby in her arms.

"Becky's cwying," Huck said.

"I know," Hope said. "It looks like she has an earache."

Huck nodded. "Uh-huh. Becky gets an eawache all the time."

Hope stopped abruptly and stared at the little boy. "All the time? Did your mom and dad leave some medicine?"

Huck shook his head. "We go to the 'Mergency Woom."

"The Emergency Room?" Hope said, alarmed at the

possibility that what was wrong with Becky might be life threatening. Surely it was just an earache.

"Uh-huh," Huck said, nodding. "'Cause when Becky's sick she might die."

The little boy said it matter-of-factly, but Hope's heart had already started to pound. She didn't want to panic and take Becky to the hospital if the baby had a malady that could be treated with eardrops. But Huck spoke as though Becky had been to the Emergency Room more than once.

If she could get hold of Jake, she could ask what to do. She called his cell phone number but got his voice mail message. Hope couldn't wait for him to get home. She didn't dare take the chance that something was wrong with Becky that might require a doctor's immediate attention.

She debated whether to leave a message, then said, "This is Hope. I'm taking Becky to the Emergency Room. I'll call again when I know what's wrong."

Hope took a deep breath and let it out, then picked up the phone and dialed 911.

CHAPTER SEVEN

ORDINARILY, JAKE WOULD HAVE WORKED from sunrise till sundown. Between the quarter horses and the cattle, there was a never-ending list of jobs that needed to be done. But today he felt antsy and out of sorts. He had unfinished business with Hope. It wasn't even noon, and he was already making mental excuses for why he ought to leave the men with some chores to do and head back to the house.

Jake had a dozen cowhands on the payroll at any given time, but he served as his own foreman, preferring the work outdoors to the administrative side of the ranching business. He left that to his brother Avery. At least, he had in the past. He couldn't help wondering what it would be like to have Hope help him out.

He saw her sitting in the big leather chair in front of his desk in a skimpy nightgown. Envisioned himself massaging her tired neck. Imagined his hands in her hair. Contemplated kissing her throat, while his hands—

"Boss, you okay?"

Jake tightened the reins at the intrusion of the voice into his daydream, and his well-trained horse backed up in response. He instantly released the pressure on the reins and his horse stopped. He patted the animal's neck, crooning his approval for its instant response, while he inwardly chastised himself for his inattention.

"What is it, Harry?" Jake said, letting the cowhand feel his irritation for the interruption.

"You said you wanted to know when that fence was mended. Me and Charlie are finished," the cowboy said.

Jake made an instant decision. "I've got some business back at the homestead. Tell the boys I want those cattle moved up into the north pasture this afternoon. Then you can take off."

"Consider it done, Boss."

Jake had already spurred his mount, heading back to where he'd left his truck and the horse trailer. It didn't take long to load his horse and head for home.

When he stepped inside the kitchen door, he was surprised to find the house quiet, until he realized it was nap time for Huck and Becky. He frowned when he saw the cereal bowls on the table. If breakfast was still on the table, what had Hope fed the kids for lunch? He headed up the stairs quietly, not wanting to wake Huck and Becky if they were sleeping.

The kids' beds were both unmade and empty. He turned and hurried back downstairs yelling, "Hey, there. Anybody home?"

When there was no answer, Jake felt a niggling of concern, but he wasn't yet worried. Maybe Hope had taken the kids on an afternoon picnic. Without a car, she couldn't have gone far. He was passing back through the kitchen when he spied a scribbled note stuck on the refrigerator.

Jake,
Called 911. An ambulance is taking us to the
hospital. Left a message on your cell phone. Will
call again when I can.

Hope

Jake felt his heart take an extra beat. Hope had
penned a message, so she was at least well enough for
that, but which of the three was hurt? And how serious
was it? He never should have left someone so young and
inexperienced with his brother's children. What had
happened? Were the kids okay?

Jake reached for the cell phone he usually carried on
his belt to retrieve Hope's message and realized he'd left
it in his truck when he'd been on horseback. He raced
out to his truck and grabbed the phone from the dash.
There were five messages, four from a number he didn't
recognize. He figured it had to be the E.R.

Jake's heart slammed against his chest. Four
messages. It must be serious. But if so, why hadn't
someone—one of his siblings—come to find him? He
jumped into his pickup and gunned the engine, aiming
his truck toward town, even as he punched the buttons
to recall the number that had been left on his phone.

"Emergency Room, please hold."

"Wait a goddamn—" But Jake had already been put
on hold. It seemed to take forever for a voice to come
back on the line.

"Emergency Room, may I help you?"

"This is Jake Whitelaw, I—"

"Oh, we've been trying to reach you."

"Not very damned hard," Jake snapped back. "What's the problem? Who's sick?"

"Hold just a moment and I'll get Miss Butler."

"I don't want to hold—" But Jake had already been put on hold. At least Hope was all right. But that meant one of the kids was sick or hurt.

"Jake?"

He heard the anxiety in Hope's voice and felt his chest tighten. "What's going on, Hope?" he said, his voice harsh in his ears.

"It's Becky, she's—"

"I never should have left you alone with her! What the hell happened?"

Jake heard silence on the other end of the phone. Hurt silence. "Well?" he demanded.

Hope's voice was measured. "Becky has an ear infection. Her fever was high and Huck said your brother usually brings her to the Emergency Room. I didn't want to take the chance it might be something serious. So I called 911. They've given her an antibiotic and she's doing fine. We've been waiting for you to come pick us up."

"Oh." Jake felt an enormous sense of relief. And then guilt, for having unjustly accused Hope. "You did the right thing," he said.

"I'm glad you think so," she said, her words clipped. "I'll wait here with the children until you arrive. Since you won't be needing me anymore, I'll call Faith to come pick me up."

Jake gritted his teeth. "I didn't say that," he muttered. He was going to be in big trouble during the next week without Hope's help. "I'm sorry I blamed you before I heard the facts."

"Yes, well, it's plain you don't think—"

"Damn it, Hope, stay where you are and don't call your sister. We'll talk when I get there." He hung up, feeling at a disadvantage arguing over the phone.

When he charged through the hospital Emergency Room doors, he found Hope sitting in a plastic chair with Becky in her arms and Huck curled up in the chair beside her, using her thigh as a pillow. He felt a swell of emotion, imagining the peacefully sleeping children were his. And the woman as well.

He eased into the empty chair next to her. He said nothing for several moments, searching for the right words. He owed her an apology. But he wasn't used to being wrong. Or admitting it.

"How are you?" he said at last.

She kept her eyes on Becky as she replied, "Fine."

He reached out and brushed a blond, sweat-damp curl away from Becky's face. He swallowed over the knot in his throat, then said, "I'm sorry, Hope."

She faced him at last, and he felt his gut clench when he saw the wounded look in her dark eyes.

"I think I should go home," she said. "I think you should get one of your brothers or sisters to—"

He put his fingertips to her lips. "I'm sorry. You did the right thing. I was scared. I spoke without thinking."

"I was scared, too," Hope said, her voice quiet but intense. "That's why I came here. I got worried when you didn't call back." She looked into his eyes and whispered, "That something might have happened to you, too."

"I used my cell in the truck and when one of the men called me out in a hurry, I dropped it there. I didn't know there was a problem until I got back to the house and you were gone."

She laid a hand on his arm. "You must have been worried sick. No wonder you yelled at me."

"I should have had more faith in you," he countered. "I should have waited to hear your side of what happened."

She promptly said, "Yes, you should have."

He found himself smiling with chagrin, and when she grinned at him, he laughed softly. "So you'll stay the rest of the week?"

Her smile faded. "I'm still not sure that's such a good idea."

"At least stay for tonight. I've got that date with Amanda and no baby-sitter."

"Amanda could come over to your house," Hope suggested. "Then you wouldn't need a baby-sitter."

Jake frowned. He hadn't even considered that option because he knew Amanda's attitude toward kids. Besides, he planned to have a serious discussion with his fiancée, and he didn't want to be interrupted, which was always a possibility with kids around.

"I'd rather not," he said. "Please. Come home with me."

She made a face, wrinkling her nose. "I'd rather—"

He didn't give her a chance to finish, simply rose and reached for the sleeping boy and slipped him up over his shoulder. "We should get these kids home to bed."

She looked up at him, opened her mouth to speak,

closed it again, then rose with the little girl in her arms. "All right. I'll stay tonight."

"After you," he said, gesturing toward the door. He didn't have baby car seats in his truck, and he ended up laying Huck on the back seat of the extended-cab pickup. He was surprised when Hope got into the back seat with Becky.

"It's safer back here if I'm going to hold her," she said.

He didn't argue, simply closed the doors and got in himself. They made the trip home in silence, although he caught Hope glancing at him once or twice when he checked on her in the rearview mirror.

He waited until they'd laid both kids down in their beds and closed the bedroom door behind them before he put a hand to the small of Hope's back. "We have to talk," he said.

She hesitated, then hurried ahead of him down the stairs to the kitchen. Once there, she began cleaning up the breakfast dishes.

"I'd like to talk," he said.

"I'm listening," she replied.

He took a cereal bowl out of her hand and laid it in the sink, then turned her around to face him, holding her by the shoulders. "I want your full attention."

She crossed her arms and stared up at him, her chin out thrust. "So talk."

"I've been thinking—"

At that moment, Becky let out a wail.

"Becky's awake," Hope said.

Jake swore under his breath. He hadn't realized, until Becky woke and it was impossible to speak, exactly what it was he'd been wanting to say to Hope. *I've been thinking about the two of us together and I think... maybe...I feel things for you that I never thought...*

She hurried out of the kitchen and up the stairs. He stared after her, grateful to the wailing child. He had no right to say those things to Hope until he'd ended his relationship with Amanda.

He looked around the kitchen, then began to clean up the mess. He didn't actually hear Hope return. It was more like he felt her presence. Yet, he was still surprised when he turned and found her leaning against the doorway, her arms and legs crossed, staring at him. "How long have you been there?" he asked.

She smiled and said, "Long enough to see you know your way around a kitchen."

"Being single can do that for you." He waited for her to cross into the room, but she stayed where she was. "Becky okay?"

"Her fever's gone," Hope said. "She was thirsty. I gave her a bottle of water and she went back to sleep."

"Did you have lunch?" he asked.

"I thought I'd wait until the kids are up and make something for all of us."

Jake emptied the water in the sink, rinsed it out, then wiped his hands on a dish towel as he turned to face her. "I think you and I need to talk."

She raised a brow. "Oh?"

Jake knew that he couldn't wait until his seven-o'clock date with Amanda before sharing his thoughts with Hope. He was a decisive man. When his mind was made up, he acted. He didn't want to wait to tell Hope what he was thinking. And feeling.

"I've been thinking about the two of us."

"Oh?" she said again, warily this time.

"Maybe I should say I've been rethinking some of the opinions I had about whether we could possibly make it as a couple."

She stood up, her indolent posture gone, her dark gaze intent on him. "And what have you decided?"

He ticked off the points he had to make, using his fingers to count them, doing it logically, the way he'd thought it all out. "First, you like and want kids—as I do—and you're young enough to have them. Second, we'd be good in bed together."

He waited for her to comment, but when she said nothing, he continued. "Third, since you've been a rancher's daughter, you understand what it means to be a rancher's wife. Fourth, you haven't changed your mind in the past three years, which suggests you're serious about wanting to marry me."

"Loving you," she corrected in a soft voice. "I haven't changed my mind about loving you. However, after that recitation, I'm not so sure I'm still interested in marrying you."

He frowned. "What the hell have I said wrong?"

"You've listed all my qualifications as a wife—all the ways I can accommodate your needs. What about what I need? What about what I want from you?"

Jake made a disgusted sound in his throat. "How the hell do I know what you want? Or need?"

"Love, for a start. I want to be loved. Do you love me, Jake?"

"What does love have to do with anything? I want

you. I'm willing to take care of you and have children with you. Isn't that enough?"

She shook her head. "No. It's not."

"I'm not going to fall in love with you, Hope. I don't think I can," he said in a harsh voice. He wasn't going to expose himself to that kind of hurt again. Especially not with someone as young—and potentially flighty—as a twenty-one-year-old girl. "But I want you. I haven't stopped wanting you since the day you cornered me in your father's barn."

He watched her eyes widen, and her mouth opened slightly as her breathing became less steady.

"That's not enough," she said. "Not nearly enough."

Her rejection stung. Especially after he'd made himself vulnerable, admitting he wanted her. Why had she pursued him so long and so hard, if she didn't want him? His eyes narrowed. "So this has all been a game? See if you can get Jake Whitelaw to kowtow, then blow him off?"

"It's nothing like that," she protested. "I told you what I want."

"To get me on my knees," he shot back. "Total surrender."

"Is that what you think love is? Capitulation? Defeat?" she cried. "I can't believe I've wasted all these years loving you, wanting you—"

"So you admit it," he snarled. "You do want me." He was across the room and seized her in his embrace before she had time to form a reply. Then, because he was afraid she would try to deny what she'd admitted, his mouth came down to capture hers, demanding the response he wanted.

She turned to liquid fire in his arms, her mouth hot and wet, as he shoved her body up hard against the male part of him that had turned to rock at the mere thought of her softness.

He squeezed her jaw, forcing her mouth open for the intrusion of his tongue. He felt his breath catch at the honey he found inside. She was sweet and soft.

And suddenly eager.

Her hands clutched his hair and she opened her mouth wide. Her tongue dueled with his, demanding equal pleasure. Her hips pressed against his and he felt the heat of her. His pulse raced, his heart pounding in his chest, the sound of it deafening in his ears.

His hands slid up from her waist and cupped her breasts, feeling the soft weight of them in his palms. His gut tightened at her guttural moan. Her head fell back and he saw her eyes were closed, her brow furrowed, her mouth open and panting, her features revealing a rapture that made him burn.

He ripped at her shirt, popping buttons as he yanked it free of her jeans, impatient to see her, to touch her naked flesh. He recognized the bra she wore. He'd seen it before. Or one very like it. Pure white, with small cups that revealed all of her breasts except the nipples. He only needed thumb and forefinger to release the catch and then shoved the scrap of cloth out of his way.

His mouth latched on to her nipple and he suckled strongly, feeling his body thrum and pulse as she writhed in his arms, her hands unsure, her body alive with feeling, her moan of desire and pain and wonder making his heart pound with excitement.

"I can't…I don't…" She gasped.

She grabbed him by the hair and pulled his mouth away. Her dark eyes were dazed, glazed, and she struggled for breath. "I want to touch you," she rasped as she yanked at the buttons on his shirt.

He let her go and ripped it off himself, buttons pinging onto the counter, then stripped his long johns off, leaving his chest bare to her gaze.

She looked at him as if he was candy, and she was a starving kid.

"Hope," he grated in a voice he didn't recognize as his own. "I—"

She didn't give him a chance to say more. She simply slid her fingers through the pelt of dark curls on his chest, then nestled her cheek against him, fitting her hips into the cradle of his own.

He felt his body harden, felt his pulse speed so his heart felt like it might pound its way out of his chest.

She looked up at him, an impish smile on her face, then reached down and began to unbuckle his belt. "I've wanted to do this for a very long time."

He stood still, afraid to move, afraid to breathe, as she unsnapped his jeans. He heard the rasp as his zipper came down. Then groaned aloud as her hand slid down the front of his briefs to cup him. It had been too long since he'd had a woman. Three years, to be exact. And if she kept touching him like she was, he'd spill himself like a schoolboy.

"Don't!" he said. He had no idea how harsh his voice sounded until he saw the hurt look on her face.

"You don't want—"

"Woman," he exclaimed with a laugh, "I want it too much!"

He saw the relief on her face, and then the return of a mischievous smile as her hand cupped him from the outside of his jeans. "I want it, too," she teased.

She shrieked with surprise when he picked her up, but he was already halfway to her bedroom by then. He threw her on the unmade bed and turned to close and lock the door. Then he yanked off his boots and shoved down his jeans and briefs. When he looked at her, she was staring at him—at one particular part of him—her eyes wide with astonishment and... anxiety.

When she met his gaze, he said, "Don't worry. It'll fit."

"I don't think so," she murmured. "You're..."

"Just right for you," he said as he pulled her boots off. He unsnapped her jeans and started tugging them off. His finger hooked her bikini panties, and they came off as well.

She grabbed at his hand, but it was too late. She was left wearing a pair of gray wool boot socks. She reached for the sheet, started to cover herself, then laid it back down again. She faced him boldly, then reached down and, one at a time, pulled off the socks as though they were black silk nylons.

The striptease worked. The instant the second sock hit the floor, he covered her body with his, settling his hips in the cradle of her thighs and lowering his chest onto hers, using his arms to keep his full weight off her.

When he sought her face again, the boldness was gone, replaced by innocence and apprehension.

He knew she was a virgin. She'd told him as much. He'd never made love to a woman who was untouched by another man. He wouldn't have believed it would make a difference to him. But he felt a sudden possessiveness and a gladness that made his throat feel tight.

He reached a hand down between her legs and she squeezed them tight to keep him out.

"Hope," he said in a tender voice. "Let me in."

"It's going to hurt," she said matter-of-factly. "I know that. Just go ahead and get it over with."

He waited for her to spread her legs and when he touched her realized that she wasn't nearly ready for him. He leaned down to find her mouth with his and kissed her. Her lips were rigid, and he realized she was too frightened to respond.

He played with her mouth, kissing one side and then the other, not touching her anywhere else, just letting her get used to the feel of his body on hers. Gradually, he felt her hands at his waist and then felt her fingertips grip his hips and slide up his back, as her body became more pliant beneath his own.

His mouth found hers again, and this time her head came up as she kissed him back. Her tongue came seeking, and he opened his mouth to her, enjoying her tentative forays as she learned the taste of him. He deepened the kiss and felt her body melting against his. His hands moved along her hip, then upward to her breast. He played with her nipples, bringing them to hard peaks, then lowered his head and suckled once more.

He felt her body arch beneath him, felt her hips pressing upward, seeking respite. He lowered his hand and this time her legs opened wantonly, as she welcomed his touch. She was slick and wet, her body ready for his intrusion.

He felt her stiffen as he penetrated her with his finger. He found her mouth with his, and felt her body quicken as he mimicked the sex act with his tongue while his finger worked inside her. But she was small. And he wasn't.

He realized he probably would hurt her, but he didn't know any way to mount a virgin that would lessen the pain.

He slid his hands beneath her hips and lifted her, angling her so it would be easier to enter her, then began to push himself inside her.

Her eyes went wide, and she gripped his arms tightly, her fingernails digging crescents in his skin. "I don't—" she cried. "You can't— I can't—"

Jake could feel her pulling away and realized that the best way to spare her pain was to broach her quickly. He took a breath and plunged into her to the hilt. She bit her lip to hold back a cry of pain, but it escaped anyway.

"Shh. Shh," he said as he lay quiescent, deep inside her. "It's done now. The worst is over."

He brushed the sweaty hair from her forehead and kissed away the tear that had slid down her temple, then soothed the hurt where she'd bitten her lip.

"Sorry I yelled," she muttered, refusing to meet his gaze. "But I felt like I was being torn in half."

"Look at me," Jake said.

She glanced up, seemed embarrassed, then looked away.

"I'm not going anywhere," he said, chuckling. "So you might as well look at me."

This time she looked at him defiantly. "I'm looking. Now what?"

"I will always treasure the gift you've given me today," he said.

Tears welled in her eyes, and she bit her lip again. "I love you, Jake," she said.

He felt the pause, the empty space in time where he should have said the words back to her. "You're beautiful, Hope," he said instead. "Lovely beyond words."

He saw the light die in her eyes and searched for what he could do or say that would bring it back. He could bring her pleasure. He could offer her that. He caught her mouth with his own and sipped from the nectar there. He found the soft spot beneath her ear. Bit at her neck and shoulder hard enough to incite both pleasure and pain.

As her passion built, she returned the savage embrace, her hands moving over him, all the more erotic for their unpracticed touch.

He used his hands and mouth to incite her desire and began to move inside her, slowly at first, then more rapidly as her desire matched his own. She arched against him, animal sounds of need wrenched from her as they climbed the peaks of satisfaction. He felt her stiffen and groan and spilled his seed inside her with a guttural sound of satisfaction.

His body was heaving, and hers beneath him, as they both sought the breath to stay alive. He slid off to the side and pulled her into his arms, fitting her hips against him. Her eyes were closed, her body slick with sweat, as was his. He kissed her shoulder, liking the salty taste of her.

He closed his eyes. Finally satisfied. Wanting to sleep. Not wanting to think about what he'd just done, or what it meant. He'd marry her, of course. And figure out a way to assuage his conscience where Amanda was concerned.

Oh, God. What was he going to say to Amanda? And how was he going to explain this to his family?

Hell. He would figure out something to say. This was right. He and Hope belonged together. He didn't know why he'd fought it for so long.

"Jake?"

"Umm," he mumbled. He'd have to teach Hope that the last thing a man wanted after sex was conversation. "Don't worry, Hope," he said. "We're going to be married as soon as I can get a license. It would have been better to wait a decent time after my wedding date to Amanda, but I didn't use a condom, and I don't suppose you're on the pill. Better safe than sorry."

"I'm not going to marry you, Jake."

It took a moment for the words to sink in. Jake sat up and stared at Hope, who pulled the sheet up to cover herself as she sat up and stared back at him.

"What the hell are you talking about, Hope? I just took your virginity. I might have started a baby inside you."

She blanched but said, "I made love to you because I wanted to know what it would be like. But I'm not going to marry a man who doesn't love me."

"I—I—I—" Jake stuttered, but couldn't make himself say the words. She ought to know how he felt without them. "Listen, girl, you'll marry me—"

Hope scrambled off the side of the bed, taking the sheet with her and leaving Jake naked on the bed. He stood and reached for his jeans and yanked them on, then turned toward her. "When I tell your father what happened here today, he'll—"

"The days of shotgun weddings are long past," Hope said. "My father isn't going to insist you marry me. I'm a big girl. I knew what I was doing."

Jake felt his face flushing. "I don't like being used," he said angrily.

"Don't worry. I'll be gone from here in an hour."

"The hell you will! I need a baby-sitter for the next week, and you're it. Like it or lump it."

"You can't make me stay."

"No. But I can tell folks you're a quitter."

He watched her eyes narrow and her chin jut. "Fine. I'll stay until the wedding. Which I trust you won't cancel on my account."

"I'm going to get married, all right. And live happily ever after, with a *grown-up* who knows better than to play games."

The color drained from Hope's face, and he could see her whole body was trembling. "Get out!" she rasped. "Get out, before I—"

Jake grabbed his boots and headed for the door. He stopped when he got there and turned to face her. "Think about my offer. A week from now, all bets are off."

She stared at him, her heart in her eyes and said, "Do you love me, Jake?"

He said nothing, the words stuck in his throat.

A tear slid down her cheek. "Good-bye, Jake."

A band tightened around his chest, until he thought he'd suffocate. "You're formidable, Hope," he said angrily. "Somewhere out there is a very lucky man."

Then he turned and left the room.

CHAPTER EIGHT

FAITH

AMANDA HAD HUNG UP THE PHONE after calling Jake's ranch early Saturday morning and dropped into a kitchen chair. Jake should have called her if he needed help with his niece and nephew. She examined her feelings on discovering that he'd called Hope Butler instead. She felt troubled, to say the least.

When the phone rang again, she leapt for it, hoping it was Jake calling. She was disappointed when she heard her principal's voice.

"Hello, Mr. Denton," she said. "How are you?"

"My arm's still broken," Denton replied. "Thought I'd take you and Rabb Whitelaw up on that offer to put together the Christmas toys for my kids. I called Rabb earlier this morning, and he came by and picked up everything. Said he could work better in his shop, because that's where he has his tools."

Amanda bit her lip. She didn't want to explain to her principal why she would prefer not to spend time in Rabb Whitelaw's company before her wedding. On the other hand, it wasn't fair to stick Rabb with the responsibility for putting together the toys for Denton's kids, when the principal's injury had occurred at her home.

"No problem," she told Denton. "Rabb and I will make sure all the toys are back at your house ready to be wrapped by the end of the day."

"Thanks, Amanda. I really appreciate it," Denton said.

He hung up without saying good-bye. Amanda took a deep breath and let it out. She could act like a rational, responsible adult around Rabb. And she owed him her help.

She decided it would be best to simply show up at his door. Otherwise, he might try to put her off, and she wanted this strangeness between them over with before the wedding.

She'd met Rabb at his shop once or twice when he'd substituted for Jake as her escort. It was located on the edge of town, on the bottom floor of a charming Victorian two-story white frame house, complete with forest-green gingerbread trim. Rabb lived on the upper floor, at the top of an exquisite winding staircase.

Amanda's heart was pounding by the time she knocked on Rabb's door. It started to gallop when he opened it, and she saw him for the first time in a week.

"You need a shave," she said.

He rubbed the short dark beard that covered his cheeks and chin and said, "Haven't had the time. I've been working."

"Oh?" She waited for him to tell her what he'd been doing, but when he didn't, she said, "I came to help with the toys for Denton's kids."

"I can manage," he said, standing in the doorway, blocking her entrance.

"It's really my responsibility."

She could see the indecision in his face and took a step forward. He stepped back rather than have her run into him. Once she was inside, he closed the door behind her and turned to face her with his arms crossed over his chest, making it clear she wasn't welcome.

She turned away from him to survey the workroom. She was aware of the sun warming the open space from large windows that surrounded the room and the rich smell of hickory sawdust. Power tools were spaced around the room, and tools hung in neat rows along one wall. She noticed the open boxes in one corner and said, "I see you've started."

"Yep. Really, I can handle this. You can leave."

It wasn't easy facing Rabb, and she kept her hands knotted in front of her so he wouldn't realize how nervous she felt. "I want this awkwardness between us gone," she said.

He snorted. "Easier said than done."

She forced herself to meet his gaze. "We're going to be in-laws. We're going to be seeing each other all the time. We have to be able to act normally around each other. Or else..." Her throat felt tight and she swallowed painfully.

He sighed and rubbed the back of his neck. "Damn it, Mandy. I don't think—"

She crossed and laid a hand on his arm. "Please, Rabb. We were friends once. I'd like us to be friends again."

He stared down at her hand, then took a step back so her hand fell away. "I don't think that's possible."

Amanda felt as if she'd lost something priceless, but she could hardly blame him. If she was this uncomfortable being around him, she could imagine how he felt, knowing she was going to marry his brother. "All right," she conceded. "Not friends, then." She managed a smile and said, "How about friendly acquaintances?"

His lips curved up on one side. "I suppose that'll have to do for now."

She felt her shoulders unbunching. She headed for the stack of boxes and said, "What all do we have to put together?"

He followed her and said, "Bicycle, tricycle, doll-house and train set."

"Doesn't sound too bad," she said. "Shall we work together on each item or split them up?"

"I've already started on the bicycle. You can have the tricycle."

"I get the train set," she said quickly.

He wrinkled his nose. "You want me to do the doll-house?"

"It'll be good for you," she said with a laugh, opening the box that contained the tricycle parts.

They worked in companionable silence for the next half hour, which was about how long it took her to put together the tiny red tricycle for Denton's four-year-old daughter. Amanda was sitting cross-legged on the floor, and she turned to observe Rabb, who was tightening the bolts on the back wheel of a racing bike for Denton's ten-year-old son.

"I would have given my eyeteeth for a bike like this when I was a kid," Rabb said.

"You didn't have a bicycle?" Amanda asked, surprised.

"I got one for Christmas when I was nine," Rabb said. "It was second-hand."

Amanda raised a brow but didn't say anything. She realized that Rabb must have gotten his first bike before he was adopted by the Whitelaws, because they were wealthy enough to buy new.

"I had my heart set on a new English racer," Rabb continued. "Of course, with my dad dead for three years and us living on food stamps, it was amazing my mother managed to get me any bike at all. The second-hand bike she found had fat tires and a big seat and wide handlebars.

"Anyway, she'd sanded it down and sprayed it with some turquoise paint I guess she thought was pretty, and added some new red plastic grips with streamers at the handlebars."

He met her gaze and said, "I was a total brat about it. I told her I'd never ride anything that looked that dumb. I wanted a new English racer, and she could take that stupid bike back to wherever she got it."

Amanda stared, uncertain what to say.

Rabb shoved a hand through his hair. "I made her cry." He grimaced and admitted, "It was the meanest thing I ever did. I never even told her I was sorry. I mean, before she died six months later."

"What happened to her?"

"She had leukemia. I didn't even know she was sick until they put her in the hospital. She went into a coma and died without me ever having a chance to say…anything."

"I'm so sorry," Amanda said.

Rabb met her gaze and said, "I learned a lesson I never forgot."

"What was that?"

"Don't wait to say what you feel. Don't count on second chances."

Their gazes held. Amanda heard herself swallow.

"I think I'm in love with you," Rabb said. He hesitated, then said, "I know I'm in love with you."

Amanda groaned. "Please. Don't."

A moment later he was pulling her to her feet and into his embrace. When his mouth sought hers, she turned her face aside, so his lips brushed her cheek. She felt the tears welling in her eyes, but the sob caught her unawares.

She hardly ever cried, because she thought tears were a sign of weakness. She hadn't shed a tear at her mother's funeral. She'd been unable to feel anything except relief—and guilt for feeling relieved. Now she was crying for the second time in two weeks. Her chest heaved, and she was racked with loud, gasping sobs.

"I don't know wh-hy I'm crying," she said.

Rabb's arms tightened around her, and he rocked her, offering comfort. "I'm a sonofabitch," he murmured. "A desperate sonofabitch," he added. "I didn't mean to hurt you, Mandy. I'm sorry."

Her hands slid up to grasp him around the neck, and she pressed herself against him. He wasn't as tall as Jake, and she noticed how their bodies fit together in all the right places. He kept rocking her and crooning to her, and she wanted to crawl inside him and hide from the reality that was staring her in the face.

She liked Rabb better than she liked his brother. She might even love him. She was unhappy and confused. And she didn't have much time—seven short days—to sort things out.

She'd never really thought too much about phero-mones and sex appeal because her mother's illness had kept her from having much experience with men. Jake was so stunningly handsome, any woman would have found him attractive. And she did.

But she'd never wanted to be held by Jake the way she wanted to be held by Rabb. She'd never felt the overwhelming desire to be kissed by Jake that she felt when she was in Rabb's arms.

She raised her head to look into Rabb's tormented eyes. She wanted to offer comfort. She needed to offer comfort.

She put her hand to his cheek, feeling the rough beard against her sensitive palm. How could such a simple touch arouse such erotic feelings? Her hand found its way to his mouth, and she felt his kiss against her fin-gertips. She stared into his eyes, feeling her insides dance at the prospect of further intimacy.

The pad of his thumb brushed at a tear on her cheek, before he dipped his head to kiss away the tear on her other cheek. "Mandy," he murmured against her lips.

Her rational mind was telling her to get out, to save herself. But a part of her desperately wanted the kiss that was only a breath away. "Rabb," she whispered.

It was a plea. A prayer. A wish that he granted.

Her heart was beating so fast she thought it might burst with fear—and with anticipation. She opened herself to him as his mouth covered hers, welcoming the urgent intrusion of his tongue. She felt his hand on her breast and arched into it, at the same time pressing her hips against his, feeling the welcome hardness and the heat.

She gave herself up to him in every way a woman can give herself to a man, body and soul, unwilling to curb the pleasure that flooded every sense. She heard his guttural groan as he deepened the kiss, and her own moan in response as his hand cupped her breast and his thumb found its sensitive peak.

Her knees threatened to give way, and she clung to him, her hands grasping his hair, her body thrust against his, wanting to be closer, frustrated by the layers of cotton and denim that kept them apart.

He dragged her sweater up over her head, while she struggled with the buttons on his chambray shirt. She pulled the shirt down over his shoulders, her hands caressing his flesh, enjoying the crisp feel of the matted curls on his chest.

She was hardly aware that her own cotton shirt had suffered the same fate as his. He was struggling with the back clasp on her bra when the phone rang.

The ring was intentionally loud so it could be heard over machinery, but it echoed shrilly in a room where their labored breathing was the only other sound.

It was a wake-up call that couldn't be ignored.

But Amanda didn't want to wake up. She wanted to stay immersed in the wonderful dream she was having with Rabb. She dropped her forehead onto his chest and gripped him around the waist. She felt his hands circle her hips as he leaned his head against the top of hers.

They let the phone ring until it stopped.

Neither of them pulled away, but it was equally impossible to continue. The trance, the mood, the utter insanity of the moment had passed.

"I don't understand why this happened," Amanda

said, still holding on to Rabb. She looked up into his face and said, "I didn't want you to stop."

"Are you going to tell Jake? Or am I?"

Amanda took a step back. "I will."

"Oh, God, Mandy. That's wonderful!" He picked her up and swung her in a circle, unable to keep the grin from his face.

She laughed delightedly, then remembered how much their happiness was going to hurt Jake, and sobered. "Put me down, Rabb."

He set her down, but his lips locked on hers at the same moment. She couldn't think. She couldn't breathe. She felt overwhelmed by love and desire. She felt herself going under, immersed in emotions that were thrilling because they were so unexpected. Kissing Jake had never made her feel like this. And no matter how much she had to hurt him, she couldn't marry him. Not when she felt this way toward his brother.

But it also wasn't right to be kissing Rabb before she'd broken her engagement to Jake. Or before a decent amount of time had passed. Enough so it wouldn't be so obvious that her feelings had been transferred from one Whitelaw to another.

She pushed herself far enough away to gasp, "Rabb, we have to—" But he took her under again, and it was long moments before her brain could function enough to remind her that pursuing a relationship with Rabb was going to have to be postponed, at least for a while.

"Rabb," she said, pushing herself away to arm's distance and searching out his eyes.

His gaze was fierce, possessive, and she felt herself responding to the desire she saw reflected in his eyes.

"Wait," she said, putting a flat palm on his chest. "We have to go slow. I'll tell Jake I can't marry him, but I don't want to tell him it's because I'm choosing you instead."

Rabb frowned. "Why not, if it's the truth?"

"It's going to be bad enough to reject him at this late date. It would be unconscionable to—"

"Jake will understand," Rabb said.

"No," Amanda said, shaking her head. "He won't. He'll be hurt. It will be bad enough if we end up together eventually. It would be cruel for us to throw our relationship in his face."

Rabb took a step back, so her hand dropped, and crossed his arms. "How long are we supposed to put our relationship on hold?"

Amanda's brow furrowed. "I don't know. This town is too small for us to risk gossip by seeing each other before a decent period has passed."

"How long?" Rabb insisted.

Amanda bit her lip. "Six months?"

"No."

"Three months."

"No."

"Any less than that and—"

"I've been waiting for you half my life," Rabb said, gripping her shoulders. "I'm not waiting any longer. Besides, Jake's no dummy. He'll figure out the truth. It'll be far worse later when he realizes you lied to him."

"What about the scandal we'd create?" Amanda asked.

"I don't really give a damn what people think."

"I do," Amanda said. "I'm a teacher. I can't be the source of gossip or scandal. I might lose my job."

"I can support us," Rabb said.

"I like my job. I don't want to lose it."

Rabb made a growling sound. "You're not going to lose your job because you broke an engagement and married another man right away."

She stared at him, shocked. "We couldn't possibly get married for *at least* a year. It would be…outrageous!"

"Bullshit."

"I don't approve of language—"

"Damn it, Amanda—"

She turned and marched toward the door. He grabbed her arm and swung her back around. His lips were pressed flat as a blade to keep from swearing again, but his eyes glittered with anger.

Through clenched teeth he said, "I don't want to lose you. I'll wait…if I have to. But I think you're being…"

She knew he was looking for the least offensive word he could find. But she got the gist of it. "I may be a fool, but this is who I am, Rabb. I can't change how I feel. I wouldn't think much of myself if I broke an engagement to one man and jumped into bed with another."

He lifted a brow.

She flushed when she realized what she'd admitted. She did want to sleep with him. All right, no more euphemisms. She wanted to have down and dirty, naked sweaty sex with Rabb, even the thought of which made her blush hotter.

She saw the smile teasing his lips and glared at him. "This isn't funny. Going to bed— Having sex," she forced herself to say, "is a big step for me."

"So you and Jake haven't—"

She shook her head. "No. I could never…I never wanted…" She shut her mouth and stared at her feet.

Rabb lifted her chin, and she forced herself to meet his gaze. "I'm glad, Mandy. So very glad."

Her heart swelled with emotion, and she managed a smile for him. "I'm glad you're glad. For the record, I'm going to be nervous. I haven't done this for a very long time." She'd implied to Jake that she was a virgin to hold him off. But she'd had that single encounter with a teenage boy in high school.

Rabb leaned over and kissed her gently on the lips. "Everything will be fine. You'll see. I hope you don't make us wait too long."

She opened her mouth to protest, but he took her in his arms and kissed her again, and she decided arguing could wait.

When he finally released her, she realized her knees were weak. She held on to his arms to keep from falling, but put some space between them. "I have a date with Jake tonight. We were planning to talk. I guess I'll have a little more to say."

"Would you rather I talked to him?" Rabb asked.

"No. If I'm going to break up with him, especially this close to the wedding, I owe it to him to do it in person."

"What about canceling the wedding? How are you planning to handle that?"

Amanda made a face. "I'll wait and see what Jake wants to do. It won't be easy. The gossip—"

He took her hands in his and squeezed them. "The

gossip will die down before you know it. People are understanding about this sort of thing."

"I dread being the object of speculation," Amanda said.

At that moment, the doorbell chimed. Amanda jerked free and turned to stare at the door. She looked at Rabb and said, "Are you expecting someone?"

He shrugged. "Could be a delivery. Could be someone in the family dropping by to visit. They know I usually take weekends off from work."

Amanda tensed as he crossed to answer the door. She would feel awkward accepting more good wishes on her marriage to Jake if it was someone in his family. She prayed it was the postman or some delivery service.

"Hey, Rabb. How's it going?"

Amanda didn't recognize the male voice. She took a step closer to see who it was. She didn't recognize the man, either, but she was stunned to see who was with him.

Rabb shot her a surprised look before he reached out a hand to the stranger. "Hello yourself, Kane," Rabb said as he backed away from the door to give the two visitors room to enter.

"This is my cousin Kane Longstreet," Rabb said as he introduced the young man to Amanda. "He went off to military school. That's why you haven't met him before now. Kane, this is Amanda Carter."

"Oh, Jake's fiancée," Kane said. "So nice to meet you, Miss Carter."

"Please, call me Amanda."

"Welcome to the family, Amanda," Kane said as he gave her a quick hug and a kiss on the cheek.

Amanda felt the blush rising on her cheeks. She shot an admonishing look at Rabb and said, "Thank you, Kane."

Rabb nodded to the woman with Kane and said, "What brings you here, Hope?"

The woman laughed and said, "My name isn't Hope. It's Charity. Charity Burnette."

Amanda's jaw dropped and she exchanged an astonished look with Rabb. The woman who'd walked through Rabb's door could have been Hope Butler's twin. But this girl had both hands, so she wasn't Faith. Charity Burnette was the same height, had the same black hair, the same dark brown eyes, the same creamy skin as Hope. Their features were identical. But how was that possible? If this girl was related to Hope and Faith, the girls would have to be triplets!

"I've been trying to get Charity up here to visit since I met her in August," Kane said, wrapping an arm around Charity's slender waist and drawing her forward. "She wouldn't come with me to the family's Labor Day picnic. And she said her mother would miss her too much at Thanksgiving. She finally took mercy on me when I begged her not to make me attend Jake's wedding all alone."

"I'm glad to meet you," Rabb said.

Charity Burnette extended her hand and Rabb shook it, his brow furrowed as he eyed her up and down.

Charity looked down at her navy wool dress and said, "Did I spill something at breakfast?"

Rabb said, "You look exactly—and I mean *exactly*—like someone we know."

"You look exactly like *twins* we know," Amanda elaborated.

Charity laughed. "Sorry. I'm an only child."

"The resemblance is amazing," Rabb said.

"Amazing," Amanda echoed. "Any chance you have a sibling out there you might not know about?"

Kane pulled Charity's arm through his and said, "Hard to believe there could be another woman like her in the world. Charity's one of a kind."

Charity had frowned, provoking Amanda to ask, "Is there a sibling somewhere out there?"

"I suppose it's possible," Charity said. "I was adopted."

"Oh, my God," Amanda said, putting a hand to her mouth. She exchanged another look with Rabb. "Do you suppose—?"

"The Butler girls were six or seven when their father moved here to manage one of the big ranches, so I don't know whether they were born as twins or triplets. But it wouldn't make sense for parents to keep two girls and give one away," Rabb said. "Would it?"

Amanda saw the pain in Charity's dark eyes and said, "Of course not. I can't imagine Hope and Faith's parents doing any such thing." She focused her gaze on Charity and said, "They say everyone has a doppelganger somewhere in the world. You simply have a pair of twins who resemble you."

"*Exactly* resemble you," Rabb muttered.

Amanda elbowed him and said, "There's an easy way to settle this. We'll introduce Charity to the Butler twins. Once we get them together, we'll see they aren't the same at all."

"Sounds like fun," Kane said. "I can't wait to meet two girls as beautiful as the one I'm trying to convince to become my wife."

Charity laughed uneasily. "Don't put me on the spot, Kane. I promised to consider your proposal. That's all."

Kane pulled her close and said, "Rabb is family, Charity. And once she marries Jake, Amanda will be, too." He turned to Amanda and said, "I've asked Charity to marry me, but she's still making up her mind whether to have me or not. I'm hoping she'll see you and Jake at the altar and decide to make me the happiest of men."

Amanda shared an uneasy glance with Rabb, then said, "Good luck to both of you."

"Charity and I are having dinner with my folks tonight," Kane said. "When would be a good time to meet these twins you say look so much like my girl?"

"Hope's spending the week at Jake's ranch baby-sitting," Amanda said.

"How about if we meet you there tomorrow after church?" Kane said. "I promised Jake I'd come by to say hello before the wedding. And I want him to meet Charity."

"I don't know what plans Faith might have," Amanda said. "But I'll call her and see if she can join us."

"Give us a call at my father's ranch if it doesn't work out," Kane said. "Otherwise, we'll see you tomorrow."

Amanda crossed her arms as Rabb closed the door behind Kane and his new girlfriend. "You realize that now I can't possibly say anything to Jake tonight."

"Why not?"

"It would make things too awkward tomorrow."

"I'll call Kane and explain—"

"What? That there won't be a wedding because you're stealing your brother's fiancée out from under his nose? Then what?" Amanda shook her head. "No. It won't make much difference if I wait another day."

Rabb stood before her and tilted her chin up, forcing her to look him in the eye. "Only one more day? Are you sure?"

She nodded solemnly.

He leaned down and kissed her softly on the mouth, and she felt her insides churn with feeling. How could he make her feel so much? Why this brother and not the other?

"I'll tell him Monday," she murmured. "I promise."

CHAPTER NINE

HOPE

HOPE STARED INTO THE BATHROOM mirror on Sunday morning and saw the ravages of the past miserable night. The eyes that stared back at her were deeply wounded. Profoundly sad. Crushed and confounded.

It had been painful to watch Jake leave the house for his date with Miss Carter on Saturday evening. His hair was still wet from the shower, and his face was fresh-shaved. He was wearing a crisply ironed white shirt, jeans with a sharp crease and highly polished black boots. He'd seemed agitated and impatient as he gave her last-minute instructions for taking care of his niece and nephew.

"Everything will be fine," she assured him.

He arched a black brow and said, "That's what I assumed when I left this morning and look what happened."

"Becky's fine. Huck's fine. I'm fine."

He snorted and said, "You look like hell."

It might have been the truth, but it hurt to have him point it out. She was feeling a stunning remorse for her decision to make love with Jake that afternoon. She'd given him something she'd been saving for a very long time, something precious, something intended for the man with whom she would spend the rest of her life.

At the time, it had seemed like the right thing to do. She couldn't deny she'd enjoyed what they'd done. She'd never felt so close to another person. Being held in Jake's arms, taking his body inside her own, had been a transforming experience she would never forget.

Hope hadn't understood beforehand how devastated she would be if Jake took the physical gift she'd offered...and rejected her love. She'd always believed that if she gave him her virginity, he would marry her. She couldn't say he hadn't offered marriage. But she wanted more. She wanted his love. She'd never imagined he'd refuse to say the words. But he had.

Hope winced at the thought.

"Are you all right?" Jake asked.

"Fine and dandy," she replied, lifting her chin a notch. She might be devastated, but she'd never let Jake know it.

He'd walked out the door for his date with Miss Carter without a backward look.

And hadn't returned all night.

She'd finally stomped off to bed at 4:00 a.m. and cried herself to sleep. This morning she looked like death warmed over.

"You have to get your act together, Hope," she said to her reflected image. "He doesn't love you. He *can't* love you. And you know you can't—won't—settle for less. It's over. Time to get on with your life."

"Hope? Are you in there?"

The sound of Jake's voice outside the bathroom door

made her heart beat faster. She looked at herself in the mirror and watched tears well in her eyes. She scrubbed them away, cleared her throat and said, "I'm in here. What do you want, Jake?"

"One of my cousins is coming over after church with someone he wants you to meet. Amanda's coming, too, and she's invited your sister Faith."

Hope jerked the bathroom door open and said, "What's this all about?"

"What the hell happened to you?" Jake asked.

"Answer the question," Hope retorted.

He eyed her skeptically and said, "Amanda wouldn't tell me. She said it's a surprise."

Hope frowned, then shut the door in his face and returned to the mirror to stare at herself. She couldn't face Miss Carter looking like this. And she didn't want Faith seeing her so wan and drawn. Her sister would worry.

The knock on the door was insistent, but she said, "Go away, Jake."

"I want to talk to you."

"We did our talking yesterday. And a lot more besides," she muttered.

"I have something to say to you, Hope. Open the damned door!"

Was he ready to admit he loved her? Hope couldn't believe he'd changed his mind over the past twelve hours.

But curiosity—and hope—made her reach for the door. She opened it an inch and peered out. "What is it?"

Jake shoved the door open and braced it with his booted foot. "I have no intention of talking to you through a crack in the door."

She took a step back, crossed her arms over the T-shirt she'd worn to sleep in, and waited. She saw his gaze caress her long legs, then slide up to her chest, where her nipples had peaked under the soft cotton. She returned his stare, her eyes focusing on the bulge behind the zipper of his jeans, then moving to his flushed face.

His mouth twisted in chagrin. "I haven't said anything to Amanda about…what happened between us. It would only hurt her. And it isn't going to happen again."

Hope lifted a brow. She wondered if Jake realized he was eating her with his eyes. Did he really believe the attraction between them wouldn't flare whenever they got near one another? He was lying to himself.

Hope realized she would be a fool to give up Jake without a fight. She still believed they belonged together. Hopeless as the situation was. Despite the fact he didn't love her. Or maybe he did love her. Maybe he just didn't want to admit it. Maybe he needed a little more encouragement. Or a little more incentive to say the words.

She grabbed the hem of her T-shirt and stripped it off in a move so quick and startling that Jake didn't have a chance to stop her. She tossed the T-shirt on the ground and pressed her naked body against Jake's fully clothed one.

She heard a harsh animal sound issue from his throat before he gathered her up in his arms and claimed her mouth with his. He took her deep and fast and she felt a surge of triumph.

Which ended when he tore his mouth from hers and stared down at her with angry eyes. "This isn't going to solve anything, Hope. Nothing's changed since last night. I'm marrying—"

Hope yanked herself free and leaned down to grab her T-shirt, pulling it over her head in jerky movements that expressed her own anger and disappointment. "You want me, not Miss Carter," she accused as she turned to face him.

"I've never denied it. But marriage is more than sexual attraction."

"Sexual attraction is important," Hope said.

"I never said it isn't," he shot back. "But it's not enough. Not nearly enough!"

Hope bit her lip, unsure where to take the argument from there. The sound of little feet pattering down the stairs brought an abrupt end to any chance of resolving the matter. "I have to get dressed," she said, backing away from him.

"I'll fix the kids some breakfast. Are you coming to church with us?"

Hope wasn't averse to praying for a miracle. "Sure. Why not?"

"Unca Jake? Where are you?" Huck called.

"I'm coming," Jake answered.

Hope closed the bathroom door on his retreating back and once more observed herself in the mirror. Her skin held a flush that hadn't been there before, and her dark eyes sparkled, the result of Jake's kiss.

God, what a fool she was! She should let him go and get on with her life.

But she hadn't given up in three years. She wasn't going to quit now. She would simply have to try harder. There must be some way to break through Jake's

reserve. There must be some way to convince him that
if he gave her his heart, she would take tender care of it
for the rest of her life.

Once she'd finished her ablutions, Hope returned to
her bedroom, opened the closet, and stared at the only
dress she'd packed, wishing she'd thought more carefully about the image she wanted to present to Jake. The
sleeveless dress was red, with a V-neck that showed a
hint of cleavage and a belted waist that emphasized her
hourglass figure. It was cut at least four inches above her
knees. She grimaced as she stepped into the three-inch
heels that made her five feet ten inches tall.

There was no getting around it. She looked like a potential bedmate, not a respectable rancher's wife. But it
was either this dress or jeans. At least in the dress, she
would provide some competition for the staid Miss
Carter.

Hope hadn't realized how self-conscious she would
feel when every eye turned to stare as she walked down
the aisle at church, Becky over her shoulder, Jake at her
side holding Huck by the hand. To her consternation,
Miss Carter was already seated in one of the pews
reserved for Jake's large family. There was barely
enough room on the same bench for her and Jake and
Huck and Becky.

Miss Carter seemed startled to see Hope, although
Hope couldn't imagine why. Miss Carter scooted down
the padded bench to make room for them. Jake ushered
Hope and the kids into the row first, then crossed past
them to sit between Hope and Miss Carter. To Hope's
consternation, Jake took Miss Carter's hand and held it
on and off throughout the service, when he wasn't

holding Huck in his lap entertaining him or sharing a hymnal with Miss Carter.

Hope had never heard Jake sing, and she was surprised to discover he had a pleasant baritone voice. Becky fell asleep during the sermon, and Hope sat with the child in her arms while the rest of the congregation rose to sing a final hymn.

Hope got another surprise when the service was over and Jake's parents approached her. At first, she thought they'd come to see their grandchildren. It didn't take long before she realized they'd come to inspect her... and perhaps to make a comparison with Miss Carter.

For the first time Hope regretted not being more subtle in her pursuit of Jake. It was obvious his parents knew of her interest in their son. It was not as obvious what they thought of the match.

"It's nice to meet you, Mr. and Mrs. Whitelaw," Hope said as Jake introduced her to them. She regretted the red dress even more, when she compared it to the dark suit, beige blouse and sensible pumps worn by Miss Carter.

"It's so nice to meet you at last, Hope," Mrs. Whitelaw said. "I've heard so much about you. Please, call me Rebecca."

"And I'm Zach," Jake's father said, extending his hand.

"Thank you...Rebecca...Zach." Hope stumbled over the names, aware of her youth, knowing how much easier it must be for Miss Carter to address Jake's parents so familiarly. And wondering exactly what it was that Zach and Rebecca Whitelaw had heard about her. And from whom?

She noticed that the greeting Jake's mother gave to Miss Carter seemed less warm than the one she'd given to Hope. Hope hadn't even considered the possibility that Jake's parents didn't approve of his prospective bride. She watched carefully to see what she could see.

"How are you this morning, Amanda?" Mrs. Whitelaw said.

"Quite well, Rebecca," Miss Carter replied.

Hope thought Miss Carter seemed nervous around Jake's folks and wondered about the source of her anxiety. She was a teacher used to dealing with the parents of the kids she taught. But she was clearly uncomfortable with Jake's mother.

"Are there any last-minute wedding details I can help you with?" Mrs. Whitelaw asked.

"Um. No. Um. Everything's…done," Miss Carter said.

Miss Carter seemed embarrassed. Hope frowned. What did she have to be embarrassed about? Hope was the one who'd been seducing the groom.

"It was nice seeing you, Amanda, Hope," Mrs. Whitelaw said. "Will you be coming over for supper today, Jake?" she said to her son. "We'd love to spend some time with Huck and Becky." She eyed Hope and said, "And it would be lovely to get to know Hope a little better."

Hope felt a chill run down her spine. Why would Jake's parents want to know her better? Unless they suspected…

They couldn't know she and Jake had become lovers. It had happened only yesterday. She wondered if she looked different. Or if Jake looked different.

She searched his features, looking for something that might give away the change in their relationship, but all she saw was cold blue eyes, chiseled cheeks, a square jaw, a slash of mouth and crow-wing black hair that had been left to grow down over his collar.

He suddenly turned his gaze on her, and she wondered if he'd felt her perusal. Then she saw what his mother might have seen. The light in his blue eyes at the sight of her. The flex of his jaw muscle as he forced his gaze away from her.

"Please say you'll come," his mother said. "It would be so wonderful to have you all there."

"Not today, Mom," Jake said as he leaned down to kiss his mother's cheek. "Kane's coming over with his new girl. And Amanda's got some sort of surprise planned."

"Will I see you before the wedding?" his mother asked.

"It's going to be a busy week," Jake said. "I don't know."

"Would you make some time for me?" his mother said. "There's something I want to talk to you about."

"Sure, Mom," Jake said.

He gave his father a quick hug, and then his parents left, along with those members of his family who still lived nearby enough to attend church together. Hope nodded to each of them as Jake gave them a handshake or a hug.

"Good to see you, Rabb," Jake said.

"You, too, Jake," Rabb said. He glanced at Hope and said, "When is Colt getting home?"

"Not till Friday, I'm afraid," Jake said. "Thank goodness I've got Hope to help with the kids."

"Yeah. That was lucky, all right," Rabb replied.

"How's it going, Avery?" Jake asked.

"Karen can't wait for the wedding reception," Avery replied. "She thinks she's going to get me on the dance floor."

"I heard you've been taking lessons," Jake said.

"There's no way to fix two left feet," Avery said with a grin.

Jake laughed, then turned to his redheaded sister Cherry, who'd been a teenage juvenile delinquent, and the last Whitelaw Brat to be added to the pack. "You're looking beautiful, as usual," he said. "How's Billy treating you?"

"Like a princess," Cherry replied.

Billy Stonecreek approached with his twin daughters from his previous marriage and his and Cherry's young son. "Seems only fair, when she treats me like a king," he said.

"I'm hungry," the little boy said.

"We've gotta go," Cherry said. "See you soon."

"Mac and I can hardly wait for Saturday, Jake," his sister Jewel said. "I never thought I'd see you marry again. I'm glad you found someone to love after that bitch—"

Mac Macready put his hand over his wife's mouth and said, "We'll be there with bells on, Jake. How are you, Amanda? Any butterflies?"

Hope turned to Amanda and saw her try—but fail—to smile.

"A few," Amanda admitted.

"Happens to the best of us," Jewel said with a friendly smile. "Don't worry. You'll make a beautiful bride. Don't you think so, Jake?"

Jake missed his cue because he was reaching for Huck, who'd made a break down the aisle of the church. He scooped the giggling boy up in his arms and turned back to ask, "What was that, Jewel?"

"I asked if you don't think Amanda will make a beautiful bride."

Jake crossed to Amanda, juggling the wriggling boy in his arms. "Absolutely," he said, and leaned down to kiss her on the mouth.

Hope heard Jewel's quiet gasp when Amanda turned her face away, so Jake's kiss landed on her cheek. Jake's brow furrowed, and Amanda's cheeks turned fiery red.

"Hey, there, you guys," Faith said. "Let's get this show on the road. I want to see this surprise Miss Carter has planned for us."

Faith's cheery interruption allowed everyone to begin moving again and smoothed over the awkward moment.

Jake glanced at his watch and said, "Kane said he'd be at the house by one o'clock and it's already after noon. You're right. We'd better get moving."

"Who's riding with whom?" Faith asked, looking from face to face in the crowd.

Hope turned to Jake and said, "Do you mind if I take Becky with me and ride with Faith?"

"Sounds fine. That way Amanda can ride with me."

"I have my own car," Amanda said.

"I'd be glad to give you a ride," Jake said.

"All right," Amanda said. "If you insist."

Hope wished Jake hadn't insisted. Or that Amanda had stuck to her guns. She followed Faith out of the church, wanting the chance to talk with her twin about her confused feelings.

Hope swiped the baby's car seat from Jake's truck and put it in the back seat of Faith's car. Becky was cranky and tired and didn't want to sit in the seat, but Hope strapped her in anyway. "It's for your own good, sweetheart," she crooned to the baby.

"You could hold her in your lap," Faith suggested.

"Jake trusts me to take care of Becky," Hope replied.

"And you're determined to prove to him what a good mother you'll make for his children," Faith said, eyeing her sister sideways.

"Exactly."

Once they were on the way, Faith turned to Hope and said, "You made love to him, didn't you?"

Hope's mouth gaped in surprise. "How could you possibly know that?"

Faith chuckled. "I didn't. Until you just confirmed it. But I didn't think Jake could resist you for long, once you were sleeping under the same roof."

"All sex did was complicate things," Hope admitted.

"The man loves you. How could sex—"

"He might have feelings for me, but he isn't about to admit to them. I think he's afraid of getting hurt again. And I don't want him without those three little words."

"*I love you,*" Faith murmured. "Sweet words indeed. Have you figured out how to get Jake to say them?"

"I have no idea what to do. The last time we spoke he said he was going to go through with the marriage."

Faith shook her head. "I don't think he's going to have much luck without a bride."

"What do you mean?"

"I mean that Miss Carter's in love with someone else.

I don't think she's going to make it to the altar with Jake."

"That's horrible! She can't leave Jake standing there alone."

Faith laughed. "I thought you wanted the man for yourself. You should be glad."

"I don't want him hurt like that. Who is Miss Carter in love with?"

"Jake's brother Rabb."

"Dear God. That's…monstrous! What kind of she-nanigans have you been perpetrating, Faith?"

"I've only pulled a few strings. None of the people involved are wooden puppets, Hope. They're all living, breathing human beings, free to make their own choices."

"If Miss Carter's in love with Rabb, why hasn't she said something? Why hasn't she canceled the wedding?"

Faith bit her lip. "I'm not sure."

"What if you're wrong? What if Rabb and Miss Carter are just friends?"

"Have you seen the way they look at each other?"

Hope frowned, trying to recall whether she'd seen any glances exchanged at church between Rabb and Miss Carter. Then she remembered Miss Carter's stutter when Rebecca Whitelaw had asked her about the wedding. Her sudden, inexplicable embarrassment. And the way she'd avoided Jake's kiss. "What kind of surprise do you suppose Miss Carter has lined up for us today?" Hope asked.

"I don't know," Faith said. "She said I'll be astounded and that it's something I won't want to miss."

"Maybe the puppet is planning to pull a few strings of her own," Hope said.

"I'll be glad when the other shoe drops," Faith said. "I can't stand to see so many people so ready to ruin their lives."

When they reached the back door to Jake's ranch house, they saw that Jake and Miss Carter had arrived before them and that an additional pickup was parked behind the house.

"That must belong to Jake's cousin," Hope said. "He's supposed to be visiting this afternoon."

Hope had gotten out of the car and turned to open the rear door to get Becky when Faith gasped.

"Oh, my God! Hope, look. Look!"

Hope turned to see what had her sister so excited. A woman stood on Jake's back porch. Hope felt her heart begin to pound.

She was looking at herself. Looking at an *exact* replica of herself and Faith. She turned to meet Faith's shocked gaze.

"Who is that?" Faith whispered.

"I don't know what kind of trick Miss Carter is pulling here," Hope said, shocked by the strange woman's startling resemblance to her and her sister. "But I sure as hell intend to find out."

CHAPTER TEN

CHARITY

CHARITY WAS SHOCKED BY THE similarity between herself and the other two women. Amanda Carter hadn't been exaggerating. They were the same height. Their eyes were equally dark, and their complexions equally creamy. Even more startling was the fact that they wore their hair the same way, shoulder length, with bangs and a part in the center. And they were all wearing gold hoop earrings and bright pink lipstick. It felt as if she was looking into a mirror—no, two mirrors.

Charity started down the back steps of the house, compelled to get closer, to see whether her eyes might have deceived her. Maybe they weren't the same. Maybe the similarities were all on the surface. She crossed to the woman closest to her and stood facing her. The woman was her spitting image, down to the mole at the base of her right ear.

"What is this?" the woman said irritably. "Who are you? Where did you come from?"

"My name is Charity Burnette," Charity said. She realized her hands were trembling and crossed her arms and lifted her chin. It was eerie to see her behavior mirrored by the other woman, whose eyes narrowed when she realized they'd both done the same thing.

"What are you doing here? Why do you look like us?" the woman demanded.

"I'm here to attend a wedding with Kane Longstreet," Charity replied. "I have no idea why I look like you."

By then, the other girl had joined her sister and Charity realized the second girl didn't have a left hand. Charity wasn't aware she was staring until the first woman said belligerently, "You can stare all you want, but Faith isn't going to grow a hand."

"Faith?" Her own name was Charity. Was it possible the third girl was named— "I suppose your name's Hope," Charity said, fighting a rising hysteria.

"Yes, it is."

"Holy shit."

Charity saw the moment the other girls realized they were part of a triumvirate, Faith, Hope and Charity.

"Holy shit is right," the girl named Hope said in a shocked voice. "Who are you?" she repeated. "How is this possible?"

"I have no idea," Charity said. Then she realized that, of course, there was an explanation for the impossible. "I'm adopted," she said. "I suppose…I guess…I suppose your mother…our mother," she corrected, "gave me away."

"Mom and Dad would never do such a thing!" Faith protested.

"Your parents are together? They're married?" Charity questioned. When she'd thought about why her mother might have given her up for adoption, she'd always imagined an unwed and pregnant teenage girl who'd made a mistake and wanted to be shed of it. Never, in her wildest dreams, had she imagined that her *married* parents might have put her up for adoption.

What was even more difficult to grasp was the fact that her parents had obviously kept two of their triplets, *yet given her away*. She couldn't imagine how or why they would do such a thing.

She stared at the other two girls, jealous of what they'd had. *Real* parents. Parents who'd wanted them. Parents who, based on Faith's defense of them, must have loved them. It was hard to accept what she now knew to be true. The pain of it was unbearable. Those same parents hadn't wanted her. Those same parents had gotten rid of her.

"Are they still alive?" Charity asked.

"Who?" Hope said.

"Your parents. *Our* parents," she corrected. She had to be related to these two girls. The identical features, the biblical names. It was too much of a coincidence. She had a sudden thought. "How old are you?" she asked, before Hope could reply to her first question. "When is your birthday?"

"November 30," Faith replied. "We just turned twenty-one."

Charity bit her lip to keep from crying out. Her birthday was also November 30. She had also just turned twenty-one. "Your...*our*...parents. Are they...alive?" she asked again.

"Mom and Dad are fine. I sat with them at church this morning," Faith said.

"I want to see them," Charity said. "I want to meet them."

She watched the two girls exchange a glance. She knew what they were thinking, because whatever empathic powers they possessed, she possessed as well. "The shock isn't going to kill them," she said bitterly. "They must know what they did. They must have wondered if I'd ever show up on their doorstep."

"They never mentioned you," Hope said. "They never even hinted at your existence."

Charity felt her insides shrivel painfully. Why had she been the one they'd given away? Why not the one without a hand? Or the pugnacious one?

All her life Charity had felt unwanted and unloved. She'd thought it was because the father who'd adopted her had changed his mind and abandoned his wife, deciding he didn't want to raise a child that wasn't his own blood after all. Her mother had let her know what an affliction she was, how she'd caused the breakup of her adoptive parents' marriage. It was a burden she'd carried all her life.

But obviously there was more to it than that.

How had her biological parents chosen which child to give away? And why had it been her? *Why?* The three girls were the same. Identical. Except Faith was missing a hand. Anyone would think they'd have given up the damaged child, not one of the perfect ones.

"I want to meet them," she repeated. "I want to ask them…" The word was stuck in her emotion-clogged throat. *Why? Why? Why?*

"Let me take Becky inside and tell Jake where we're going," Hope said. She looked Charity in the eye and said, "I want some answers, too."

Hope was back a moment later, but Jake's cousin

Kane Longstreet was with her, his face white with shock. He was loose-limbed, with long strides that ate up the ground. His dark-eyed gaze focused intently on Charity, as though no one else existed. "What's going on, Charity? Who are these women?"

Kane's hands—large, callused, powerful—reached for her own and he waited for her to speak, his tall, lithe body taut. She was grateful for his strength in the storm that swirled around her. The weather had turned bitterly cold since daybreak, and she shivered as an icy gust whipped at her bare face and hands.

Kane slid an arm around her shoulder and their hips bumped together. She welcomed his closeness and felt warmer because his body blocked the frigid wind.

"Did you have any inkling of this?" he asked.

"None," Charity replied.

"Who are they?" he asked Charity as he looked at the two girls that resembled her.

"I believe they are my sisters. I'd like you to meet Faith and Hope," Charity said.

"Good God," Kane said, dropping his arm and crossing to examine each of the girls.

Charity noticed that Faith had slipped the prosthetic device behind her back, concealing her defect. "We're identical," she told Kane. "Down to the moles beneath our right ears." She hesitated, then added, "Except Faith doesn't have a left hand. Did you lose it in an accident?" she asked.

"She was born without it," Hope shot back. "It never grew."

"Oh," Charity said.

"I'm stunned," Kane said with a laugh that was half shocked, half amused. "Three of you, Charity. It's…"

"Appalling," Charity said. "My parents are alive, Kane. They gave me away and kept the two of them."

He crossed and embraced her, offering comfort. "Oh, sweetheart, I'm so sorry."

Charity hadn't wanted to come to Kane's home in north Texas for Christmas because she knew it was one more step toward a commitment. He'd already asked her once to marry him, and she'd refused. She couldn't see the point. There was no such thing as love, really. If parents could abandon their own children, what hope was there that two people who weren't even related could spend a lifetime loving one another? Better not to promise love in the first place. Or believe in the promises of others.

But she was feeling fragile, and Kane's strong arms felt good around her.

"I think I've figured out what must have happened," Faith said. The arm with the device at the end of it was no longer hidden, and she crossed to stand beside Hope. "I think it's all my fault."

"What are you talking about?" Hope said, frowning. "What could you have to do with Mom and Dad's decision to—"

She held out the prosthetic device at the end of her left arm and said, "These don't come cheap. Mom and Dad have made sacrifices for years to pay for the best care for me."

Charity found herself looking into the same pained dark eyes that she saw in her own mirror every morning.

"I wasn't in a position to refuse as a child," Faith said.

"They did what they thought they had to do. It must have been too great a financial burden for them to bear. I mean, three children all at once. And one of them... deformed."

"Don't *ever* use that word," Hope said, turning on Faith. "You're *perfect* in every way. You're simply missing a hand."

Charity felt another lurch of emotion. How lucky they were to have each other. She'd been so alone.

But she wasn't alone anymore. She had sisters. Two sisters, like her in every way. Except that they were strangers to her. And from the look on Hope's face, not likely to forgive her anytime soon for the monkey wrench she'd thrown into their lives.

"Maybe you girls ought to give your parents a call to prepare them before—" Kane began.

"No," Charity interrupted. "I want to see their faces. I don't want to give them a chance to make up some story."

"My parents don't lie," Hope said.

Charity saw the bleak look that crossed Hope's face when she realized that, of course they had lied—by omission—neglecting to tell their twin daughters that they were, in fact, merely two of three triplets.

"Why don't the three of you come inside—" Kane urged.

"No," Charity said, shaking her head. "For twenty-one years I've wondered who my parents were. I don't want to wait a minute longer to find out."

"They're good people," Faith said. "Good parents."

"Not to me," Charity retorted.

"If that's the way you feel, why bother meeting them?" Hope shot back.

"I want to know what happened," Charity said. "I think I'm entitled to know."

"I've told you what must have happened," Faith said.

Charity shook her head. "So why didn't they get rid of you?" she said to Faith. "You were the one who was going to cost them a lot of money. Or you?" she demanded of Hope. "Why was I the one who got dumped?"

"Maybe they drew straws," Hope said angrily. "What difference does it make now?"

She was right, Charity realized. What possible difference could it make to her now, if she finally knew why her parents had given her away? The fact was, they had. She was a grown-up. Her childhood was in her past. She would soon be a college graduate with a degree in economics. She was going to join the Peace Corps and serve in some foreign land for two years. At least, that had been her plan before Kane had proposed.

She hadn't been able to say yes to him. But she'd been tempted. Despite her feelings about the unreliable nature of love. Because the thought of belonging, of being loved by someone, was seductive.

Charity knew why Kane had invited her to attend his cousin's wedding. He was hoping the romantic atmosphere would induce her to want a wedding of her own. He'd told her about his cousins, eight adopted kids who'd all been loved and treasured by their parents, most of which, once Jake was hitched, would be happily married with families of their own.

He'd wanted to prove to her that love could last. He'd

wanted to prove to her that when he said, "I do," he meant it for a lifetime.

"Meeting your parents this way sounds like a bad idea," Kane said to Charity. "I think you should wait—"

Charity pulled herself free of Kane's embrace. "I'm not waiting. I intend to confront them now."

Since she'd met Kane in August, she'd learned all his moods. Worry lurked in his dark eyes now. But she knew he wouldn't try to change her mind. He respected her intelligence. He admired her spirit. He'd said he loved her.

She didn't trust such a fickle sentiment, but that didn't mean she hadn't realized the difference between Kane and the other males she'd met during her university years.

When Kane had asked her out after class one night, she'd been reluctant to go with him, because she'd found him much too attractive. He had hair as dark as her own and deep brown eyes that made her emotions feel jumbled when she looked into them. Against her better judgment, she'd gone with him to have a cup of coffee.

The "date" had been nothing like anything she'd previously experienced with the college boys she'd gone out with. There was no leering. No groping. No boasting of athletic exploits or sexual conquests.

Of course, Kane was six years older, twenty-six to her twenty, so maybe that explained the difference in his behavior. It had been a welcome relief when he spent the entire evening encouraging her to talk about herself. He'd seemed genuinely interested in finding out what she wanted to do with her life. He'd even hinted that he'd be willing to join her, if she really wanted to spend two years in the Peace Corps.

He'd never pressed her to be more than his friend. She'd found herself gravitating toward him, having conversations about subjects she'd never discussed with a man. She hadn't felt the need to distance herself from him, the way she had with the men who'd wanted more from her. But she hadn't totally let down her guard with him, either. She hadn't let herself fall in love with him.

Because all she'd known was abandonment.

It had taken her a long time to admit to Kane that she was adopted. And that her experience hadn't been anything like a TV fairy-tale-of-the-week.

Because she'd learned to trust and rely on him, it had come as a shock when she discovered that Kane wanted to be more than her friend.

Just before Thanksgiving break, he'd led her to a stone bench beneath one of the towering live oaks that dotted the University of Texas at Austin campus and urged her to sit. He'd taken her books from her and set them on the bench, then sat beside her and said, "I have something important to ask you."

"What is it?"

"I was going to wait and take you to dinner tonight. But there's been a family emergency and I have to leave right away, in the next few minutes, actually, if I'm going to catch my flight."

"What's wrong?" she asked anxiously.

"My sister, Karen, has been expecting her first child, and it arrived a little early," Kane said. "She and the baby are both fine, but there were some complications and she has to stay in the hospital. She asked me to come and spend some time with her husband. He's driving her nuts trying to wait on her hand and foot."

Charity had felt her heart clutching at the thought of Kane leaving so soon. She'd agreed to join him at his home in northwest Texas over Christmas for his cousin Jake's wedding, but she had no idea what Kane was doing after that. He was completing his graduate work this semester. She wouldn't be done for another six months.

She laid a hand on his arm and said, "Of course you have to go, if your sister needs you." She hesitated, then said, "Will I see you again before the wedding?"

"Of course, but there's something I want to say before I leave."

She looked at him expectantly and was surprised when he took her hands in his.

"I've been putting this off because I didn't know quite how to say what I'm about to say."

Charity felt the breath being sucked from her lungs. *He's changed his mind and is spending the Christmas holiday in Timbuktu. He's found a job in the Middle East. He's fallen in love with someone and—*

"I've fallen in love," he said.

"Oh, no!" Charity yanked her hands free to cover her face, which had contorted unexpectedly in despair.

He pried her hands loose and held them once more in his. His gaze was tender, and she was already missing him. Already regretting the loss of her best friend. She wanted to wish him well, but the words stuck in her throat.

He looked at her with concern, and she felt the tears brim in her eyes. "Please, Charity, don't cry."

"I can't help it," she sobbed. "How could you fall in love with—"

His mouth covered hers so swiftly, so completely, that she was too astonished to resist. His lips softened almost immediately against hers, coaxing a response, rather than demanding it. She was aware of the warmth of his mouth, of his tongue gliding along the seam of her lips seeking entrance. When she gasped at the erotic feeling, his tongue found its way inside to taste her and to offer pleasure.

She felt the kiss in her breasts, which ached, and in her loins, which drew up tight, responding to the exploding need inside her. She felt herself lean closer, open her mouth wider, welcoming the desire that fought its way past barriers that had been erected so high and so strong that no man had found a way past them. Barriers that had kept her safe from betrayal. Safe from suffering abandonment yet again.

Her growing desire was slowly but surely crushed by the terror that rose along with it.

She jerked away and stared, stunned and disbelieving, into the dark eyes of her best friend.

"How could you?" she gasped, wiping her hand across her mouth, as though she could erase what had happened.

"I've fallen in love with you, Charity."

"No," she said, shaking her head. "Don't say that. We're good friends. That's all."

He grasped her hands, which she realized were trembling badly. "You're the best friend I've ever had," he agreed. "But friendship isn't all I need from you. Or all I feel for you."

The terror was growing, a beast that threatened life and limb. "You can't love me."

He looked at her, his heart in his eyes. "Why not?"

"Because." *I'm unlovable.* She didn't say the word. But she felt it in the deepest core of her being.

"I do love you." He took a shaky breath, then said, "And I want to marry you."

She stood abruptly, jerking her hands free, agitated, confused. He rose and put his hands on her shoulders, which was all that kept her from bolting.

"I'm sorry this is such a surprise," he said. "But I didn't want to leave for the holiday without telling you how I feel."

"I have to go," she said. "I have to study."

She grabbed her books and had already whirled to run when his arm snaked around her waist, and he turned her to face him again.

"I thought you might feel the same way I do," he said. "I thought—"

"You thought wrong," Charity said. "I don't love you. And I have no intention of being married. Ever!"

His eyes clouded and his face looked strained. "You sound pretty certain about that."

"I am. You of all people should understand why I could never trust a man to…to…"

"To stick around for the long haul?" he finished for her.

"Yes," she said breathlessly. "Yes."

Because he'd been her friend, she'd told him how her drunken mother had admitted that Andy Burnette had left her because she couldn't have children. Charity wasn't even their baby. She was adopted, and Andy hadn't been able to love a baby that wasn't his own flesh and blood. He'd left her mother high and dry, stuck with a baby to raise and feed and clothe.

Once her mother had sobered up, she'd apologized and assured Charity that she was no burden, but rather the light of her mother's life. Sometimes, Charity had even believed her.

But she'd already been dumped twice in her life. Once by her real parents, and once by the father who'd adopted her. She was no glutton for punishment. She'd looked with a jaundiced eye at every man she'd dated, wondering if there was one who would ever stick around. She took what they offered—sexual pleasure— then walked away before they could leave her. They'd taken what they wanted and left without ever getting to know her.

All except Kane. Who'd become her friend.

She looked at him with troubled eyes. "How could you do this? I trusted you. I lo—" She felt a spurt of panic as she realized what she'd been about to say. She didn't love him. She was never going to love anyone. Because she couldn't count on anyone to love her back. She'd jerked free and run as fast as she could.

Away from temptation. And from pain.

Her whole life had been shadowed by the choice her biological parents had made to give her up for adoption. At last, she was going to have the chance to face them. At last, she was going to find answers for the unanswerable questions that had plagued her all her life.

She turned to her sisters and said, "I'm going. Right now. With or without the two of you."

Once again, Hope and Faith exchanged a look that

Charity found easy to read. They were coming along to protect their parents. And why not? When it had really mattered, their parents had protected them.

"Let me come with you," Kane said to Charity.

"I think this is something better resolved with just family," Hope said before Charity could answer him. "Don't worry," she reassured him. "We'll bring her back in one piece."

Charity was amazed that Hope could find humor in the situation. She felt shattered by what she'd discovered. Perhaps the answers she sought would provide a healing balm.

"Will you wait here for me?" she asked Kane. "I don't think this will take long."

"I'll be here," he said.

In his eyes she saw what he hadn't said. *To pick up the pieces.*

"Let's go," she said to her sisters. "The sooner this is done and over with, the better."

Charity slipped into the back seat of the car, while Faith slid behind the wheel and Hope buckled herself into the passenger seat. Charity stared at Kane as they drove away.

She wanted this confrontation. Her biological parents couldn't hurt her any more than they already had. In fact, she was looking forward to the opportunity of getting a few things off her chest. At long last, she could tell them how she felt about what they'd done. Hope turned in the seat to face her and said, "You'd better watch what you say. If you attack my mom and dad, I'll—"

"They're my parents, too," Charity reminded her. "I can say anything I please."

That shut Hope up, but Charity could see both girls were worried about the coming showdown.

"I can't wait to meet Mr. and Mrs...." Charity frowned and asked, "What's your last name?"

"Butler," Hope replied.

"I can't wait to meet Mr. and Mrs. Butler."

CHAPTER ELEVEN

FAITH, HOPE & CHARITY

FAITH FELT SICK INSIDE. SHE DIDN'T need her parents' confirmation to know that she was the reason Charity had been kicked out the door. She wasn't responsible for the way she'd been born. But that didn't mean she didn't feel guilty for the sacrifices her parents had made to provide the medical care she'd required. That remorse paled in comparison to the shame she felt knowing that, because of her, Charity had been given away.

She met Charity's gaze in the rearview mirror but couldn't hold it for long. "I'm sorry, Charity."

"What do you have to be sorry for? You didn't do anything."

"If you knew how hard Mom and Dad have worked to pay my medical expenses, you'd understand—"

"They should have worked harder," Charity shot back.

"There are only so many hours in a day," Faith argued.

"Maybe, in a million years, I might understand the reasons for what they did, but I'll never, ever forgive them for it."

"That's not fair," Faith said.

Charity snorted. "Fair? Was it fair for me to have to spend my life with people who didn't want me?"

Faith gasped. "Why would they adopt you if they didn't want you?"

"My 'father' decided an adopted daughter wasn't good enough and left my mother because she couldn't deliver him a child of his own. And my mother never let me forget it."

"I'm so sorry," Faith said.

"I don't need your pity," Charity snarled. "I managed fine."

"Sounds like sour grapes to me," Hope interjected.

"Don't you dare—" Charity began.

"Please don't fight," Faith said. "We'll be home soon and Mom and Dad can explain everything."

"I can't wait to hear what excuses they make," Charity muttered.

"Put yourself in their shoes," Faith said. "Can you imagine how they must have felt? I know they couldn't have wanted to give you up."

"How can you be so sure?"

"Because when Hope and I were about nine years old, Mom miscarried a baby. If you'd seen her grieve for that lost child, you'd know—"

"You're telling me that after she gave me away, she got pregnant again? She was actually going to have another baby when she'd given one away?" Charity asked incredulously.

"I overheard Mom and Dad talking, so I know it wasn't a planned baby," Faith explained. "But by then the worst of my medical expenses had been paid. I think they genuinely wanted another child. Mom was…devastated…when she miscarried in the fourth month."

Faith suddenly realized that her mother hadn't been losing a child for the first time. Knowing her mother as she did, she might even have believed God was punishing her for giving up the first child by taking the second from her. Faith didn't think God worked that way, but a grieving woman might be willing to place blame where it didn't belong.

Faith had done it often enough herself.

She'd grown up living in Hope's shadow, always careful to keep her deformity hidden, which she could do easily by sliding her arm behind her back. With that slight change in posture, she and Hope became identical twins.

Except, they'd never quite been that. There had been no hiding that missing hand in school. About an inch of flesh had grown beyond her left wrist and was tipped by tiny pink knobs that should have become fingers. The other children had looked and laughed. Nervously. Anxiously. Meanly.

Hope had been a militant protector, and over the years her behavior had become more and more outrageous so people were more likely to comment about "that wild child" Hope Butler, than to remark about Faith's missing hand.

But there had been times when some boy had mistaken Faith for Hope, and she'd seen what it might have been like to be perfect, like her twin, to find admiration in a boy's eyes, and sometimes even titillating sexual interest. But it never lasted longer than it took for the boy to realize she was the "other" twin.

Until Randy Wright had come along.

Faith hadn't believed Randy could be interested in her. She'd actually brought her arm out from behind her back, to show him the prosthetic device. He'd claimed it didn't matter to him, that he wanted to spend time with her, maybe go to a movie. But she'd seen the huddle of teenage boys nearby laughing and pointing and figured Randy might have been dared to ask her out. She'd learned to protect herself, and she'd almost said no.

But there was something about the look in Randy's eyes that said he wasn't playing a trick on her. And they'd started seeing each other. She could still remember the first time he'd taken her imperfect hand— or what there was of it—and laid it against his cheek, proving to her, and maybe to himself, that it didn't matter to him.

Their romance had survived the long distances that had kept them apart while they attended different colleges. But it hadn't been difficult to stay faithful to Randy, when he made her feel so cherished and loved.

She'd very much wanted Hope to find that kind of love, and though she'd never understood Hope's attraction to Jake, she'd been willing to support it. She hadn't had an opportunity to speak with Hope lately, but things didn't seem to be going as well as she'd hoped.

Charity's arrival was a shock. Faith still felt awestruck by the realization that she and Hope were not twins, that there had been three of them in the womb.

It struck her suddenly that the presence of the third child in the womb might have been the reason that she hadn't been born whole. It was that much more difficult for an egg to split perfectly three times, rather than twice. She glanced in the rearview mirror once more and studied her newly found sibling. And thought that a hand was a small price to pay for another sister.

HOPE HAD BEEN DYING OF CURIOSITY ever since she'd first laid eyes on Charity. She angled herself in the front seat so she could look at her sister—she was still having trouble accepting how exactly Charity looked like her and Faith—and asked, "Have you been living in Texas all this time?"

"I was raised in the hill country near Kerrville."

"Do you have brothers and sisters?"

"My mother couldn't have children, that's why she adopted me. And I've told you how that turned out."

"What kind of toothpaste do you use?" Hope asked.

Charity frowned. "Why in the world do you want to know that?"

Hope had always been fascinated by the studies that had been done on twins and triplets and quadruplets. She was curious to know whether the results she'd read about would hold true for herself and Faith and Charity.

She explained, "A lot of twin studies say that heredity has as much, or more, to do with who you are as environment. It sounds crazy, but twins separated at birth show remarkable preferences for the same toothpastes, soaps, cars, occupations, stuff like that. I wondered if we're all using the same toothpaste," she finished.

"I use Crest toothpaste and Ivory soap," Charity said. "I don't have a car. But I'd buy a Saturn if I had the money."

Hope glanced at Faith and then burst out laughing. "What's so funny?" Charity asked.

"We use Crest toothpaste and Ivory soap, too," Faith said. "And this is my mom's Chevy I'm driving. Hope and I have a blackberry-colored Saturn that we bought with our baby-sitting money when we were eighteen."

Charity shrugged. "Pretty superficial similarities, if you ask me. Those are popular brands."

"But still fascinating, don't you think?" Hope said. "What about your career plans? What did you study in college?"

"Business," Charity replied.

"Me, too," Hope said. "Faith went into hospital administration. She's already lined up a job at the local hospital."

"I'm going on to law school," Charity replied.

"Oh?" Hope said. "What kind of law do you want to practice?"

Charity hesitated, then answered, "Family law." Almost defiantly she added, "I plan to work with adoptive parents and children who need representation."

Hope settled back into her seat facing forward. "That's certainly environment at work," she muttered.

"What did you say?" Charity asked sharply.

"I was saying your choice makes a lot of sense, considering what you've been through," Hope said. "I've been wondering what it would have been like growing up as triplets. Faith and I made a splash as twins. We'd have created a tidal wave of comment and speculation as triplets. I don't think I'd have enjoyed being gawked at wherever I went."

"I'm glad to have spared you the trouble," Charity said.

"I suppose that sounds selfish," Hope conceded. "I'm sorry—"

"Don't," Charity interrupted. "I don't want your pity, either."

"It isn't pity," Hope said. "It's…empathy. Or sympathy. Whether we like it or not, the three of us are connected and always will be, especially now that we know you exist."

"I have no intention of hanging around here after I confront…your mother and father," Charity said. "I'm not even sure I'm going to hang around for the wedding."

Hope could feel Faith's eyes on her. With any luck, there wasn't going to be a wedding, so that was no loss. She hadn't given up on Jake. But she was troubled by what she'd allowed to happen between them.

Hope might have a degree in business, but she wanted to use her skills helping Jake on his ranch. At a time when it wasn't politically correct to focus on being a wife and mother, that was the most fulfilling goal she could imagine.

Maybe later she'd want to do other things—and maybe that was what had Jake so spooked. She had to admit she hadn't thought beyond having babies and raising them. But that could take twenty years, and along with all the ranch work that had to be done, keep her life full and satisfying.

What had been worrying her lately was what she would do with her life if she *didn't* marry Jake. She couldn't imagine herself with any other man, couldn't imagine the man that could measure up to Jake.

She glanced over her shoulder at the miraculous third sister who'd arrived so unexpectedly, and who planned to become a lawyer specializing in family law. Hope didn't have a traumatic childhood pushing her in any particular direction. She'd grown up happy, knowing her parents loved and cherished her, and with a sister who was her best friend and confidante.

What would life have been like if her parents had kept Charity? For one thing, Hope wouldn't have been the only "perfect" child. Would she still have been Faith's protector? Or would she and Charity have teamed up and shut Faith out?

Of course, they might all three have become bosom buddies if they'd grown up together.

What was going to happen now? What kind of havoc was Charity going to wreak on their parents' lives by showing up and accusing them of being heartless and cruel? Especially when she planned on exiting as abruptly as she'd entered.

"What is it you hope to gain from this confrontation with our parents?" Hope asked.

"Answers," Charity said.

"You already know the answers," Hope said. "Knowing what you do about Faith's situation, it's pretty obvious what must have happened."

"I want to hear it from them," Charity said.

"You want to reproach them for what they did," Hope said. "You want to rub their noses in the mess they made of your life."

"So what if I do?" Charity said. "They didn't give me a choice. They made it for me. I want them to see the results of what they did."

"You look pretty normal to me. You've got a boyfriend and a college education and you're not in jail or pregnant," Hope said.

Charity snorted. "That doesn't nearly sum up my life."

Hope turned to Faith and said, "I'm not so sure we should take her home, especially without giving Mom and Dad some warning. She's liable to upset them both."

Faith frowned. "You want me to take her back to Jake's place?"

"The more I think about it, the less certain I am we should just show up with her like this," Hope said.

"You can't keep me from seeing them," Charity said.

"No," Hope said thoughtfully. "But we can make sure they aren't ambushed by your visit."

Charity pulled out a cell phone and said, "Here. Call them. Tell them I'm coming."

Hope took the phone and punched in her home number. Her mother answered. "Mom, Faith and I are on our way home with…" Hope realized it wasn't going to be any less of a shock if she told her mother over the phone who was in the car with them "…someone who wants to meet you.

"It's a surprise," she said when her mother asked who it was. "We'll be there in about ten minutes. Is Daddy home? Good. Well, Faith and I wanted to give you fair warning. You'll see who it is when we get there. Yes, you've met her before. But it was a long time ago and she's…changed. See you soon. Love you, too."

Hope disconnected the call and handed the cell phone back to Charity.

"Why didn't you tell her?" Charity asked.

"I don't know," Hope admitted. "I suppose I was afraid of how she'd react."

"I'm glad you didn't tell her," Charity said. "I want to see her face when she recognizes me."

"You want to see her hurt," Hope said.

"She hurt me," Charity said.

"Not on purpose," Faith reminded her. "They're good people, Charity. You should give them a chance. Take some time to listen when you meet them. Let them explain."

"And apologize?" Charity said bitterly. "It's too little, too late."

Hope felt a sense of foreboding. Her mother's heart hadn't been good for some years. What if Charity's appearance caused a heart attack? She had to get into the house ahead of her. She had to give her parents warning. Losing a parent was too high a price to pay for a new sister.

CHARITY'S EMOTIONS WERE TUMBLING over one another. Anger. Excitement. Resentment. Anxiety. Bitterness. Relief. *Relief.* That was the one thing she hadn't expected to feel. But she finally had an answer for the nagging sense of abandonment she'd felt all her life.

It wasn't simply that she'd been forsaken by her parents. She'd been torn from siblings with whom she'd shared nine months in the womb. It must have been some lingering consciousness of that connection that had left her feeling so bereft.

Her anger was palpable, a barely controlled rage she hadn't even realized had been simmering all these years. It frightened her to realize she must have hidden the pain she'd felt even from herself. Now, like a scab ripped off of an oozing sore, those festering feelings were exposed.

Her heart hurt. Her chest physically ached. She'd wondered for so many years who her parents were, why they'd given her up. The truth was harder to bear than she'd expected. They'd had to choose which child to give up. And they'd chosen her. There must have been something horribly wrong with her for them to make that choice.

Maybe they'd gone eenie, meenie, miney, moe.

God. It couldn't have been like that. Or maybe it had been exactly like that. She thought of the war movies she'd seen, where who lived and who died seemed purely arbitrary. A bullet found you, or it didn't. Why had she been given away and not Hope? Honestly, it would have made far more sense to give away Faith.

She glanced from Hope to Faith. She had two sisters who looked exactly like her.

That reality was still too hard to grasp. She'd been alone since her mother had died last year from an embolism. Her mother's death had made her wonder even more about her biological parents. She'd gone on the Internet, started to search, then gotten scared and quit. What if her birth mother didn't want to meet her? That would mean a third rejection.

Two was plenty.

She wouldn't have been human if she hadn't imagined a powerful, emotional reconnection with her biological mother. She'd seen the reunions engineered on *Oprah* and *Maury* and *Ricki Lake*. In her own private scenario, her mother would have realized her mistake years before and would have searched fruitlessly for the daughter she loved. She'd miraculously find her at last, and they'd smile and hug each other hard and tremble with joy.

She was too anxious to smile. Too bitter to want to hug them. And if she was trembling, it was with rage.

Because it hadn't been a case of a young, unwed mother unable to care for her child. Her parents had been married, so both mother and father had made the decision that had changed the course of her life. She hadn't imagined a mother *and* a father. She'd never had a father. And she hadn't allowed herself to picture him in her mind.

But he existed.

And meet him she would. Confront him, rather. Demanding answers. Seeking some explanation for the restlessness that had tormented her for so many years.

"What are they like?" she asked.

Hope turned to face her. "Our parents? Like a mixture of us. Or rather, I suppose we're a mixture of them. Mom has dark eyes and brown hair. Dad has gray eyes and black hair. Mom is short. Dad is several inches over six feet."

"That's a physical description," Charity said. "I meant, what kind of people are they? What kind of parents were they?"

Hope pursed her lips. "Dad never went to church, but Mom took us every Sunday. We lived by the Golden Rule—Do unto others—"

"As you would have them do unto you," Charity finished. "But they didn't live it, did they? Not really."

"They were loving parents," Hope said stubbornly. "Dad taught us everything about how to run a ranch. That's what he does, manages other people's ranches."

"Not his own?" Charity questioned.

Hope shook her head. "Mom and Dad never had the money to buy a ranch of their own."

"My medical expenses kept them from saving enough for a down payment," Faith said.

"You make them sound like saints," Charity said sarcastically.

"I'm not saying they never wrangled. All parents do," Hope said. "But they loved each other. And they made it plain they loved us."

"How did they do that?" Charity asked.

"By setting limits for us. By giving us responsibilities and making us meet them. By teaching us to take care of each other. By—"

"No kisses when they tucked you into bed?" Charity interrupted.

"That, too," Hope said. "I don't think a day has gone by when Mom or Dad or both of them haven't said 'I love you' before I left the house."

Charity scoffed. "Yeah, right."

She saw the flush on Hope's cheeks that signaled her anger before her sister replied, "Actually, it was always more like, 'Love ya, kid,' or 'You know we love you, honey.'"

Charity felt the tears filling her eyes and the sting in her nose and turned to stare out the window, so Hope wouldn't see her lose control. She blinked hard and gritted her teeth to stop the wobble in her chin. The knot in her throat made it hurt to swallow.

"Are you okay?" Hope asked.

Charity kept her eyes out the window, where Santa Gertrudis cattle dotted the grassy plains. She swallowed, cleared her throat and said, "I'll be glad when this is over, and I can get the hell out of here."

Confronting a set of parents who'd given her away was an awfully high price to pay for her peace of mind.

CHAPTER TWELVE

CHARITY

CHARITY'S HEART WAS BEATING SO hard it hurt. At the end of the dirt road, she could see the ranch house where her parents and siblings lived. It was far nicer than she'd expected. The white, two-story wood-frame ranch house had large, shady porches on both levels, and pink impatiens hung in baskets at intervals, giving it a homey look.

She almost gasped when she realized a man and woman were sitting in rockers on the lower level porch. She tried to see their faces, but she was in full sunlight and they were in shade, and she couldn't make them out.

They had covered half the distance to the house when Hope suddenly said, "Stop the car, Faith."

Faith hit the brakes so hard Charity was thrown forward. Her nose was an inch from Hope's when Hope turned and said, "Maybe you ought to stay in the car while Faith and I tell Mom and Dad about you."

"No. I'm here. I'm going to talk to them."

"I didn't say you couldn't talk to them," Hope said. "I just think it might be better if we give them some warning before we spring you on them."

"Is one of them sick? Have a heart problem, or something?" Charity asked.

"Actually, Mom's heart isn't in the best shape," Hope said. "And I'm sure you're going to come as quite a shock."

"I'm not about to give either one of them a chance to run away without facing me," Charity said.

"I don't think they'd do that," Faith interjected.

"Oh, yeah? What's to stop them?" Charity saw Hope reaching for the door and reached for her own door, shoving her way out of the car about the same time Hope did. The two of them looked at each other past the glare off the hood, before Charity began striding across the dandelion-infested lawn, Hope a half step behind her. She heard another car door slam and realized Faith was following them.

Charity saw her mother raise a hand to shade her eyes, focusing on them, and then saw the hand drop, as she rose from her chair and moved to the wooden rail that surrounded the porch. Her hands gripped the rail, and she stared at them as they approached.

Charity's gaze was focused on her mother, and she saw her own dark brown eyes staring intently back at her from a pale face. She saw her mother's gaze flicker to Hope, and then to Faith, and then back to her. A second later, Charity saw her father slip an arm around her mother's waist to support her as she slumped back against him.

His gray eyes were piercing, narrowed, unwelcoming.

She felt her heart skip a beat, felt her step falter, then forced herself to continue forward. She walked up the three steps onto the porch, not willing to let the porch rail remain between them, not after all this time, not after finding her parents at last.

Charity could feel Hope's hot breath on the back of her neck, felt the touch of Faith's comforting hand briefly on her arm before she jerked it away. She took a step forward, distancing herself from her sisters, so she was standing directly in front of her mother and father.

She wanted to say something, but her throat had swollen completely closed. She felt her eyes welling with tears and blinked hard. She crossed her arms under her breasts, a defensive gesture in case her parents tried to embrace her. She didn't want them to touch her. If they did, she wasn't sure she could keep from falling completely apart.

Her breath came in short, openmouthed pants, and her stomach was knotted. Her knees were trembling and she stiffened to keep them from buckling. She wanted desperately to speak, wanted to accuse, to vilify, to blame.

But nothing came out.

Her mother had let go of the rail and turned to face her, one hand grasping her father for support, the other reaching out to Charity. "Oh. Dear God. Charity."

Charity felt the urge to throw herself into her mother's arms. But that would mean forgiving her. She wasn't ready to do that yet. Or maybe ever.

"So you know who I am," Charity said with a sneer.

"Of course we know who you are," her father said.

His jaw was so tight a muscle jerked, and his eyes were still narrowed. He, at least, was honest about his feelings. It was clear he didn't want her here now. Just as he obviously hadn't wanted her when she was a baby.

"Why?" The word was torn from her throat, a cry of unutterable pain and helpless rage.

"Let's go inside," her father said, starting to move her mother toward the front door.

They were going to escape. They were going to run without answering the questions she'd been harboring all of her adult life. "No!" she snarled. "You're not moving an inch until I get some answers."

She felt Hope grab her arm and yank her around.

"You can see Mom's ready to collapse," Hope said. "She needs to sit down."

"She can sit later."

But while Hope had distracted her, her father had moved her mother into the house.

"Now look what you've done," Charity cried. She started after them, but Hope stood in her way, putting out a hand to brace her shoulder, while Faith grabbed her hand.

"Please," Faith pleaded. "Give Mom a minute to get back her color."

Charity wanted to shove them both out of the way and run after her parents. But their hold was inexorable, and when she looked toward the open front door she saw her parents had already disappeared into the shadows inside.

"All right. They're gone. Now let go of me," she said.

Hope dropped her hand, but Faith held on.

"I know what you're feeling," Faith began.

"No, you don't!" Charity snapped. "Let go of me," she said, yanking herself free.

"Hey," Hope said, putting herself between Charity

and Faith. "Watch what you're doing. Faith never did a thing to hurt you. There's no reason to take out your frustration on her."

"You're in my way," she said to Hope, pushing herself forward.

She saw the indecision in Hope's eyes, the yearning to make a fight of it, and the quick glance at Faith, before she finally stepped out of the way. "Go on in," she said. "You'll probably find them at the kitchen table. That's where we have all our serious discussions."

It wasn't hard for Charity to find her way to the kitchen. It was at the back of the house, straight down a central hallway. As Hope had predicted, her parents were there. Her mother was sitting at one end of a long trestle table, a glass of water, dripping with icy condensation, on the table in front of her. Her father stood protectively behind her mother, his hand on her shoulder. Once again, he was staring at her with narrowed eyes.

"Never expected to see me again, did you?" she said. Her voice was harsh, angry, taunting.

"No," he admitted. "We didn't."

Oh, it hurt to hear him admit it. The knot was back in her stomach. And in her throat. She knotted her hands as well, to stop them from shaking.

She watched as Hope and Faith crossed into the room and stood together by the kitchen sink. Hope had grasped Faith's prosthetic hand. She didn't seem to notice the missing flesh and blood and bone.

Charity turned her attention back to her parents. She focused her gaze on her mother and managed to say with hard-won calm, "Why? Just tell me why."

"It is so wonderful to see you," her mother said haltingly. Tears dripped down her cheeks, and she brushed at them with her hand.

"Skip the sentimental crap," Charity said, feeling her heart melting in the face of her mother's obvious distress, and fighting the urge, once again, to comfort her. "Just answer the damned question."

"Watch your tongue, young lady," her father said. "You will respect your mother."

"She's not my mother! My mother is dead!"

In the silence that followed her outburst, Charity felt the blood thrumming in her head, felt the heat of a flush running up her throat to stain her cheeks.

In a hard, implacable voice her father said, "You will address my wife respectfully, or you will leave this house. Is that understood?"

Charity managed a tight nod.

"We tried to keep all of you," her mother said in a voice hoarse with emotion. "For two years we struggled to make ends meet. And then…" She shrugged defeatedly. "We realized we might lose all of you—" she glanced from Charity to Hope and Faith "—if we didn't give up one of you."

Charity didn't quite believe what she'd just heard. Was afraid to believe what she'd just heard. "Are you telling me that I lived with you—" She swallowed past the painful lump in her throat and continued. "As part of this family—" She swallowed again. "For *two years* before you gave me away?"

Her mother couldn't meet her eyes. She stared down at her hands, which were twisted together on top of the table. "Yes," she croaked. She looked up briefly, the shame rife in her eyes, before she looked down again. "Yes. I'm sorry."

Charity couldn't speak. No wonder she'd always felt bereft. Bereft didn't begin to cover it. Torn from the bosom of her family at *two years old!* Tossed out like a dirty dishrag. Her brow furrowed painfully as she searched for some memory, any memory, of the time she'd spent with her biological family.

There was none.

But now she knew why she had such a deep-seated fear of abandonment. She'd been ripped from her family at an age when she had enough memory of her parents and siblings in her subconscious to know they existed, but was too young to consciously remember them. Only the pain of separation, and the fear of ever enduring it again, had remained.

She sank into the nearest chair, her knees no longer able to keep her upright. "How could you?" she grated in a hoarse voice. "How could you?"

She heard Faith's sob, and Hope's soft, quiet words of comfort to her. She glanced up at her father, expecting the narrow-eyed, disapproving look that was all she'd seen since she'd arrived.

Tears glistened in his eyes.

"I knew you might come looking for us someday," he said. "I was afraid you would," he admitted.

"Sorry to inconvenience you," she said, her scornful voice tear-choked.

"Oh, baby," he said. "Oh, baby, you have no idea…"

He crossed to her in two steps, pulled her up out of the chair and surrounded her with his strong arms, pulling her tightly to him, rocking her as though she were a child who'd skinned her knee.

But there was more wrong with her than a skinned knee. Much more.

"Oh, baby," he crooned. "Sweetheart. We've missed you so much."

Some part of Charity must have needed the solace he offered, because she didn't try to free herself, simply allowed him to rock her in his arms. She couldn't hear what he was saying, because her heart was beating too loudly in her ears. She could smell tobacco and laundry detergent and male sweat, her father's scent. *Oh, God. She remembered it!*

He stopped rocking her and put his hands to her shoulders to move her far enough away that he could look into her eyes. "We regretted our decision later. But there was nothing we could do to reverse the adoption. The papers were sealed, and we couldn't find you."

Charity stiffened. "I lived in the same town my entire life, and you couldn't find me?"

"We tried," her mother said.

Charity shook herself free of her father's hold. The fact remained that they'd given her away. "Why me?" she demanded. "How did you choose me?"

For a moment, she was afraid to hear the answer. Her mother rose and joined her father. They faced her with their arms around each other, their expressions sad, their eyes tragic.

"I'm waiting," Charity said, her voice edgy with fear. "Was I the bad one? The ugly one? I certainly wasn't the deformed one," she added belligerently.

She heard Faith's soft cry and was immediately

ashamed of herself. She wasn't a mean person, but it was easier to lash out at others than to face the pain she felt.

"How did you choose?" she demanded. "I want to know."

Her mother and father exchanged a glance before her father turned to her and said, "Of course we kept Faith, because we would always love her as she is, when others might not. Hope was the troublemaker, the one who howled all night with colic. You were the most beautiful of our three lovely daughters."

"Bullshit," Charity countered. She saw her father's mouth flatten to a thin line, flushed, and continued. "We're triplets. We look exactly alike."

"You were the prettiest, with deep brown eyes that saw so much," he continued. "Such a perfect baby, always laughing, always smiling."

"Newborns don't laugh or smile," Charity countered.

Her parents exchanged a troubled glance and she remembered what he'd told her. She'd been two years old when they'd given her away. Had spent two years being loved by them, held by them, a part of them.

"We tried so hard to keep all three of you," her father said, "Finally, the medical bills were so overwhelming—"

"Which you paid to keep me," Faith said miserably.

"Oh, honey," her mother said, crossing to hug her. "It wasn't your fault. None of this was your fault."

Charity felt her insides twist as both Hope and her mother embraced Faith, enfolding her in their arms.

"Charity," her father said, drawing her attention to him once more. "We knew whoever became your parents would have to love you, because you were such a good child, such a happy baby. We gave up our most precious child. The one most certain to be loved by strangers."

Charity felt the tears spill from her eyes and stifled a sob with her fist. She had been the best baby, the most beloved. And therefore, the sacrificial lamb.

"I have to get out of here," she said. "I have to go."

She hurried from the room, unable to look at any of them any longer, and raced down the hall toward the front door. This family was the fantasy she'd always imagined in her dreams, loving parents and fun-loving siblings. But the dream had always ended when she'd woken to a nearly empty house and a mother who was there physically, but not otherwise.

The keys were in the Chevy and she gunned the engine and spun the wheels, spitting dust and gravel. The Butlers weren't going to turn her in for stealing their car. After all, she was their daughter.

She wheeled the car and headed it back toward Jake Whitelaw's ranch, where Kane waited for her. Kane, who had never understood why she wouldn't marry him.

Her vision was blurred by tears and she scrubbed at her eyes, veering over the center line once and hearing the angry blare of a car horn warning her back onto her side. Finally, she had to pull over, as the ululating howls of pain and anger shoved their way out through her mouth.

She wrapped her arms around herself as though to keep her flesh from splintering like ice smashed by a hammer. She needed someone to hold her, someone to warm her. She was so cold inside.

She forced herself to start the car again and drove

more sanely the rest of the way to Jake's ranch. She didn't want to see anyone but Kane, and she was lucky enough to find a cowhand who told her he was in the barn.

She found him there currying a saddle horse. "Hi," she said. It was all she could manage. The smile she attempted wobbled and then disappeared.

He took one look at her, dropped the currying comb and opened his arms to her. "Come here, sweetheart."

She ran into his arms, wrapping her hands tightly around his neck, pressing herself against him, sobbing and sobbing, as though her heart was broken.

Because it was.

"Love me," she begged. "Please, love me."

"I do love you," Kane murmured against her ear.

"Make love to me," she pleaded. She was tearing at his shirt, trying to get it unbuttoned.

He caught her hands and gripped them tightly. "Charity, honey, what happened? What's wrong? What did they say to you?"

She tried to free her hands, wanting to be closer to him, wanting him inside her, wanting to hide inside him. But his hold was inexorable. She felt the pressure of his hands, demanding an answer.

"You know I want to make love to you," he said in the gentlest voice she'd ever heard him use. "But not like this."

After Thanksgiving, he'd kissed her often, but she'd always called a halt when their lovemaking had gotten too intense for her, when it had seemed that if she gave herself to him fully she would be breaching some unbreachable chasm. She would tear herself from his embrace at the last moment, even when she knew he would be in pain if they stopped. And he'd never pressed her for more. Never forced her to fulfill the promise of those early kisses and touches.

His eyes had questioned why she stopped, but he'd allowed her to keep her secrets. She knew he must have wondered why she wouldn't make love to him, especially when she'd made it clear she was no virgin. She'd made love with boys in high school and in college. She'd given herself to them physically. But she'd never gotten emotionally involved with any of them. Not the way she'd let herself get involved with Kane.

She hadn't wanted to fall in love with him. She'd resisted the attraction. But he'd done what no other man in her life had ever done. He'd become her friend first. She'd learned to like him more than anyone else she knew. She'd learned to rely on him.

She'd trusted him. Which, when she thought about it later, was something she hadn't allowed herself to do with any of the men with whom she'd been physically intimate.

She'd been shocked the first time Kane kissed her, because it had been so unexpected. And because she'd been caught off guard, she'd been assaulted by feelings she hadn't expected. Tumultuous feelings. Jumbled-up feelings of love and like and to her surprise…enormous desire.

She'd been so upset, she'd refused to speak to him for a week after he'd returned. She'd wanted to talk to her best friend about what she was feeling, but Kane was her best friend, and she'd shut him out of her life. She'd expected him to walk away, as every other man had when he'd gotten what he wanted from her. She'd expected him to give up, to abandon her, as it seemed everyone always did.

But Kane had not given up. He'd persisted in calling her until at last she'd agreed to see him again.

"I don't expect you to feel for me what I feel for you," he'd said. "At least not right away. But I'm not going anywhere. I've got all the time in the world for you to change your mind. I've got the rest of my life."

She hadn't believed him. She'd figured he would get tired of waiting for her to put out—because she'd made up her mind she wasn't going to have sex with him— and drift away in the wind.

But he hadn't gone anywhere. He'd hung around, loving her, offering himself to her, stopping when she would remember that she didn't want to give herself to him—even though she wanted to. Very much. She'd wanted him for a long time.

She just wasn't going to let herself have him.

Because the moment she did, she feared he would be gone. Like all the others.

Only, now she knew why she believed she would be abandoned by anyone she allowed herself to love. Because it had really happened. Her parents had sent her from them. She couldn't help wondering what her thoughts might have been as a child of two. What had that two-year-old imagined had caused her to be thrust from her family? What had she been told by those who had given her to another family to be raised as their own?

Your parents love you, but they had to give you away because they can't afford to keep you. Probably not.

Your parents love you, but another family wants a baby and since your parents have two others just like you they offered to share you with this other family. Sounded possible.

Your parents are dead. This family really wants a baby and they chose you. Sounded probable.

But that didn't really explain why her own parents would give her up. Charity still couldn't imagine any scenario where she, personally, would give up a child.

But they'd said they might have lost all three children if they hadn't given up one. What if she were the one on the verge of bankruptcy, with the prospect of becoming homeless and having to live in a car...or on the streets? What sort of life would that be for her child? A good family, a different family, would surely provide a better life for a child destined to grow up in abject poverty.

She could understand. But she could not forgive.

"Charity?" Kane said, his eyes studying hers. "What happened?"

"My parents didn't give me up as a newborn," she said bitterly. "They kept me around until I was two years old."

She saw the shock and horror in his eyes before he pulled her close and clutched her tight.

"Sonofabitch," he muttered. "So that's it. I always figured... Damn them. Damn them to hell."

"No." The protest surprised Charity. She lifted her face to look into Kane's eyes. "They...had no choice."

"I find that hard to believe," Kane said.

Charity frowned. "I believe they thought they had no choice," she said. "They had three babies and one of them needed a lot of expensive medical care."

"Still, that's no excuse—"

"It's all right, Kane. It doesn't matter."

"Doesn't matter? How can you say—"

"Make love to me," she said, looking him in the eye. She could see the confusion in his eyes, the distrust of her motives.

"Why now?" he asked. "What's changed?"

She found herself putting into words what she'd begun to feel inside ever since her parents had explained to her what had happened when she was a baby. "My whole life I've never felt like I could really trust a man not to walk away if things got tough. I always thought it was because my father—my adoptive father—abandoned me and my mother.

"But that wasn't it at all. He came and went so quickly in my life that I don't think his leaving had much effect one way or the other. It was losing my family—my sisters and my mother and father that made me so distrustful. Children are resilient. Everyone says so. The wound healed, all right. But it left a deep scar."

"Are you saying you can trust me now?"

She managed a smile. "I wish I could. I want to, very much." But she didn't. She couldn't.

His kiss was gentle at first, but that lasted as long as it took for her tongue to slide into his mouth. His passion rose quickly, and she could feel the hard ridge pressed against her belly.

"Wait," he said breathlessly, holding her head between his hands so she was forced to look at him. "Wait."

"What is it?"

"Will you marry me? Say yes, Charity. We can have

the ceremony this week, while all my relatives are here for Jake's wedding."

Charity felt a familiar flare of panic. "You're moving too fast. I—"

"What are we waiting for?"

She searched his eyes and realized why he was in such a hurry. He was afraid her fear of commitment, for which she finally had an explanation, would rear its ugly head. "I'm not going to run anymore, Kane. I'm not going to hide from what I'm feeling. I'm not going to be afraid of loving you."

Although she wasn't yet ready to say the words to him.

He kissed her again, and she felt a yearning to be joined with him, to become one with him forever. Her hand slid down the front of his jeans and she heard him groan before he reached down to cover her hand.

"We've got all the time in the world," he said. "A lifetime. Let's do this right."

She grinned and said, "I thought I was doing it right."

"I mean, let's make sure we have privacy and a soft feather mattress instead of a bed of straw."

"What's wrong with straw?"

"It's itchy as hell."

She laughed and slid her hand back up his chest until she was cupping his cheek. "I do...want you, Kane." She could see from his face that it wasn't what he'd been hoping to hear. But it was the best she could do.

"You haven't given me an answer to my proposal," he reminded her.

"So much has happened—"

"Say yes," he urged.

She wanted to say yes. She wanted to marry him and be committed and be over the fear of abandonment that had followed her all her life. She opened her mouth to agree, but what came out was, "I'll give you an answer soon."

"Tomorrow?"

"Soon," she promised. She rose on tiptoe and kissed him lingeringly, fitting her body to his, feeling the rightness of it, enjoying the pleasure that rose inside her. "Are you sure I can't tempt you right now?" she murmured in his ear.

His hands cupped her buttocks and he pulled her tight against him. "Lord knows I want you. But I think I'm going to hold out till our wedding night."

She stared at him in astonishment, then burst out laughing. "Why, you...tease!"

He grinned at her and said, "I'll use whatever works. If you want me half as much as I want you, we'll be married by the end of the week."

She took a step back so he was forced to let her go. She eyed him seriously and said, "I'm moving as fast as I can, Kane. I want to believe we can live happily ever after. I just..."

"Don't," he finished for her.

She grimaced. "I wish I could tell you what you want to hear."

"But you can't. It's all right, Charity. Believe me, it will be all right. Now, where are these sisters of yours?"

"I...kind of ran out on them," she admitted. "I'm not sure they're going to want to have much to do with me."

"Why is that?"

"Because I gave their parents—my parents—such a hard time."

"They'll get over it."

She raised a brow. "How do you know that?"

He put an arm around her shoulder and headed out of the barn. "Between my twin sisters Karen and Kayla, and my older brother Kyle, I've had lots of experience with sibling rivalry."

Charity took a deep breath as they left the fecund smell of the barn behind and stepped into the sunlight. She saw a blackberry-colored Saturn parked at Jake Whitelaw's back door. Her sisters hadn't wasted any time coming after her.

"Maybe you're right," she conceded.

She saw her sister Hope—she knew it was Hope because she had both hands—coming toward her, lips clamped tight, arms swinging angrily.

And maybe he was all wrong. She would know pretty damn quick one way or the other.

CHAPTER THIRTEEN

HOPE

"I HOPE YOU'RE HAPPY!" HOPE SNARLED at Charity as she closed the distance between them. "Mom collapsed after you left, and Dad had to rush her to the hospital."

Hope was as angry with herself as with Charity, whose face drained of color. She should have known better than to spring that kind of surprise on her mother, who'd been taking heart medication for the past three years. But she'd been half in shock herself, discovering she was actually a triplet, and had wanted answers from her parents as much as Charity had.

"Is she going to be all right?" Charity asked.

"How the hell do I know? She was gasping for breath and holding her chest and white as a sheet."

"Then what are you doing here?" Charity demanded. "Why aren't you at the hospital?"

"Because..." Because she couldn't bear seeing her mother in pain, gasping for breath. Because she needed someone else to blame for what had happened.

"If you're not going, I am," Charity said sharply. "What hospital is she in?"

"There's only one in town," Kane said. "I'll take you."

A moment later, Charity was gone. Hope stared at the dust kicked up by Kane's pickup, wondering at her sister's abrupt about-face. Charity had said she didn't care, that she would never forgive her parents for what they'd done. Yet, her first thought had been to race to the hospital.

"Is everything all right?" a female voice asked. "Where did Charity go in such a hurry?"

Hope turned to find Jake on the back porch with Miss Carter by his side, his arm around her waist.

Hope felt a stab of pain at the sight of them together. He was going to go through with the wedding. He was going to marry the wrong woman. Infernal man!

"Hope?" Miss Carter prodded. "Is something wrong?"

"You bet something's wrong!" she shot back. She couldn't say what was really wrong, that she was in love with the other woman's fiancé. But Miss Carter had left an opening for attack, and Hope thrust hard. "Thanks to you, my mother's in the hospital. She could die!"

The stricken look on Miss Carter's face gave Hope little satisfaction. She felt as though she'd been sucker-punched when Miss Carter broke into tears and Jake opened his arms to her, offering comfort.

The reproachful look Jake gave her over Miss Carter's shoulder made Hope want to dig a hole and climb into it. She felt like screaming with frustration, but she wasn't about to do it in front of her rival. She could see Jake expected her to let Miss Carter off the hook. But she couldn't do that, either.

"It *is* her fault!" Hope protested to Jake. "She's the one who got us all together."

"Whose idea was it to confront your parents?" Jake asked.

Hope gritted her teeth to keep her chin from quivering.

"It's all right, Jake," Miss Carter said, looking up at him with tear-streaked eyes.

How could Miss Carter look so pretty when she was crying? Hope wondered. Hope always looked terrible when she cried, her face patchy, her eyes red and swollen. She watched, her stomach knotted, as Jake used the pad of his thumb to gently wipe the tears from Miss Carter's cheeks.

"What happened isn't your fault, Amanda," Jake said. "It was the girls who decided to surprise their mother."

"I could have said something. I could have told the girls' father, so he could have prepared their mother in advance. I could have—"

Jake turned to Hope, his look stern—like a *father,* not a *lover,* not a *husband,* and damn it, not an *equal*—and said, "Hope, I think you owe Amanda an apology."

"Not in this lifetime!" she spat. "You're not my father, Jake. You're not my husband. You're not… *anything* to me. You don't have the right to give me orders."

She whirled and marched toward her car in high dudgeon. She hadn't gone two steps before Jake grabbed her arm and swung her around.

"You need someone to teach you basic, common courtesy," he snapped.

"You can go to hell!" she retorted.

"Watch your mouth, little girl, you—"

She hadn't known she was going to slap him. Her arm

seemed to rise and swing on its own, cracking against his cheekbone with a satisfying *thwack!*

He looked at her for an instant with eyes as stunned and angry as her own.

"You asked for it," she said breathlessly. "You shouldn't have called me a little girl. Because I'm not, Jake." She could feel the tears welling in her eyes, feel her chin begin to wobble. "I'm not a little girl, Jake. I'm not. I'm not!"

She was crying in earnest when she felt his mouth on hers, offering succor, offering solace. She felt his strong arms wrap around her and pull her tight, her breasts crushed against the hard wall of his chest. She rose on tiptoe to fit their bodies together, her hands clutching at his hair, holding him with all the desperation she felt, her mouth opening to meet the urgent thrust of his tongue.

She moaned.

He made a guttural sound in his throat, and she felt his hands behind her hips and then under her knees, lifting her up into his arms.

"I'm sorry," he murmured against her mouth. "I'm sorry, Hope."

He turned to walk into the house with her and froze.

Hope felt him stiffen and opened her eyes. And saw Miss Carter staring at them, her eyes wide with dismay. Well, more like shock. All right, horror. And something else that made Hope feel ashamed. *Humiliation.*

Hope made a little move in Jake's arms, indicating that he should put her down. He released her knees and she slid to her feet. He took a step to the right, his hand falling off her shoulder.

Hope straightened her shirt and lifted her eyes defi-antly to Miss Carter's, but she couldn't hold the other woman's gaze. She had wanted to strike back. But not like this.

Jake spoke first. "Amanda, I—"

"There's no need to explain," Miss Carter said in a high, clipped voice. "I think the situation is perfectly clear."

"Amanda, I—"

"Please, Jake. I'd like to go home now."

Hope's stomach sank to her toes. Of course. Jake had brought Miss Carter here from church, so he was going to have to take her home. The two of them were going to have to get into a car together and spend the next half hour in uncomfortable silence.

"We need to talk," Jake said.

Hope didn't like the sound of his voice. It grated with pain and self-disgust. She knew how he felt. She wasn't feeling very proud of herself at the moment.

"I'm sorry, Miss Carter," she blurted.

"Are you really, Hope?" Miss Carter challenged. "I think you got exactly what you wanted. Exactly what you've wanted for the past three years."

Hope felt the blood leave her face. The accusation made her sound wanton. Like some sort of female vampire sucking blood from an unwilling victim. But Jake had kissed her. All she'd done was... provoke him.

"That's enough, Amanda," Jake said. "We'll discuss this in the car."

Hope was surprised to hear Jake come to her defense. Or maybe he just didn't trust her not to make another scene.

"I'll get my purse and meet you at the car," Miss Carter said. She turned and walked inside, her back ramrod straight, her shoulders squared, letting the screen door slam behind her.

Jake thrust both hands through his hair and groaned.

Hope wasn't sure what to say, what to do. She wasn't going to apologize to him. He was in the wrong. He knew how she felt about being called a *little girl*. They'd been lovers. She was his equal in every way—except age. And there was nothing she could do to change how old she was.

"I didn't want to hurt her like that," Jake said. "I'm going to have to grovel pretty hard to get her to forgive me."

Hope's heart jumped to her throat and nearly choked her. He was going to ask for forgiveness? He was going to make amends? He was going to marry Miss Carter even after what had just happened?

"You are the biggest fool I ever met, Jake Whitelaw," she said in a scathing voice. "You seem bound and determined to ruin your life. She's not the woman for you. I am. But if you're too stubborn to realize what's staring you in the face, I give up. I'm done. That's it. I'm out of here."

She headed for her car, expecting him to grab her arm and stop her.

But he didn't.

Her eyes were so blurred by tears, she could hardly see to drive to the hospital. She wanted Faith. She needed to pour out her despair to a pair of sympathetic ears. And she needed someone to hold her up if the news about her mother was bad.

She had always marveled how everyone thought she was the strong one. Faith was stronger. Faith had faced more adversity and overcome it. Faith had always been her rock. Faith would comfort her. Faith would understand and sympathize.

Then she remembered that Faith wouldn't be at the hospital alone. Charity would be there. Charity, who'd wreaked havoc by her appearance, revealing that Hope was not the favored child she had always believed herself to be.

Her father's words to Charity were burned in Hope's memory. *You were the most beautiful of our three lovely daughters.... You were the prettiest...a perfect baby, always laughing, always smiling.... We gave up our most precious child.*

It was quite a shock to discover that her parents had favored one child above the others. Alarming to realize that the child they'd favored was her sister Charity. Of course, it had cost Charity. She'd been given away because of it. Hope was still struggling to acknowledge her father's description of her. *Hope was the trouble-maker, the one who howled all night with colic.*

Hope wondered what her parents had thought as they'd watched her grow. Wondered if they'd ever regretted the choice they'd made. Even if she'd stopped howling with colic, she hadn't stopped being a trouble-maker. But she couldn't help who she was.

Yes, she pushed back when she was pushed. Yes, she went after what she wanted. Yes, she wasn't above conniving to get it. Did that make her a bad person?

Maybe her parents had given away the wrong child. On the other hand, would she have been able to survive the life Charity had described? Or would her brashness and stubbornness and sometimes unscrupulous behavior have been magnified into something truly mean-spirited? Hope wasn't sure she would have been as sympathetic to an adoptive mother who didn't love her. She would have run away. She would have fought back. Somehow. Because she wasn't tolerant. She wasn't patient.

She would have hated her life. She would have hated her mother. She would have hated everyone around her.

It wasn't a thing she would have admitted to anyone else. It wasn't anything she would have said aloud. But she knew her parents had chosen rightly. She couldn't have survived what Charity had survived.

That admission gave her a new respect for her sister.

Hope felt her heart begin to beat a little faster when she entered the hospital. It smelled like one, nose-curling ammonia and antiseptics. It sounded like one, the rattle of carts and the impersonal intercom calling doctors. It looked like one, pale green walls halfway up and spick-and-span linoleum that must be buffed every hour on the hour.

She asked at the reception desk where she could find her mother and discovered she was in the intensive care unit. That didn't sound good. She headed upstairs and found her father and two sisters sitting on colored plastic chairs in the waiting room outside the ICU.

"How is she?" Hope asked her father.

His expression was grim. "She's had a heart attack. They don't know yet how much damage there is to the heart. All we can do is wait and see."

"Oh, God." Hope felt her knees begin to buckle and

then felt Faith's arm slide around her waist. Her sister led her to an orange plastic chair and urged her into it.

"Mom's stronger than you think," Faith said as she met Hope's guilty gaze. "And she has a great deal to live for."

Faith glanced toward Charity.

"You mean her," Hope said, her gaze settling on Charity.

She realized Kane wasn't with her sister. "Where's your boyfriend?" she asked.

"He went to see his sister's baby in the neonatal ICU. He'll be back," Charity said.

"Then maybe this is a good time for us to talk," Hope said.

Charity lifted a brow. "About what?"

Hope turned to her father and said, "I feel bad about what happened to Mom, but I still don't understand how you could have done what you did to Charity. I can't help thinking it could just as easily have been me."

"Or me," Faith said as she sat on a yellow chair beside Hope.

They stared at their father, waiting for his response.

He turned away, parting the slatted venetian blinds and staring out, as though he could find the words to explain somewhere out there on the desolate prairie. "We didn't make our choice lightly," he said at last.

"We had a right to know," Hope said. "Why didn't you tell us?"

Her father turned and met her gaze. "It wouldn't have changed anything."

Hope exchanged a glance with Faith, wondering if they should reveal the secret they'd kept for so many years. The words came blurting out before she could stop them. "Faith and I have known for a long time that…some part of us…was missing."

Her father made a low, grunting sound.

"What did you tell us back then?" Hope asked. "How did you explain Charity's disappearance from our lives?"

She watched her father's hands ball into fists, watched the muscles cord in his forearms, saw the blue veins that strained against his skin. He made a surprising villain. But villain he was. Along with their mother, he'd kept this dastardly secret for nearly twenty years.

Hope's stomach was churning, and she felt sick. Although she bore no responsibility for what had happened to Charity, her sister had nevertheless paid a price for the life Hope had been allowed to lead. She and Faith had always wondered why their parents had named them Hope and Faith when there was no Charity. They'd puzzled over it but never imagined another child in the womb with them, never imagined a sister who'd spent the first two years of her life in their home.

They'd known, all the same, that something was wrong. And had done nothing, said nothing, to try to dispel the feeling. How might things have been different if they'd confronted their parents sooner?

"Why couldn't you find Charity when you went looking?" Hope demanded. "If she's been in the same place all these years, it should have been easy."

"It wasn't as easy twenty years ago as it is today for adoptive parents and children to find one another," her father explained. "I wish your mother…"

He was clearly uncomfortable making the explanations Hope had demanded. She watched his Adam's apple bob as he swallowed, then continued, "We did try to find her, but couldn't. After a while, we thought it would be cruel to force ourselves back into Charity's life. It would only be confusing and perhaps make her unhappy. And we didn't want to cause pain for her adoptive parents."

"We're *triplets*," Hope said. "We belonged together!"

"You've got each other now," her father said, looking from each girl to the next.

As though that excused what had gone before, Hope thought. "You haven't told me what lies we were told," Hope reminded him.

Her father paled, then flushed. "We told you she died. We told you she'd gone to heaven."

"Oh, God." Hope put a hand to her mouth to hold back a moan of pain. She heard Faith's wail and felt it to her core.

"I have to get out of here," Hope said, rising abruptly. "I need some air, some time to think," she said to her father. "Come on, Faith."

She never questioned that her sister would come with her. They'd been inseparable since birth. Best friends. Confidantes. They could almost read each other's minds. She knew Faith felt as devastated as she did by their parents' betrayal.

And yet, Faith hesitated.

They might have been born of the same egg split in two—make that three—but they were not the same. Faith's missing hand had given her a different perspective on life, had made her more patient, more tolerant, more compassionate.

Hope's jaw jutted. "Are you coming?" she asked Faith.

She saw the moment when Faith realized that Hope needed her as much as their father and mother did. When push came to shove, Faith was always going to put Hope's needs first. Their parents could take care of each other.

"I'm coming," Faith said.

"Where are you two going?" her father asked.

"Why do you care?" Hope retorted.

"I'm still your father," he said implacably. "I want an answer."

Faith met her gaze, then turned to their father and answered, "We'll be at home."

That was as good a place as any to lick their wounds, Hope thought.

It wasn't until they were on the highway that Faith said, "I'm not going home with you."

"Why not?"

"I don't want to talk about this right now. I'm still feeling too…raw. Especially after what we found out today. I mean…"

"It wasn't your fault," Hope said angrily. "They made the decision to give her away. You couldn't help the way you were born."

"It doesn't make me feel any less guilty," Faith admitted. "Can you drop me off at Randy's house?"

"I can. I'm not sure I should."

"Please, Hope. I want…I need…"

Hope eyed her sister. Because she and Faith had always been so close, it had never occurred to her that it wouldn't always be that way. She'd been in love with

Jake for three years and should have bonded with him. But Jake hadn't been there for her. She still needed Faith.

Faith had loved Randy for the past three years…and he'd loved her back. It had never dawned on Hope— until this moment—that her role had been usurped. Randy had become the most important person in Faith's life. Faith wanted…and needed…him now.

Hope saw the apology in Faith's eyes. Yet she still felt unaccountably hurt. It wasn't fair. She'd lost Charity a long time ago. Now she was losing Faith. And she was a long way from having Jake as a permanent part of her life.

"Sure," she said, her throat tight. "I'll be glad to drop you off at Randy's place."

"I thought you'd understand," Faith said quietly. "Because of how much you love Jake."

"I do," Hope conceded. "It's just…hard not to be first anymore."

She felt Faith's prosthetic hand on her arm. Words weren't necessary. The bond was there and always would be, but love for one's sister, even when they'd started life together in the womb, was no match for the love of one's soul mate.

Hope was happy for her sister. And envious of her.

Her soul mate still planned to marry another woman six days from now.

Randy was repairing the porch railing when they arrived. With bleak eyes, Hope watched Faith run into Randy's open arms. Her sister glanced back at her once, then followed Randy into the house.

Hope's nerves felt raw. She backed the Saturn and headed home, knowing full well there was no one waiting for her there.

It was hard to keep fighting for the love of a man who seemed so determined to throw himself at another woman. Hope wanted to be chased, instead of doing the chasing. She wanted Jake to want her badly enough to come after her.

Which meant she had to stop pursuing him. Which meant she had to let nature take its course.

That wasn't going to be easy. Hope had always gone after what she wanted—and always gotten it. Until Jake Whitelaw had come along.

Hope stopped the car at her parents' back door but didn't turn off the engine. She needed a plan, but nothing was coming to her. The knock on the closed window startled her. She rolled it down and said, "What are you doing here, Jake?"

"We need to talk."

"What did you do with Miss Carter?"

"Rabb stopped by. He's dropping the kids at Mom's and then taking her home."

"So you came running here to see me," Hope said.

"Amanda called off the wedding," he said.

Hope felt the breath stop in her chest. "So what do you want from me?"

"I…" He pulled off his Stetson and slapped it against his jeans then set it back low on his head. "Damned if I know."

Hope's chest ached. Her throat was raw. "I can't do this anymore," she said. "It hurts too much."

She shifted the car into reverse, but before she could back up, Jake reached in, turned off the ignition and pulled out the keys.

"Let's go inside and talk," he said.

"What is there to say? Miss Carter turned you down, and you still don't want me."

"Oh, I want you, all right."

Hope's eyes went wide. "You want to marry me?"

"I didn't say that," Jake said.

Hope grabbed the door handle and shoved her way out of the car, knocking Jake off balance. "Go away, Jake. Go home. Leave me alone. I don't ever want to see you again."

She could feel the heat of him at her back as he followed her to the kitchen door. It wasn't locked, and she shoved it open and stepped inside, turning immediately to close the screen door and lock it. Not that that would have kept him out, if he'd forced the matter.

But he didn't. It was one more sign that he didn't care enough to fight for her.

Jake's image was distorted by the mesh screen and blurred by the tears that brimmed in her eyes. "You had your chance, Jake. I would have made you a good wife, but I'm tired of waiting around for you to make up your mind. I'm going on with my life. Without you. Goodbye, Jake."

She closed the kitchen door until she heard the latch click. And then turned the lock.

CHAPTER 14

FAITH

FAITH WALKED STRAIGHT INTO RANDY'S open arms, gripping him around the waist and holding on tight. He was naked from the waist up, his beltless jeans slung low on his hips. His skin was salty against her lips, and he smelled of hard-working man.

"Hey, babe," he murmured in her ear. "You all right?"

She didn't answer him, just shoved her nose harder against his chest and tightened her grasp.

He knew her well enough not to say anything more. She gasped when he picked her up, but slid her arms up around his neck as he carried her inside. Randy's sister Jenny and her husband Colt were still on vacation, and Jake was taking care of their two kids, so she and Randy had the house to themselves.

"I've been hoping you'd come by," Randy said as he carried her into his bedroom. He laid her on the navy-blue chenille bedspread and lay down beside her, pulling her close again. "We haven't taken advantage of this empty house the way we should."

Faith raised her face for his kiss and felt the gentle touch of his lips. But she needed escape, and gentleness wasn't what she wanted right now. She thrust her tongue into his mouth and wrapped her jean-clad leg around his hip.

He grasped her rear end and pressed their bodies together so she felt his arousal. She forced her hand down between them and inside his jeans.

"Whoa, babe," he said breathlessly. "I want you too much to—"

"Take off those jeans," she ordered, freeing her hand and reaching for the buttons of her shirt. He yanked off his boots while she stripped away her shirt and unsnapped her bra. She took a second to unstrap her prosthetic device and dropped it over the edge of the bed onto the rug.

He was out of his jeans and underwear before she was, so he reached for the snap of her Levi's and zipped them down, sliding his hand down inside her panties. He inserted a finger inside her as his mouth latched on to hers, catching her gasp of surprise and pleasure. A last shove and her clothes were gone.

Naked flesh met naked flesh as their bodies pressed together. She slid her arm around his neck and reached for his genitals with her hand. They were both too excited to spend time on foreplay. She wanted him inside her and guided him there.

He grunted softly as their bodies merged, and she groaned as he seated himself to the hilt. She put her feet flat on the bed and tilted her hips up to angle her body into his, as he began to move inside her. He sought her mouth and their tongues dueled, mimicking the thrust and parry of male and female seeking sexual satisfaction.

Their breathing became labored as he moved over her and she writhed beneath him. She grasped his hair and moved her arm over his back, bucking against him, meeting his savage thrusts. The moan of pleasure grated in her throat as her body began to spasm, and he made a guttural sound as he emptied his seed into her welcoming womb.

She felt the weight of him on top of her and unwrapped her legs from around his hips, unaware when or how they had gotten there. They were breathing hard, their bodies like bellows, as he laid his cheek against hers.

"I'm too heavy," he muttered.

She held him where he was. "Don't move. Please. I like the weight of you on top of me."

He groaned loudly. "I'm too tired to move anyway."

She ran her fingers through his thick hair and held on to his back, now slick with sweat, with her arm. "I have something I need to tell you," she said.

"Umm," he murmured.

"We're going to have a baby."

She felt his body stiffen, before his head jerked up. Then she felt his upper body lift from hers as he braced himself on his arms.

Faith kept her eyes closed, afraid to see what effect her news had. She wanted Randy to be happy, because she was. They both still had another year of college to finish, but the baby wouldn't be coming until summer. They hadn't planned to have a baby right away, and she'd been taking the pill. But she'd been sick with the flu over Halloween, and everything had come up for a few days—including, apparently, her birth control pills.

Now she was pregnant.

"How…? Open your eyes, Faith," he said.

She hesitated a moment, then squinted up at him. When she saw he was smiling—grinning, actually—she opened her eyes and grinned back. "Remember when I was sick with the flu? I guess I lost my pills along with my lunch."

"I can't say I'm sorry," he said.

"You look pretty proud of yourself."

"I'm going to be a father," he said in wonder. He slid to her side and laid his hand on her belly. "There's a tiny little Wright growing inside you."

"A tiny little Butler," she corrected.

"We're not going to let Miss Carter's wedding preparations go to waste, are we?" he said, still grinning. "Somebody should get married on Saturday."

Faith sighed. "I've been a sorry failure as a matchmaker. Last I heard, Jake was still planning to marry Miss Carter on Saturday."

"Really?" Randy said. "I thought Hope—"

"Despite all my machinations, I don't think Hope is going to be able to stop the wedding."

"Hope may still get some help from Rabb. I wonder who I need to see to arrange a wedding."

Faith arched a brow. "I don't remember agreeing to marry you."

He shot her a chagrined look. "Gosh, Faith. I've proposed so many times over the past three years I've lost count. You've always said you wanted to wait until we graduated. But surely, now that—"

"Yes, I'll marry you," Faith interrupted. "But I don't know if I want to do it at the end of the week. I just realized I haven't told you yet that my mom's in the hospital."

Randy sat upright. "What? When did this happen?"

Faith sat up across from him and said, "I was at the hospital before Hope dropped me off here. Mom had a heart attack."

"Holy cow! Just like that? Out of the blue?"

Faith made a face. "She had a shock. It put too much stress on her heart."

"What kind of shock?"

"There's something else I haven't told you. I have another sister named Charity." She put a hand over Randy's mouth to prevent his interruption and continued. "Hope and I aren't twins. Hope, Charity and I are triplets."

Randy's jaw gaped. "Good God."

Faith felt the weight of guilt again and lowered her chin to her chest. "It was all my fault Mom and Dad gave Charity away. She showed up at Jake's ranch with Kane Longstreet—they're dating. It was so amazing—she looks just like us. She wanted to meet Mom and Dad, so Hope and I got in the car right then and there and took her home with us."

Faith shuddered. "She was horrible to them. And Mom... After Charity ran out, she collapsed."

She felt Randy's hands at her waist, lifting her into his lap. He cradled her in his arms, and she laid her cheek against his chest. She felt the tears filling her eyes and felt one spill over.

"Don't cry, babe. You know I can't bear it when you cry."

She sniffled and then sobbed. "I can't help it. I can't stand it. It's all my fault."

"Shh, babe," he soothed, rubbing his hand against her back and pulling her close. "Shh. How could it be your fault?"

"If I hadn't been born like this—" She held out her handless arm. "Taking care of me was so expensive, my parents couldn't afford to keep all three of us. So they gave Charity away."

She felt Randy's arms tighten around her. "You couldn't help how you were born. And it sounds like your parents were in a tough spot and did what they thought was best. Why don't you blame them if you have to blame somebody?"

"It wasn't their fault I was born this way."

"It wasn't your fault, either," Randy reminded her.

"I feel sorry for Charity."

"Did she end up getting adopted?"

"Yes, but I don't think she had it too easy. The worst of it was, she wasn't given away at birth. Mom and Dad kept all three of us for two years before they decided they had to give one of us away. They chose Charity."

"How on earth do you make that sort of choice?" Randy asked.

Faith put a hand to Randy's cheek and said, "They said they picked the best of us to give away, 'the one certain to be loved by strangers.'"

Randy said nothing. Faith finally looked up and saw his eyes were glistening with tears. She watched his Adam's apple bob as he swallowed, then said, "You can't be mad at them, Faith. And you can't blame yourself. It must have been terrible for them. I can't imagine..." He swallowed again. "I can't imagine giving up a child of ours. The pain must have been awful. And they've had the two of you to face every day, all these years, knowing they have a third child who looks exactly like you out there somewhere."

"I can understand what they did," Faith said. "I can even forgive them. But I haven't been able to forgive myself."

"You have nothing to forgive yourself for," Randy said, kissing her brow. "You're not responsible, Faith. If anyone bears the burden of what happened, it should be your parents. And even if Charity didn't have a perfect life, it appears she survived and has finally found her way back to your family."

"I don't think she's going to forgive Mom and Dad anytime soon," Faith said. "Although she did show up at the hospital when she heard Mom was sick, so she must care a little."

"How do you feel about having another sister?" Randy asked.

"It's strange," Faith admitted. "Hope and I have always felt like there was a part of us missing. Now we know why. But Hope and I have also been inseparable all these years. I don't know how another sister is going to affect that. I mean, we haven't shared our lives with Charity. She's a stranger, even though she looks like us."

"Do you want to get to know her?"

"I'm not sure I'm going to get the chance. She lives in the hill country near Kerrville. On the other hand, she came here with Kane Longstreet. It would be amazing if she ended up marrying him. Then we'd all live close to one another."

"What are the chances of that?"

"I have no idea," Faith admitted. "He had his arm around her when they entered the waiting room, but he didn't stay with her, so I don't know quite what their relationship is."

"Maybe they need some matchmaking help, too," Randy suggested.

Faith's eyes narrowed. "You're kidding, right?"

Randy shrugged. "I don't think you've done such a bad job with Jake and Hope or Rabb and Miss Carter. Frankly, if a match with Kane Longstreet will keep your sister nearby, why not?"

"I hardly know Kane. And Charity is a mystery to me. It would be pretty presumptuous to get involved in their lives."

Randy grinned. "Remember who you're talking to. Interfering is what you do best—especially on behalf of those you care about most."

"Like I said, I hardly know Charity."

"She's your sister," Randy said. "Don't you want the chance to get to know her?"

"Of course I do."

Randy leaned over and kissed her on the nose. "Then go to it." He slid to the edge of the bed and reached for the clothes he'd discarded, pulling on his shorts and jeans in quick succession.

Faith stretched across the bed and reached down for her prosthesis. Randy beat her to it.

"Let me," he said, picking up the hooked device.

Faith never stopped marveling that Randy accepted her as she was. She held out her arm so he could slip the prosthesis onto it. He paused long enough to kiss her wrist before doing so, and then attached the strap around her shoulder. She went up on her knees to embrace him. "I love you," she said.

"And I love you," he replied. "And I want to marry you on Saturday. What do you say?"

She pushed him to arm's length and looked into his eyes. "It's awfully short notice."

"Who else would you invite that isn't already invited? And my sister and brother-in-law will be back by then."

"What if my mom is still in the hospital?" Faith asked.

"Do you really think she'd want you to postpone getting married once she knows you're pregnant?"

"That's not fair," Faith protested.

Randy grinned. "I'm right. Admit it."

Faith laughed. "All right, you're right." She sobered and said, "I'll marry you so long as her condition remains stable or improves. If she gets worse…"

Randy put his arms around her and said, "That's not going to happen. She's a strong woman. And she has a great deal to live for—a long-lost daughter *and* her first grandchild."

"I hope you're right." She pulled his head down to kiss him, and their lips caught and held. He tumbled her back onto the bed and she went willingly with him.

She would do what she could for Charity and Kane. Later. After she'd made love once more to the father of her child.

CHARITY

CHARITY PACED THE HOSPITAL CORRIDOR waiting for the opportunity to see her mother. The nurse had said she was resting peacefully but couldn't have visitors. Charity feared that her mother would die before she had a chance to know her. Which surprised her, since she hadn't realized until the opportunity was nearly stolen away that she wanted to get to know her.

"How is she?"

Charity turned and walked into Kane's arms. "I think she's going to be all right. At least, that's what the doctor told my father an hour ago."

"Where is he?" Kane asked, glancing around the empty ICU waiting room. "For that matter, where is everybody?"

"They left when the nurse said my mother couldn't have visitors."

"And you've been waiting for me," Kane said, giving her a hug. "Sorry to be gone so long, but my sister wanted to talk and show off my tiny new nephew. She asked about you, and I told her about your mom."

"I should have gone with you," Charity said. "I'm sorry."

"No need to apologize. She understood that having found your mom, you'd be worried about losing her again so soon."

Charity's eyes widened. "Amazing that she realized how I felt, when I've only just discovered it myself."

"It's hard for me to imagine what you're going through. Finding your biological mother would be amazing enough, but discovering that you're one of a set of triplets must be pretty overwhelming."

"It is," Charity admitted. She glanced toward the door to her mother's private room. "What if she dies? I'll never forgive myself—"

"Hey," Kane said, rocking her in his arms. "She's going to be fine."

"You don't know that," Charity said, jerking herself free of his embrace. "If I could just talk to her, tell her I'm sorry—" At that moment a nurse left the room, closing the door behind her, smiled at Charity and Kane, then headed down the hall.

Charity watched her go, then glanced back at the closed door. "I'm going in there."

"You said she's not supposed to have visitors," Kane said. "She's probably not even awake."

"If she's sleeping I won't disturb her," Charity said. "But I need to see her."

She felt Kane's hands on either side of her face as he lifted it to look her in the eye.

"All right, sweetheart. I'll be waiting here for you."

She kissed him quickly on the mouth. "Thank you, Kane." She turned and hurried to her mother's room, pushing the door open and sliding inside.

Her mother's room was considerably darker than the waiting room, since the venetian blinds were closed, shutting out the sunlight. Charity waited for her eyes to adjust to the difference in light before she moved into the room. What seemed like a dozen monitors were lit up beside the bed, and she could hear a steady beep that she realized must be the cadence of her mother's heartbeat.

Charity wasn't even aware she was walking on tiptoe until she reached her mother's bedside and settled onto her feet. Her mother's eyes were closed and Charity was glad to see there was no tube down her throat to help her breathe. But an IV was taped to the back of her hand and a plastic container of some liquid was being slowly dripped into her veins.

Charity sank into the chair beside the bed and leaned her forehead against the sheets beside her mother's hand. She was surprised a moment later to feel her mother's hand stroke her hair.

"I'm glad you came," she said.

Charity resisted the urge to lift her head and look into her mother's eyes, because she didn't want her caressing touch to stop. "I'm sorry," she said.

The caress stopped anyway. When she felt her mother's hand move away, Charity lifted her head and looked into her mother's dark brown eyes, which glistened with tears.

Charity's throat was thick and painful, but she had to speak, had to apologize. "I'm sorry," she said.

One of the tears slipped from her mother's eye and ran down her cheek. "You have nothing to be sorry for," she said.

Charity reached over and wiped the tear from her mother's face with her fingertips. The touch felt electric. She pulled her trembling hand away and said, "I've wondered my whole life where you were, why you gave me away. I needed answers. I'm not sure what to think of the ones I got."

"You were loved," her mother said in a whisper. "You were cherished."

Charity couldn't speak, so she nodded.

"I won't ask you to forgive me," her mother said. "I—"

"I missed so much," Charity cried. "I can't ever get back what you took from me."

Another tear slid down her mother's cheek. Charity could feel her hands shaking and kept them locked in her lap. She realized suddenly the heart monitor was beeping more rapidly.

She rose abruptly. "I should leave. This isn't good for you."

"Wait," her mother said, reaching out to grasp at her arm. She missed, but Charity returned to her bedside, allowing her mother to grasp her hand. Her hand was rough, callused. Her life hadn't been easy, either, Charity realized.

"Won't you stay for a while?" her mother said. "Give us a chance to know you?"

"Stay where?" Charity said.

"With us. With your family."

Charity bristled. "The family that threw me out? No thanks!" She felt like marching from the room, but her mother still had a strong grasp on her hand.

"Give us a chance to know you. Let us give you a chance to know us. I may not… That is, I don't know how long…"

"You mean you might die," Charity said flatly.

Her mother nodded. "My heart isn't in very good shape. The doctor has promised that if I take care of myself, I could live a longer life. I want to know you're happy before I go."

"And knowing you is supposed to make me happy?" Charity challenged.

"Getting to know your sisters, getting to know your

father—he suffered so much. You were his favorite. It nearly killed him to—"

"That's enough," Charity said. "You've said enough."

Silent expectation filled the room.

Charity wasn't sure what she wanted. She couldn't help thinking that getting to know her "perfect" family would only make her more bitter over what she'd never had. On the other hand, she had a long life ahead of her that might be more fulfilling if she included her sisters and her father and mother.

She had never really had a father. Only she did have one. A father who had loved her best of all. The thought was painful…and wonderful.

"I'll think about it," she said at last.

"I'll do my best to get better and get out of here so we can have a family dinner by Christmas," her mother said.

"You rest and get better. I'll—"

"What are you doing in here?" a nurse scolded as she hurried across the room. "This patient needs her rest."

"I'm leaving," Charity said, sliding her hand free of her mother's grasp.

"Talk to your father," her mother whispered. "He needs to know you forgive him."

Charity barely managed to avoid blurting *Why should I?*

But she'd already forgiven her mother. Why shouldn't she forgive her father? "I'll speak to him," she conceded.

To her dismay, he was waiting for her just outside the door, Kane at his side. He looked worried and upset, but what she heard in his voice was anger.

"The only reason I didn't come in there after you, young lady, is because your boyfriend here assured me you wouldn't upset my wife."

She wanted to snap back at him but managed to bite her tongue. "Mrs. Butler is fine," she said at last. "All we did was talk."

"If you hurt her—"

"Hurt *her?* What about *me?* What about the way I was hurt?" she cried.

She felt Kane take a step toward her and shrugged off the arm that came to rest on her shoulders. She kept her gaze focused on her father, not certain what she wanted from him. Maybe that he feel her pain. Maybe that he realize the enormity of the wrong he'd done to her. Maybe that he acknowledge the fact there was no way to change the past. He had made a choice and there were consequences as a result.

"I realize you're not my daughter in any way except by blood," he said. "But you said you didn't have a father, that he left your mother. If you'd let me, I'd like to be a father to you in any way I can."

Charity was surprised by the offer and unsure how to respond to it. She'd wanted a father all her life, and here was her *real* father offering to fill that role. *Why not?* a voice inside her said. *See what it feels like. You can always walk away if it doesn't work out.*

"I'm going to be here until Saturday," she said. "Mrs. Butler said we might get together for dinner once she's out of the hospital. If that happens before Saturday, I'll join you."

"That would be nice, Charity. If there's anything I can do—"

"I have everything I need until then," she said, cutting him off. She turned to Kane and said, "I'm ready to go now."

He nodded to her father and said, "We'll be seeing you."

Charity hadn't realized how much she wanted Kane with her when she met her family for dinner until he invited himself along. "Kane and I are engaged," she said, to clarify their relationship.

She watched her father assess Kane Longstreet before he said, "Congratulations, Kane. Do you plan to make your home here when you're married?"

Charity knew what he was asking. Would she be around so they could have a father-daughter relationship? She and Kane hadn't discussed where they would be living, but he'd told her he had work here for one of his cousins if he wanted it.

Kane met her gaze, then said, "We haven't decided where we're going to live."

She felt grateful for his thoughtfulness. If things didn't work out with her parents and siblings, she'd want to be a thousand miles from here. And it seemed he was willing to arrange his life to make that possible. Which was one more reason for loving him.

I love him. She hadn't realized it until this moment.

"Let's go," she said, slipping her arm around Kane's waist. "I think we need to do some talking."

Kane lifted a brow, but said nothing. "So long, Mr. Butler," he said. "I hope your wife is feeling better soon."

Charity realized he wasn't budging until she'd made

her own courteous farewell. She lifted her gaze to her father's and said, "Good-bye, Mr. Butler. Please ask your wife to contact me when she's feeling better."

"We'll both be in touch, Charity," he said. "You can count on it."

CHAPTER FIFTEEN

HOPE

FOR A LONG TIME JAKE STARED AT THE door Hope had slammed in his face, torn between the urge to pound on it until she opened up and the longing to turn on his heel and run in the other direction as fast as he could go. The blood pounded at his temples as he fought a war between reaching for what he wanted and doing the sensible thing.

He'd been confounded time and again when his craving for Hope Butler had caused him to lose control. Here he was, a grown man, standing at her door, needing her like hell, wanting her as he hadn't wanted a woman in years, and she'd told him she was over him. She was going on with her life. Good-bye, so long, farewell.

He reached out a fist to knock, then pulled it back. Nothing had changed, really. She was still too young. Even if he didn't marry Amanda, which was looking more and more likely, he'd be better off alone than with a woman who was going to wake up one of these days and realize she'd made a mistake marrying him.

But he was finally ready to admit that Amanda wasn't the right woman for him, either. He just didn't *want* her physically. At least, not the way he wanted Hope. And it was foolish to marry a woman he didn't desire in bed.

Jake turned and headed back to his truck. It was time he settled things with Amanda. She'd already made the break, but he wanted to apologize for his behavior with Hope and let his former fiancée know he was sorry things had ended this way.

On the way to town, he passed the entrance to his father's ranch. He owed his mom a thank-you for taking Colt's kids until he could make other baby-sitting arrangements. Rubber squealed as he turned the wheel and shot through the wrought-iron entrance to Hawk's Pride.

He found his mother in the kitchen putting the last of the dishes from lunch into the dishwasher.

"Jake, how wonderful that you stopped by," his mother said. "Your dad's putting Huck and Becky down for a nap. Can I get you something to eat?"

Jake's stomach growled, but he realized he didn't want food. He wanted to talk. He pitched his Stetson onto the antlers mounted just inside the door, then crossed to the fridge and found the half-gallon jar of sun-brewed iced tea that his mother kept there. "Can I pour you a glass of tea?" he asked.

"Thanks. I could use one." His mother wiped her hands on a dish towel, then sank into a chair at one end of the enormous kitchen table that had once seated ten of them—Zach and Rebecca and eight adopted kids.

Jake realized he wasn't going to end up with any kids at all, not the way things were going. He hadn't even finished pouring tea when he said, "What was it like for you and Dad when you realized you'd never have kids of your own?"

He carefully set the two glasses of tea on the table before he looked at her. Her face had paled. "Forget I asked," he said quickly.

She reached for his hand and pulled him into the chair beside her. "Before I answer that question, I'd like to know why you asked it."

"Really, Mom, it's not—"

"What's happening between you and Amanda?"

Jake made a face and slumped in his chair. "She's called off the wedding."

"What a relief!"

Jake sat up straight and stared. "What?"

"You were never right for each other. That young woman needs…another kind of man."

Jake's eyes narrowed. "What's wrong with me?"

"Nothing. Except you don't love her. You love someone else."

"Who would that be?"

"Hope Butler, of course."

"There's no 'of course' about it, Mom," Jake said, controlling the anger over Hope's rejection that still bubbled under the surface. "How can she be right for me, when Amanda's not?"

"Oh, Jake," she said, laughing. "Those two women couldn't be more different. Amanda's… prim and proper and reserved and refined. And Hope's…"

"A hellcat. A troublemaker. A wild child—with *child* being the operative word," Jake retorted.

He studied his mother's face, as she studied his.

"If you can't think of her as a woman—in every way," his mother said slowly, "then of course she's not the one for you."

"She's more woman than I've had in—" He cut himself off and felt the furious flush race up his throat.

"Ah," his mother said. "So that's the way it is." She tilted her head, like a small bird eyeing him, then asked, "What's stopping you from marrying her, Jake? I've always thought Hope loved you. Am I wrong?"

"She cares, all right," he said. "Or at least, she did."

"Then why aren't the two of you getting married on Saturday?"

Jake shoved both hands through his hair. Then everything came blurting out, the way it had when he was fifteen and first had sex with a girl and had sought out his mother, terrified that his girlfriend was pregnant because they hadn't used any kind of protection, and how he'd meant to but had gotten so excited that he'd just…done it.

"I want her, Mom. Physically, I ache for her. But you know my history. I've already had my heart broken once. With Hope… The feelings I have for her are so much stronger, so much more powerful than what I've felt for any other woman, that losing her would be… I'm not sure I could survive it."

"So you'd rather pass on the chance of happiness than take the risk of loving—and being hurt—again?"

"That's about it," he admitted bleakly. "Not only that, but I think she's given up on me."

"Hope? Given up? I don't think that's possible."

"You didn't see the look in her eyes when she shut the door in my face thirty minutes ago," Jake said.

"What did she say?"

"That she was tired of waiting around for me to make up my mind, and she was going on with her life— without me." .

"Can you blame her?"

"Whose side are you on?" Jake demanded.

"I'm surprised she kept pursuing you as long as she did. You've been a pretty reluctant beau. What's amazing is that she didn't give up, even when you got yourself engaged to Amanda to keep yourself from going after Hope."

"That isn't why I got engaged to Amanda," Jake protested.

"Isn't it?" his mother said, spearing him with her gaze. "Amanda's spent more time with Rabb over the past three years than she has with you."

Jake frowned. "That can't be true."

"You might have brought her to every family gathering, but you abandoned her to Rabb's care the instant you arrived."

"He didn't mind. Neither did she."

His mother lifted a brow. "Doesn't that tell you something?"

"They have more in common—" Jake cut himself off, remembering what Rabb had said a week ago about doing his best to stop the wedding, because Jake didn't love Amanda. His eyes narrowed. "That low-down, sneaky—"

"Don't blame Rabb," his mother interrupted. "You're the one who threw the two of them together so often. Rabb can't help loving Amanda. Any more than you can help loving Hope."

"Rabb loves Amanda?"

His mother nodded.

"For crying out loud! And by the way, I never said I was in love with Hope."

"Aren't you?"

Jake felt the knot in his gut twist. "God, yes. I am."

"Then you're a fool if you don't marry that girl."

"You make it sound so simple. It isn't."

"It is," she countered. "I can't believe how much like your father you are," she said, shaking her head.

Jake gave her a quizzical look. "My father?"

"Like Zach. Everything's black and white with you, just like it is with him. He was hurt by his first love, too, so badly that he decided he wasn't going to fall in love again. So he advertised for a wife."

Jake grunted in surprise. "How did you two end up together?"

"I answered his ad," she said with a grin. It quickly faded as she continued. "He didn't want a wife, really. What he needed was a broodmare, a mother for his children that he could stand to look at across the breakfast table and couple with in bed."

"My God," Jake said. "You're kidding, right?"

His mother shook her head. "We married with the understanding that if I wasn't pregnant within a year, we'd divorce."

Jake's jaw gaped. "But you never did have any kids. And Dad's crazy in love with you."

His mother's gaze looked faraway as she recalled, "Six months or so after we married, I had a riding accident. Your father had to face the fact that he could have children of his own blood with some other woman—or he could have a life with me and a family of adopted children."

Jake felt his throat constricting. He knew the choice his father had made. "I never imagined...I didn't realize..."

"He took the risk of loving again, Jake. He never realized his dream of having children of his own blood. But no father could love his children more than your father loves all of you."

Jake grasped the hand his mother extended to him and nodded, because he couldn't speak.

"The choice is up to you," she said. "You can spend your life alone. Or you can take the risk of loving that young woman. What is it going to be?"

Jake pulled his hand free and rose. "I don't know, Mom."

"Life is short, Jake. And unpredictable. Don't wait too long to make up your mind."

He crossed the room and grabbed his hat, settling the Stetson low on his brow. "I want kids of my own, Mom. Lots of them. So does Hope. Maybe it wouldn't be such a bad thing to marry her with the understanding—"

"Is that really fair to her, Jake?"

"It worked for you and Dad," Jake said pointedly.

"I wouldn't wish the pain and uncertainty I went through with your father on that poor girl. If you love her, why not tell her so?"

"I...can't."

He turned away from the pity he saw in his mother's eyes. She made it sound easier than it was to give his heart into someone else's care. He wasn't about to expose his soft underbelly and have it ripped out again.

But he did owe Amanda an apology. The sooner they confirmed their wedding wasn't going to happen, the better. There were vendors to be contacted, guests to be informed, a church to be canceled.

Why let all those preparations go to waste? You could marry Hope on Saturday.

And live happily ever after? Jake didn't believe in fairy tales. Besides, Hope didn't want him anymore. She'd given up on him before they'd even gotten together. What chance was there her feelings would last for a lifetime?

When Jake pulled up behind Amanda's house he saw Rabb's car was still parked in the driveway. Which reminded him what his mother had said. *Rabb can't help loving Amanda.*

Was it true Amanda had spent more time with Jake's brother than with him? Had Amanda noticed his inattention? How could she not? More important, did she return Rabb's feelings? And if she did, why hadn't she said something?

Jake stared up toward Amanda's bedroom window, where the curtains were drawn, then knocked on the back door. It took a long time for her to come to the door, and when she opened it, she was wrapped in a white terry cloth robe, which she clutched together at her throat. The belt swung at her sides and the robe fell open above her knees, making it clear she was wearing little—or nothing—underneath. Her hair was mussed, her eye makeup smudged.

Jake suddenly realized he'd never seen Amanda looking like…like she'd just gotten out of bed.

She only opened the door far enough to stick her head out, and her eyes were anxious as she asked, "What is it, Jake?"

Jake was astonished to hear himself demand, "Is my brother in there?"

Her eyes went wide and her cheeks turned rosy. "I… He…"

A male hand reached around and pulled the door wide, and Jake found himself staring at Rabb, whose hair was equally disheveled, and who wore only an unbuttoned pair of Levi's that hung on his hips.

"I'm here," Rabb said. "What's it to you?"

Amanda turned to Rabb, laid her palm on his naked chest, and said, "Please, Rabb. He's your brother. Let's talk this out."

"It didn't take you long to get her flat on her back," Jake said.

Amanda gasped and stared at Jake with stricken eyes.

Or what was left of Jake as he landed on the ground, flattened by Rabb's blow. His brother straddled him, his hands knotted, his teeth bared, his eyes narrowed.

"Damn you," he raged. "She doesn't deserve that from you. Take it back!"

There was no taking back that sort of comment, but Jake was ashamed enough of himself to say, "I was wrong, Rabb. I'm sorry."

"I ought to pound you into next week. In fact—" He reached down to grab Jake by the shirt, and Jake tossed him over his head, then rolled over and bounded up to fight. He'd wanted to hit something ever since he'd kept himself from pounding on Hope Butler's kitchen door. His brother was a fair target.

But he never got the chance.

An avenging angel, her eyes flashing, her hair a riot of curls, her robe flapping, threw herself between the two men, sticking out an arm in either direction. "Stop it! Both of you. That's enough!"

Jake could see how Amanda might have learned the technique as a teacher breaking up fights at school. Her voice was sharp and commanding, and her posture was ramrod straight, like a pillar of concrete set in the middle of a raging sea. You might wear it down eventually, but at the moment, it wasn't going anywhere.

"Rabb, how could you hit your brother? He has a right to be upset. Imagine how you'd feel in his shoes."

Jake took one look at his chastised brother and made the mistake of laughing.

"And you," the avenging angel said as she turned on him. "You have no right at all to be casting stones. At least our engagement was over before I turned to someone else."

"So it *is* over?" Jake asked, looking from Amanda to Rabb and back again.

"I thought we settled that at your house," she said. "At least, I considered it settled. Didn't you?"

She looked at him earnestly, apparently ready to make whatever amends were necessary. Jake noticed that Rabb moved up behind her, ready to support her in whatever way was necessary.

"I only came by to say I'm sorry things ended between us the way they did," he said.

"But not sorry things ended," Amanda said, to make the situation perfectly clear.

"No," he admitted, eyeing his brother. "Not sorry they ended." He was no dog in the manger. He didn't want Amanda for his wife, but Rabb apparently did. And it seemed, this time, the feeling was mutual.

"Do you love her?" he asked his brother.

"I've loved her most of my life," Rabb said simply.

"Then I wish you both happiness."

Rabb's arms surrounded Amanda from behind, and

Jake noticed how her body swayed comfortably back into Rabb's, in a way it never had when she'd been with him.

"You two go on back to bed," he said with a wry smile. "Sorry I interrupted you."

"You're okay…with us?" Rabb asked.

Jake saw the anxiety in his brother's eyes. "It looks to me like you belong together. When's the happy day?"

Rabb exchanged a sheepish look with Amanda, then said, "I've been trying to talk her into following through with a wedding on Saturday—to me."

"Why not?" Jake said. "No sense letting all those arrangements go to waste."

"You could join us," Rabb said.

"As your best man? I'd be glad—"

"We could make it a double ceremony," Amanda said. "Rabb and me…and you and Hope."

"Thanks, but no thanks," Jake snapped.

"But, I thought—"

Jake cut off Amanda with a snarl. "I wish people would stop trying to manage my life for me. If you two want to marry on Saturday, fine. Do it. Just don't include me."

"Fine," Rabb said. "We won't say another word about it. But I'd still like you to be my best man." He gave a chagrined look and said, "That way folks will know for sure there's no hard feelings about…"

"About the switch in grooms?" Jake finished for him.

"Yeah."

"I'll be there. Same time, same place?" he asked Amanda.

She nodded. "Are you sure you don't mind?"

Jake felt like saying he considered himself lucky to be out of the situation, but he figured that would earn him another smack in the nose from his brother, so he kept his thoughts to himself.

Rabb and Amanda had already gone back inside by the time Jake revved his truck engine. He wasn't certain how he felt about what had happened. Two hours ago he'd been an engaged man, on his way to marriage within a matter of days. Now he was free again. Alone again. With no plans for the future.

He turned his truck around and headed back toward his ranch. But he never got that far. His truck seemed to turn itself down the dirt road that led to the Butler home.

When he got to the house, he pitched open the door to his truck and raced to the kitchen door, pounding on it until it opened.

"What's wrong? What's the matter?"

Jake found himself facing Hope's father. "Where's Hope?" Jake asked.

"She doesn't want to see you," her father said.

"I need to talk to her."

"You're too late. She's gone."

"Gone where?" Jake demanded.

"She specifically said not to tell you."

Jake bit back an epithet. This was Hope's father. He wanted answers, but browbeating the man wasn't likely to get them. He just wasn't sure what would. "I need to see her. I need to talk to her," he repeated.

"Sorry," her father said, shaking his head. "She said she's had enough. She can't take any more."

"I want to marry her," Jake blurted.

The man blocking the doorway narrowed his eyes. "You're a little late," he said at last.

"It can't be too late. I love her," he said.

"Do you really think you can make her happy?"

"I can try," Jake said.

"That's not good enough," her father said, and began to shut the door.

Jake stuck his boot in to keep it from closing. "Look here, Butler. I—"

"Get out of my house, Whitelaw. Don't ever darken my doorway again."

"Where is she?" Jake pleaded. "Just tell me where to find her."

"You had your chance," Hope's father said. "Now be a good boy, and leave her the hell alone!"

Jake stared at the cracked paint on the Butlers' kitchen door for the second time in a day. Where was Hope? Where could she possibly have gone? How could he find her? Who would know where she was?

Faith would tell him. She'd always believed he and Hope belonged together. He'd have to figure out how to get Faith out of the house and meet her somewhere. But where?

The obvious place was at Randy Wright's ranch. He'd see Randy right now and work something out. Faith was a big believer in happily-ever-after. He needed a fairy godmother to step in and help. Especially since Cinderella had flown the coop.

CHAPTER SIXTEEN

AMANDA CLOSED THE DOOR BEHIND Jake and turned to face Rabb. "I wish he hadn't—"

"I'm not sorry he found us like this," Rabb said. "Not when it made you admit that you love me. And that you'll marry me."

Amanda shook her head, still stunned by the events of the past few hours. She placed a palm against Rabb's stubbled cheek and said, "I never expected... I never thought I was capable of..." She lowered her eyes shyly. She'd made passionate love with Rabb Whitelaw like some wanton woman. She'd relished all the things he'd done to her and done things back to him that she'd never imagined herself doing.

The reason she'd never gone to bed with Jake in all the years they'd been engaged was that she hadn't expected to enjoy it. She'd kissed Jake when he'd insisted and hadn't worried too much when he hadn't insisted that often. In hindsight, she realized they'd used each other to avoid having to move forward with their lives.

Seeing her fiancé ravish another woman in front of her eyes had forced Amanda to admit the truth. Jake had never wanted her like he wanted Hope. And, she was ashamed to admit, her feelings for Jake didn't come close to the passion Hope had offered him. Still, shattered by what she'd seen, she'd leapt at the chance to have Rabb take her home.

Once they'd dropped Huck and Becky with his parents, Rabb said, "I can see you're still upset. What happened back there with Jake?"

"He comforted Hope," she said.

Rabb glanced sideways at her and asked, "That doesn't sound so bad."

"He kissed her senseless," Amanda said agitatedly. "And she kissed him back. He was so worried about her, he completely forgot I was standing right there."

"That jackass!" Rabb pounded the steering wheel. "I ought to go back there and give him the kick in the butt he deserves."

"I'm glad it's over," she said, shoving her bangs away from her eyes. "Really. I am."

"It's over between you two?" Rabb asked cautiously. "For good?"

"I don't think I ever loved him," Amanda admitted. "I'm not proud to say that. When he proposed to me I…I'd just been through a difficult time, and I suppose I was flattered that someone like Jake would want to marry me."

"You mean someone intelligent and—"

"No," she said, cutting him off. "I'm embarrassed to admit this, but it was…" She flushed. "The fact he seemed so determined never to marry again. Catching a man who didn't want to get caught was like riding the full eight seconds on an outlaw mustang. Does that make any sense?"

Rabb nodded. "So it wasn't…that you were attracted to him physically?"

"Of course he's handsome," Amanda said. "But not as good-looking as you are."

Rabb snorted. "Get real."

"I mean it. Your face has so much more… I don't know how to describe it, except to say that I can see what you're feeling. It's there in your eyes and in your smile. With Jake… His face was like a stone wall that I couldn't get past. I never knew what he was thinking."

"And that was bad?"

"He shut me out," Amanda said. "I don't know why I never noticed how carefully he kept me at arm's length. Emotionally and physically."

"I'm glad," Rabb said as he pulled up in the driveway behind her house.

"So am I, since things turned out the way they did. I mean—"

That was as far as she got before Rabb leaned over and kissed her. Senseless. His tongue slid along the seam of her lips until she opened to him. After that, she was lost. He dragged her across the seat and into his lap, so she could feel his arousal beneath her hip. His hand closed over her breast through her beige silk blouse, and her nipple budded beneath his coaxing fingers.

"Rabb, I—"

He never gave her a chance to protest, not that she would have been able to put together a coherent sentence. Her driveway was secluded, a white wooden fence on one side and a row of forsythia bushes on the other.

She heard Rabb grunt in satisfaction when he realized

she was wearing real nylons with a garter belt. She was ravenous to touch him, to be touched by him, and in no state to protest when he hiked up her skirt to the waist, then pulled off her lacy black bikini panties and tossed them onto the dash.

"Come here, woman," he said in a guttural voice.

Amanda had never straddled a man in her life and never imagined doing it in the front bench seat of a pickup truck. She could feel the hardness beneath her as he pressed her naked pubis down against his jeans. She reached between his legs, and he bucked upward when she touched the fullness of him. She reached between them and unbuckled his belt, then unsnapped his jeans and unzipped them, shoving them down off his hips along with his underwear.

He thrust upward at the same time she sank down onto him.

"Oh," she said, the word drawn out and full of feeling. She was surprised at how good it felt. How right it felt.

He was gripping her hips tightly, holding her in place, not moving. "Are you all right?" he asked, his eyes intent on hers.

"I'm great. I'm wonderful. This is wonderful."

"It gets better," he said with a grin. And began to move inside her.

"Oh." She gasped. "Oh, yes."

Their mouths meshed as their tongues mimicked the thrust and parry below. Rabb's hands were never still, touching her in places that increased her pleasure, that took her higher, that made her want more, and want to give more.

Suddenly her body was convulsing and she felt such

pleasure it was almost unbearable. She heard Rabb cry out as he gripped her hips and held her still and spilled his seed inside her.

Her body trembled as she sank against him, her lungs bellowing. She felt totally enervated, unable to move, unable to speak.

She wanted to tell him how good it had been. She wanted to ask him if it had been as good for him. She realized that it was a silly question. His breathing was as labored as hers, and his expression in those last moments before they had come together had been tortured with the same pleasure/pain she'd felt herself.

Their bodies were still connected when he spoke at last. "I've wanted you for so long...and thought for so long that I'd never have you for my own."

She kissed his throat and said, "I'm yours."

"Will you marry me?"

She lifted her head and looked into his eyes. "I want to. I just don't think—"

"Say yes, Mandy. We've already lost so many years we could have spent together. I don't want to waste another day apart."

"You know how I feel about—"

His hand caught her nape and he pulled her down for a kiss that made her toes curl. She felt a thrill of feminine satisfaction as he hardened inside her. "Again?" she said with a smile against his lips.

"Constantly," he replied. "I want you all the time."

She giggled, a girlish, totally unAmandalike sound. "We're not kids anymore, Rabb."

"That's no reason we can't have fun like kids, or play together like kids," he said as he moved slowly inside her.

She closed her eyes and moaned, arching her body into his, her hands gripping his shoulders. "I can't believe... It feels so good."

"Now that I've had you once, I'm going to want you all the time," Rabb said. "I'll be at your house night and day. Marry me, Amanda. Make an honest man of me. And shut up the neighbors' gossip."

She laughed, and realized she felt carefree and... young. "You make me want to be irresponsible. And I'm *never* irresponsible." She gasped as his mouth latched on to her throat and he began to suck with a pressure that was strong enough to cause shivers to run down her spine.

She thrust her hands in his hair and yanked hard enough to force him to let her go, and when she could reach his mouth, thrust her tongue inside and ravaged him. She felt his body convulse and caught his guttural groan in her mouth.

Then her body joined his, spasming as she threw her head back and arched her body to reach for the joy that loving him promised.

It took them longer the second time to recover from their lovemaking. She had experienced a few awkward moments when Rabb withdrew from her and tucked himself back into his jeans, while she searched for the package of tissues he kept in the glove compartment and wiped away the semen that had spilled onto her thighs.

He didn't even ask if he could come into the house, simply came around to her door and opened it for her, handed her down, and walked her inside.

She hadn't realized she wanted him to stay, but she was glad he had. She hadn't eaten lunch and neither had he, so she fixed him a hamburger and offered him some leftover potato salad. He came up behind her at the stove and put his arms around her waist and kissed her neck and she'd realized he was ready for her again.

"You're insatiable," she teased.

"I'm been saving myself for you," he teased back.

After lunch he insisted on washing the dishes and she came up behind him and put her arms around his waist and let them slide down the front of him. She heard the hiss of breath as she traced the length of him and felt his shaft grow hard beneath her hand.

"To hell with the dishes," he said.

To her surprise he shook the water off his hands, turned and picked her up and headed for the stairs.

"Where do you think you're going?" she asked breathlessly.

"I'm going to make love to you in your bed, where I can get a good look at you. I want to see your breasts and your belly and your legs and—"

"Oh, God. What if you're disappointed?"

He laughed. "I couldn't be. Don't you understand yet? It's you I love, Mandy. Every part of you is perfect to me."

He laid her on the bed and undressed her, taking his time, kissing the flesh as he exposed it. "You are so beautiful," he said, when she was naked at last.

She lay beneath his adoring gaze, her throat swollen tight. "I wish..." She'd never known what it was like to be loved by a man. Never imagined how honored she'd feel to have his devotion. Never imagined how excited she'd be to have his eyes devouring her or his hands exploring her.

"Mandy, I—"

She put her fingertips to his lips and said, "I want to do something impulsive. I want to say something that's as stunning to me as it may be to you." The words were there. All she had to do was say them. But it was an enormous, irrevocable step to take.

"I love you, Rabb."

His eyes closed, and she heard him swallow noisily.

She let her fingertips drop from his mouth and leaned over to kiss his lips gently, tenderly. "I love you," she whispered. "I love you."

When he opened his eyes they glistened with tears. He managed a smile and said, "I love you, too."

They said nothing more for the next hour while he made love to her. And she made love to him. She took her time undressing him, discovering all the male parts of him that made him different from her.

She realized she could make him burn. And she did. She realized she could make him groan. And she did. She realized she could take him to the edge and leave him hanging. And she did. She had her wanton way with him.

And he returned the favor.

They were both exhausted, pleased and happy with themselves, when the doorbell rang. And reality returned.

Amanda begged Rabb to stay upstairs when she glanced out the bedroom window and saw Jake's truck outside. But as she threw on a robe, he pulled on his jeans and followed her downstairs. He stood behind the door as she greeted her former fiancé.

Former by about three hours.

Amanda felt flustered and uncomfortable and embarrassed and ashamed. And defiant. Jake hadn't wanted her. Rabb did. Jake had chosen another woman. Rabb had chosen her.

Then Rabb had opened the door and exposed their indiscretion. And she realized she'd already made her choice. She loved Rabb. She wanted to marry him.

Aloud, she'd deplored the violence that erupted between the two brothers. Inside, she'd felt a swell of savage satisfaction that Rabb was willing to fight for her. She hadn't imagined she could be so bloodthirsty. But she'd relished seeing her man lay his brother out in the grass.

The commitment she'd been reluctant to make in bed had been easy to make after Rabb's fierce defense of her. She could hardly believe they were going to be married at the end of the week. She stared at the door that had closed Jake out of her life, then looked at Rabb once more.

"Say it again," he said, holding her hand against his cheek with his own.

She noticed the webbed feet at the corners of his eyes where he'd squinted against the sun, followed the lines on either side of his mouth that professed how much time he spent smiling, then looked into his warm brown eyes and said, "I'm in love with you, Rabb." She brushed away the lock of hair that had fallen on his brow and said, "I want to spend my life with you."

He brushed at her furrowed brow with his thumb and said, "Something's still bothering you, Mandy. What is it?"

"You realize I don't want to have children. Not right away. Maybe not for a long time."

"We've got plenty of time," he said. "I'm in no hurry."

"You're sure?"

"You're all I want, Mandy. All I need."

She stepped into his embrace, knowing it was right. "Then we're agreed," she said. "I'll marry you on Saturday."

He whooped and picked her up and swung her in a circle.

His celebration was so loud, she almost didn't hear the doorbell. He stopped and they looked at each other, then stared at the door.

"Who the hell could that be?" he muttered as she slid down the length of him.

"I don't know. Stay back out of sight," she said, tightening the tie on her robe and holding out a flat palm to ward him off.

He grinned and crossed his arms. "I don't think anyone would blame us for anticipating the wedding."

"Shh," she said as she opened the door. And then, "Why, Faith. What are you doing here?"

"I need to talk to you," the young woman said.

Before Amanda could stop her, Faith had stepped inside.

"Oh," she said, staring wide-eyed at Rabb.

Rabb scratched the hair on his chest and grinned at Amanda. "Do you want to tell her, or should I?"

Faith looked from one to the other and said, "You're getting married!"

"Bingo," Rabb said. "On Saturday, as a matter of fact."

"That's wonderful!" Faith said.

"It is?" Amanda said.

"Of course. Now Jake and Hope—" Faith cut herself off and said, "I'm sorry, Miss Carter."

"No need to be sorry," Amanda said. "Jake knows about me and Rabb. He's agreed to be best man at our wedding."

"I'm so glad everything's turned out all right," Faith said.

"How's your sister?" Amanda asked pointedly.

"Which one?"

Amanda had forgotten about Charity. "How's Hope?"

"Unhappy," Faith admitted. "Unfortunately, Jake's being—"

"A jackass," Rabb finished for her.

Faith smiled. "That sounds about right."

"Anything we can do?" Rabb asked.

"To be honest, I came here to see if I could help you two along," Faith said. "But you've managed things just fine on your own."

"I can't imagine you're going to have much luck with Jake and Hope," Rabb said. "He seems pretty determined to make himself miserable."

"Oh, I hope not," Faith said. "But I'd better get going. There's not much time left till Saturday."

"You really think you can get the two of them together by then?" Amanda asked. "He's resisted your sister for three years."

Faith shrugged, grinned and said, "Hope springs eternal."

FAITH

FAITH DIDN'T BOTHER EXPLAINING to Rabb and Miss Carter that it wasn't Hope and Jake she was worried about at the moment. She was much more concerned with Charity and Kane.

If at all possible, Faith wanted Charity to live nearby. That way, Charity would have the opportunity to get to know their mom and dad, and Faith and Hope would have a chance to get to know their sister. If Charity left now and went away, there was no telling when they'd see her again.

Faith was delighted things had turned out so well between Rabb and Miss Carter, especially since that left her more time to finagle things between Kane and Charity.

She used her cell phone to call Kane's house, hoping that's where she would find Charity.

"Kane and Charity are at the hospital," Kane's mother said. "They've been there all day."

"Together?" Faith asked.

"As far as I know," his mother said. "From what Kane said, Charity's worried that Mrs. Butler might not come through all right, so she's been checking in on her through the day."

"Thank you, Mrs. Longstreet," Faith said.

"Can I take a message?"

"No, thanks. I'll see them at the hospital," Faith said, disconnecting the call.

It was a good sign that they were together, Faith thought. But she had no idea how to encourage them to stay that way. She called Randy and said, "Hi, honey.

Thought you'd like to know Miss Carter and Rabb are getting married on Saturday."

Randy laughed and said, "What did I tell you? What's going on between Jake and Hope?"

"Nothing at the moment," Faith said. "I'm heading to the hospital. It seems Charity's been there all day with Kane."

"That sounds promising," Randy said.

"I think so, too," Faith said. "I'm going to the hospital now to check on Mom. With any luck, I'll run into Charity and Kane."

"Got any hot matchmaking ideas?" Randy asked.

"Nope. Not one," Faith admitted. "But I'll do my best to come up with something on the way to the hospital."

"Hey, babe," Randy said, his voice lower, softer, more seductive. "I love you."

"I love you, too," Faith said.

"Do you want me to join you at the hospital?"

Faith shook her head, then realized Randy couldn't see her. "I think I can do this better alone," she said.

"Call me if you need me."

"I will."

Faith disconnected the phone, marveling at how nice it was to have someone who believed she could manage the situation, but was there if she wanted help. That's what a marriage should be, she thought.

And wondered how Hope ever imagined she and Jake could make a go of it. Did Jake trust her? Could Hope depend on him? Were they really right for each other?

Faith forced her thoughts away from Jake and Hope. It was Kane and Charity she had to focus on. Her life could easily continue without Charity being a part of it, but now that Faith knew about her sister, the deep sense of loss she'd always felt would be magnified if Charity left again.

The solution to that problem was to keep Charity nearby.

Faith wasn't above manipulating another marriage, especially if she could be certain her sister was in love with Kane Longstreet.

And if she wasn't? She'd worry about that problem when it arose.

CHAPTER SEVENTEEN

CHARITY

CHARITY SAT ACROSS FROM KANE AT a table in the hospital cafeteria, where they'd been most of the afternoon. They'd gone there for a cup of coffee and had never left.

"I have a feeling I need to be here," Charity had explained to Kane. "Something might go wrong and…"

"You don't have to explain yourself," Kane said. "I understand."

"You do?" Charity couldn't understand her feeling of foreboding, she only knew it was strong enough to make her heart palpitate when she thought about leaving the hospital.

"You've just found your birth mother and you're afraid of losing her," Kane said. "I'm happy to stay with you as long as you need to be here."

She reached across the table and squeezed his hand. "Thanks, Kane."

"There is something I'd like to discuss, since we're going to be here for a while."

"What's that?"

"You told your father we're engaged," Kane said.

"I'm wondering if you'd consider getting married on Saturday."

Charity laughed. "You're kidding, right?"

Kane shook his head. "My whole family's here. And now we know your family—your original family—is here, too. Why not marry me and stay?"

"I have a semester of college to finish."

"I'm sure we can find a way to work around that. Don't you want to stay here with me? And with them?"

Charity made a face. "I should hate my biological parents for what they did to me. I don't know why I don't. Not that I'm not angry with them. I am." She made a disgusted sound in her throat. "I don't understand myself."

"It explains a lot, doesn't it?" Kane said.

"What do you mean?"

"Being abandoned like that. It explains why you don't trust me not to do the same thing."

She stared at him. "I've agreed to marry you, haven't I?"

"Yes, you have. Don't get me wrong, I'm glad. But I'm also aware that your feelings can't have changed overnight."

"Why not?" Charity challenged. "Now I know *why* I've always felt like you might leave me someday. I've been left before, and not just by my adoptive father."

"I'm not ever going to abandon you, Charity," Kane said, looking into her eyes.

"Stop saying that. You don't know what's going to happen in the future. You might change your mind about being married to me. It could happen!"

He shook his head. "Nope. I'm a sticking kind of guy."

Charity shook her head. "There's no way to tell—"

He grabbed both her hands. "I want to marry you so much I ache inside. But this isn't going to work unless you're as committed to making it last as I am. I don't want you watching over your shoulder, waiting for the other shoe to drop, holding part of yourself back, saving yourself from whatever pain you think might be lurking out there somewhere. I want all of you, every blessed inch of you, with me."

"I can't give you that," Charity said, feeling panicky at the thought. "You can't expect me to trust you—"

His hands tightened on hers painfully. "I do expect it. I insist on it," he said. "I want a wife who loves me the way I love her, heart and soul. No half measures. No holding back."

"I'm doing the best I can," Charity cried. "I do love you, Kane. I do want to be with you. I just… I'm afraid."

"Look at me," he said, his eyes focused on hers. "If you never believe another thing I tell you, believe this. When we speak those vows in church—to love and to cherish, in sickness and in health, for richer or for poorer—I will consider myself committed to you for as long as I live."

"People make those promises every day. And break them," Charity said bitterly.

"Not me," Kane said. "I will always love you."

"Oh, Kane. How I wish I could believe that."

"Give me your heart, Charity. I'll protect it and cherish it. I'll keep it safe."

She was so tempted to take the giant leap of faith he was asking of her. "I want to," she said. "I want to so much."

He leaned over and kissed her lips, his mouth lingering on hers. "Trust me," he whispered. "I love you."

"How can I know you mean what you say? How can I know you'll live up to what you promise?"

"You have to believe in the power of love," he said.

She made a face. "My parents loved me and look what they did. How can you say the circumstances would never arrive that would make you give up on marriage to me?"

Kane let go of her hands and sat back with his arms crossed. "You're never going to let go of the past, are you?"

"How can I?" she protested.

"At least you're honest," he said.

Charity felt her heart sinking. "Does this mean you don't want to marry me after all?"

"I want you any way I can get you," he shot back. "I just wish there was some way to convince you that the past is just that—the past."

"In my case, the past has become my present. I've just met my biological parents and discovered I have two sisters with whom I shared the womb. I need time to absorb it all, Kane. What's the hurry? Why do you want to marry so soon?"

"My cousin has offered me a job here that starts right after the new year. If you go back to South Texas we won't see each other for months. I want our lives together to start sooner, rather than later. Is that asking too much?"

"It's only a few months."

"It's time enough for you to start doubting yourself. And me."

"I won't—"

"You will," he interrupted. "I want to wake up with you in the morning. I want to come home to you at night. I want us to start a family of our own."

Charity had often imagined having children of her own. She would love them and protect them and make sure they knew they were wanted. "I want all that, too," she said softly. "I want it so much."

"Why wait?" Kane said.

"Why hurry?" she countered.

"Life is short. And uncertain," he said. "None of us knows how long we have. I want the rest of my life with you to start right now."

What Kane said resonated with Charity. Enough that she reached out and intertwined her fingers with his. She met his gaze, took a deep breath, and said, "All right. My heart is yours. Take care of it. Please."

The smile on his face was dazzling, and caused her to smile in return. "Thank you, darling," he said. "Saturday can't get here soon enough for me."

He was on his feet a moment later.

"Where are you going?" she asked.

"I've got a million things to do if we're getting married on Saturday, not the least of which is to see if I can reserve the church and make sure the minister's available."

"I want—I need—to stay here," she said. "Can you understand that?"

"Stay," he said. "I'll be back as soon as I've made all the arrangements."

He took off without a backward look.

Charity searched inside to see what she was feeling.

There was no regret. No feeling of anxiety. Nothing but joy. And anticipation. And hope.

Even the feeling of foreboding that had been with her all afternoon seemed to have disappeared. She wondered if her mother truly was better, or if the joy she felt at having committed herself to Kane was interfering with her perception of the true state of affairs with her mother.

She rose abruptly and headed for the ICU. She had to see her mother's condition for herself. She was going to live close enough to see her mother and father and sisters often. She was going to have a chance to get to know them.

If only her mother recovered from this heart attack.

FAITH

FAITH WAS SURPRISED TO FIND Hope and Charity in the waiting room at the hospital when she arrived. She was glad she'd come when she realized her sisters were circling one another with stiff legs and raised hackles, like two big cats stuck in a tiny cage.

"Hello, you two," she said, putting a smile on her face.

Faith watched as the night nurse did a triple-take when she realized the three girls had identical faces. "What's going on?" Faith asked.

The nurse answered her. "I've been trying to explain to these young women that Mrs. Butler needs her rest."

"I need to talk to her," Hope said.

"And if she's going in, I'm going in," Charity said.

"I need to see her, too," Faith said as she put a hand over her womb, where her child was growing. She turned to the nurse and said, "Believe me, our mother will feel better once she hears what I have to say."

"If she's going in, I'm going in," Charity said.

"She's not going in without me," Hope said, jutting her chin in Charity's direction.

"I can't stay here and guard the door," the nurse said in exasperation. "I have work to do. Just remember, your mother needs her rest."

"We won't bother her for long," Faith promised. "And we won't upset her," she said as she met each of her sisters' gazes.

"Very well," the nurse said. "Be as quick as you can."

She headed down the hall, leaving the three girls staring at one another.

"Shall we?" Faith said as she gestured toward the open door to their mother's room.

She watched Hope and Charity abortively stop and start a couple of times, vying to be first inside, then stepped into the room in front of both of them. A small fluorescent light above her mother's bed was on, illuminating her face—and the fact she was awake.

"Did you hear any of that?" Faith asked as she stepped up beside her mother.

"You mean Hope and Charity hissing at each other like she-cats?" her mother said.

Faith smiled. "Guess you did."

Hope and Charity appeared a moment later, Hope joining Faith on one side of the bed, while Charity crossed to the other.

Faith saw the smile on her mother's face as she eyed the three girls. "I'm glad to see all of you here together," she said.

"I need to talk to you privately," Hope said, eyeing Charity.

"Has something happened between you and Jake?"

"You could say that," Hope said.

"I need to talk with you privately, too," Charity said. "I'm sure what I have to say—"

"I'm pregnant," Faith announced.

All eyes turned to stare at her. She made herself stand still for their scrutiny, aware of the moment when everyone's eyes left her face and lowered to her still-flat belly.

She splayed her hand across her stomach and said, "I don't show yet. I'm only six weeks along. But I've been to see a doctor, and he confirmed I'm pregnant. Randy's proposed and I've accepted."

"Come here, sweetheart," her mother said, opening her arms.

Faith crossed to her mother and hugged her, receiving a hug in return. "We've decided to get married on Saturday," Faith said. "Randy's already called the church to make arrangements." She eyed Hope as she said, "It seems Jake isn't going to be using it."

"Oh? Really?" her mother said, her gaze skipping to Hope.

"But Miss Carter is," Faith continued. "She's marrying Rabb Whitelaw on Saturday."

Hope gasped.

Faith turned to Charity and said, "And it seems there's been another request for the minister's services that day."

Charity turned to their mother and said, "That's why I'm here. Kane and I are tying the knot. Since all his relatives are gathered for Jake's wedding, we decided to take advantage of the opportunity to marry this Saturday."

"Good heavens!" her mother exclaimed. She turned to Faith and said, "Both of you are getting married the same day?" She looked from Faith to Charity and said, "Would you consider a double wedding?"

Faith hadn't considered the idea, but she thought of her mother sitting through two ceremonies and realized it would be easier on her if she and Charity married at the same time. "I don't think Randy would mind," she said tentatively.

Charity eyed Faith, then turned to their mother and said, "If it would make it easier on you, I'd be willing. I'll have to talk with Kane, but when he hears the circumstances, I don't think he'll mind, either."

Faith felt relief as she watched the smile widen on her mother's face.

"Two of my girls getting married together. I feel like dancing!"

"Save that for Saturday," Hope said. She turned to Charity and said, "I suppose congratulations are in order."

"Don't knock yourself out," Charity retorted.

Faith crossed around the foot of the bed and put herself between her sisters. "Congratulations," she said, hugging Charity as though they'd spent their lives together. She was pleased to feel Charity hug her back. Then she turned to Hope, whose eyes looked troubled, and whose heart, she knew, must be aching.

She put her arms around Hope and whispered, "He's yours, if you want him. Just go get him!"

Hope ended the hug and snapped, "If he wants me, he's going to have to come after me."

"I'm right here."

HOPE

HOPE TURNED TO FIND JAKE STANDING in the doorway.

"Hello, Jake," Mrs. Butler said.

"Hello, ma'am," Jake replied. "How are you?"

"Just fine," Mrs. Butler said, beaming.

"I'd like to borrow Hope for a few minutes, if that would be all right."

"I'm visiting my mother," Hope said.

"I can spare you for a little while," her mother said, "while Charity and Faith and I work on plans for their double wedding."

"You and Randy are getting married?" he asked Faith.

"On Saturday. Along with Charity and Kane," Faith supplied.

Jake turned his attention to Charity and said, "This is a surprise."

"We're going to make it a double wedding to save Mrs. Butler from having to sit through two ceremonies," Charity said.

"Hold that thought," Jake said, "while I talk to Hope."

Jake caught her by the arm and started out of the room, but Hope balked.

"Whatever you have to say to me, you can say right here."

"What I have to say is between you and me," Jake said implacably.

Hope's heart was beating erratically, and her pulse had jumped at Jake's appearance. She wanted to believe he was going to propose to her at last, that they were going to have a triple wedding. But she'd been wrong too many times in the past.

"Come with me, Hope," Jake said. "Please."

It was the "please" that got her moving. Jake wasn't used to asking for what he wanted. If he was asking, rather than ordering, maybe he was going to say something she wanted to hear.

She didn't answer him, merely tugged her arm free of his grasp and headed out the door ahead of him. She heard her mother's hospital-room door swish closed behind Jake and turned to face him, her arms crossed over her chest. "Well? I'm listening. What is it you want to say?"

"It appears you've heard that my brother Rabb is marrying Amanda on Saturday."

"I heard."

"So you know my engagement to Amanda is over."

"It appears so."

"You're not making this easy for me," Jake said, adjusting the collar at his throat as though it were tight, even though the top two buttons were undone.

"What is it you have to say to me?" Hope said, unwilling to bend even an inch to accommodate him.

"We could make it a triple wedding," Jake blurted.

"Who is we?"

"You and I could get married on Saturday, too."

"Could we?"

"What's going on, Hope?" Jake said irritably. "You've got what you wanted. I'm willing to marry you."

Hope felt the ache spread across her chest, feeling the pain of Jake's halfhearted offer as a physical thing. "No thanks," Hope said.

"Damn it, Hope. What in hell is wrong with you?"

"What's wrong with me? Nothing. You're the one with the problem."

Jake grabbed her arms in a hold so tight she would have bruises when he let go, and his blue eyes sought hers in a look so piercing she gasped. "You've been wagging that tail of yours in my direction for three years, and now that I've finally come to heel, you're giving me the bum's rush. I want to know why."

"You're *willing* to marry me? At last? When you've run out of other options? Why, Jake? What's different today from yesterday, or even this morning? Miss Carter's dumped you, that's what's different. I'm not willing to be second choice. I want a man who wants *me,* who can't live without *me,* who loves *me!*" Hope cried.

"I love you, goddammit! I wouldn't be marrying you if I didn't. I've loved you since the day you lured me into your father's barn and did that damned striptease. I haven't been able to get you out of my head—or my heart—no matter how hard I've tried. Is that what you wanted to hear?"

Hope stared at Jake, dumbfounded by his declaration. "Then why—"

"I've been—"

"Afraid," she said.

"An idiot," he said at the same time.

"Yeah, that too," she said with a smile.

His mouth found hers as he gathered her up in his

arms and pulled her tight against him. Hope slid her fingers into his hair and held on as he kissed her silly.

"I love you, Hope," he said when they both came up for air. "Marry me. Spend the rest of your life with me."

Hope grinned. He was back to imperatives. He would never be the sort of man who asked for what he wanted. He would always demand it. But she was the sort of woman who could handle that sort of man. "Ask me nice," she murmured against his lips. "And maybe I'll say yes."

He took her deep again, asking with kisses, rather than words. She could feel the urgency in his hands, as they wrapped around her, in his heart, which beat hard against her own, and in his mouth and teeth and tongue, which made an eloquent plea on his behalf.

"Yes," she said as he kissed her cheeks and her nose and her eyelids.

"Yes, what?"

"Yes, sir?" she said with an impish grin.

He framed her face with his strong hands and forced her to look him in the eye. "Will you marry me, Hope? Will you have my babies?"

Hope felt the lump in her throat, felt the sting of tears in her nose, felt the tears well in her eyes and spill.

He caught the tears with his tongue, then kissed her so she tasted the salt of her tears. "I love you, Hope. I'll always love you."

"Yes," she managed to rasp. "I'll marry you, Jake Whitelaw. I love you...so much."

He put his arms around her and hugged her tight.

"Hey, you two. Are you going to join us on Saturday?"

Hope turned to find Faith in the doorway to her mother's room. She glanced at Jake, who nodded. She grinned and said, "You bet."

CHAPTER EIGHTEEN

FAITH, HOPE & CHARITY

"I CAN'T BELIEVE WE'RE ALL GOING TO be married thirty minutes from now," Faith said as she stared at herself in the full-length mirror behind the door of the church vestry.

"I can't believe it, either," Hope said sardonically. "Especially since one of us isn't here."

Faith grimaced. "Charity will be here. She probably—"

"She probably changed her mind. Again," Hope said.

"I'm convinced she loves Kane," Faith said.

"That isn't the problem, and you know it," Hope said.

The three sisters had spent enough time together over the past week to begin to know one another. It had been apparent from their first conversations that Charity found it difficult to trust in anyone or anything. She moved on tiptoe, as though with every step she expected the rug to be pulled out from under her.

It had been difficult for Hope to identify with her sister's problem. If anything, she had too much self-confidence. Faith had been more understanding—she always was—and had tried to make Charity feel more comfortable sharing her life story with them.

It hadn't made easy listening.

Hope had been more and more grateful that she'd been spared the life Charity had led. She found herself admiring her sister tremendously, especially when she heard how Charity planned to spend two years with the Peace Corps.

"Kane has agreed to put his career on hold for a couple of years so we can spend time overseas together," Charity said.

"Can you join the Peace Corps if you're a married couple?" Hope asked.

"I haven't checked the rules," Charity said. "But if there's some restriction, we'll find another way to spend time working with the poor. It's something I'm committed to doing."

"I haven't thought about anyone but myself over the past few years," Hope admitted. "You've made me realize I need to give back a little of what I've gotten over my lifetime."

"You shouldn't feel obligated—"

"I want to," Hope interrupted. "It's just that over the past three years my goal has been to…"

"Grow up in a hurry," Faith supplied for her. "And you've done a good job of it. Which is more than I can say for myself."

"What are you talking about?" Hope said. "You're going to be a mother and a hospital administrator."

"In that order," Faith said with a laugh. She patted her belly. "And delighted with the situation."

"I can't wait to be a mother," Hope said. She turned to Charity and said, "I suppose you'll have to postpone having babies until you get back from overseas."

Charity blushed. "I planned to. I have to admit I haven't been as careful…about things…as I should have been this past week with Kane. I really…well…we've spent a great deal of time together since I agreed to marry him."

Faith grinned. "I suppose what you're saying is there's a good chance you'll be working with the poor right here at home."

"It's true I don't have to go overseas to help," Charity said.

"All right, girls," Mrs. Caruso interrupted, "let me see the three of you together. Perfect! You're beautiful. I know three young men who are going to feel very lucky on Saturday."

"It wasn't luck that two of these dresses were already made and ready to go," Hope said. She gave Faith a hug. "I have you to thank for planning ahead and having Mrs. Caruso make these fabulous wedding gowns."

Hope didn't have to look at herself in a mirror, she only had to look at Faith and Charity, since they were dressed exactly alike. "We look like three Cinderellas, ready for the ball," Hope said with a laugh.

"Once I knew I was pregnant, I figured I'd be getting married over Christmas," Faith said. "I knew sooner or later Jake would realize he loved you—"

"Right," Hope said, making a face.

"Well, he did!" Faith said. "I wasn't sure how much I'd show, so I wanted a dress that fit around the waist but wouldn't reveal my growing belly—"

"So we got Cinderella ballgowns," Hope finished with a grin.

The dresses might as well have been created by Disney, they were so fantastical, with heart-shaped bodices, capped sleeves, fitted waists and bell-shaped skirts.

"I'm just glad Mrs. Caruso could finish a matching gown for me so quickly," Charity said.

"I've been working on your dress for almost a week," Mrs. Caruso said.

Charity's brow furrowed. "But—"

"I asked her to get started on it," Faith said. "Just in case. Then I did what I could to help things along between you and Kane. I hope you don't mind."

Charity laughed. "How can I mind, when I'm going to be part of a triple wedding with my long-lost sisters?"

She'd seemed pretty certain about going through with the wedding then. But she hadn't shown up at the church this morning.

"What shall we do?" Faith asked. "Who should we call? Where could she be?"

"I'm right here."

Hope and Faith turned to see Charity in the doorway.

"You're not dressed!" Faith said.

"That's because I'm not getting married."

"Why not?" Hope demanded.

"Because it won't last," Charity said. "Because I'd rather not be one of those who 'loved and lost.'"

"Too late to avoid the pain now," Hope said. "You've already admitted you're in love. Why not grab for some of the joy?"

"Easy for you to say. You're not the one who—"

"Faith and I know what you've been through. You've gone to great pains to tell us. I admire how well you survived your past," Hope said. "But here's a news flash. All that admiration's going out the window if you throw away this chance at happiness."

"I look on it as self-preservation," Charity said.

"Cowardice is what it is," Hope retorted.

Charity's nostrils flared and her lips pressed flat.

"That's a little strong," Faith said, ever the mediator.

"Maybe not strong enough," Hope said. "How about, you're chicken." She made a sound like a chicken and flapped her elbows like wings.

"Cut it out," Faith said, watching Charity's face turn red with anger.

"Sticks and stones—"

"Give me a break," Hope interrupted. "And get out. Go ahead and go! Just don't come around here looking for sympathy when you get back from darkest Africa. It's going to be in short supply."

Charity had already whirled to leave when Faith grabbed her arm and said, "Don't go! Please. Mom is looking forward to this—"

Hope realized in two seconds that Faith had used the wrong argument.

"She's your mother, not mine!" Charity snapped.

Faith let go of Charity's arm as though it had turned into a pit viper. "What did you say?"

"You heard me!"

She pointed her hook at Charity and said, "You're not the only one who paid a price for the fact there were three of us in that womb. I did, too! So don't think you're the only one who's made sacrifices. Mom deserves your consideration. You can't blow off this wedding without hurting her, too."

"She's not involved in—"

"Get real," Hope interrupted. "It doesn't take a genius to figure out Mom and Dad have suffered every day since they gave you away. Charity begins at home," she snarled.

"Oh, that's a good one," Charity snapped back. "Just what exactly did you have in mind?"

She was glaring at Hope, but Faith answered, "Put on your wedding dress and join us at the altar."

"I'm supposed to get married so your mother doesn't feel bad about giving me away? Forget it."

"Then get married because you love Kane and it's the best way to make yourself happy," Hope said.

"Because it is!" Faith added.

"It won't last," Charity said.

"Talk about neurotic behavior," Hope muttered.

"What did you say?" Charity asked, crossing to confront her.

"When circumstances change, you have to change right along with them," Hope said. "Your adoptive father abandoned your mother. So he was a creep. What does that have to do with you? And you know why Mom and Dad gave you away. Not because they didn't love you. In fact, *they loved you best!*"

"That just proves my point!" Charity said. "They loved me and yet they abandoned me. Kane could do the same thing."

Hope threw up her hands. "I give up. You talk to her," she said to Faith.

Faith grimaced. "She does have a point. In fact, what guarantees do any of us have? Randy could decide he doesn't want to take a chance that his children will be born…like me."

"That isn't going to happen," Hope said. "Don't even think it!"

"Of course it could happen," Faith said. "And Jake could decide that after worrying so long about whether you'd be satisfied living with him, *he* isn't satisfied living with *you*."

"Perish the thought!" Hope said, crossing herself, even though she wasn't Catholic.

"And Kane could decide somewhere down the road that he doesn't want to be married to Charity," Faith said, her eyes locked with Charity's.

"You're chock-full of fun speculation," Hope muttered.

"Don't you see?" Faith said, looking from one sister to the other. "Marriage is a gamble. It's a risk. It's a good bet, if there's love and mutual respect. But there are no guarantees. You grab hands and leap off the cliff and hope there's a soft landing somewhere below."

"And if there's not?" Charity said bleakly.

"Then you pick yourself up, glue the pieces back together and go on with your life. Like you've been doing all along." Faith crossed and hugged Charity. "I have Faith in you."

"And I've got a lot of Hope," Hope said, smiling as she crossed and hugged her sisters.

"You two are awful," Charity said. She looked from one to the other and said, "And I'm looking forward to offering both of you a little Charity over the years."

Hope and Faith both groaned. And grinned.

"So where's your dress? Somewhere close, I hope," Faith said.

"In the car. I was going to return it—"

"Get it and get dressed," Hope said. "We don't have much time."

"Oh, God. This is such a giant leap—"

"Of faith," Faith said. "I know. Get your dress. We'll all grab hands and jump together. It'll be easier that way."

While Charity was outside retrieving her wedding gown, Hope slid an arm around Faith's waist and turned them so they were looking into the mirror. Faith automatically slid her prosthetic hand behind her back.

"Don't," Hope said. "Just let it hang by your side. You don't ever have to hide again, Faith. We're back together again, the three of us, and we're going to be that way for the rest of our lives."

"Not tonight, I hope," Faith quipped. "Randy and I have plans—"

Hope pinched Faith's waist and Faith yelped. "You deserved that," Hope said.

"Hey, what's going on?" Charity asked, stepping into the room with her dress in hand. "Leave her alone."

Hope wanted to say they were just teasing, but she realized Charity didn't understand what that was like. She would. As time went on.

"We were just playing," she said in explanation. "Which ends now. We need to get you dressed."

It didn't take more than five minutes to get Charity out of her clothes and into her wedding gown. Faith and Hope sat her in front of a mirror, made sure she ran a brush through her hair and dabbed on some lipstick and powder. Then the three of them stared at each other.

"My God. We look so much alike, I think we could fool our prospective husbands," Hope said.

"Don't you dare suggest that we try it!" Faith said. "I want to end up with the right groom at the end of the day."

"But wouldn't it be fun—"

"Some other time, girls. Not today."

The three girls turned to find their mother sitting in a wheelchair as their father pushed it farther into the room.

"Mom," Hope said. "You look so well."

"Thanks. I think," her mother said with a smile. "Stand there together, so I can look at all of you."

The three girls slid their arms around one another and stood in a line.

"If I hadn't heard Hope speak, I wouldn't have known the three of you apart," her mother said. "You are all so very beautiful."

"I'll second that," her father said.

"I have something for each of you," her mother said. "I bought them shortly before you were born, after I knew there would be three of you.

"A cross for Faith," her mother said, holding out the fragile gold chain with a gold cross on it. "Who has always been the strongest of us all."

Faith took the few steps to her mother and bent down to kiss her, then stood as her father clasped the necklace around her throat. Hope noticed Faith's hand trembled as she reached up to caress the necklace before stepping back.

"A circle for Hope," her mother said. "Which has no beginning and no end."

Hope felt her heart beating erratically as her father clasped her necklace around her throat. She kissed his cheek, then turned and said, "I love you, Mom."

"And a heart for Charity," her mother said, "with a wish that her life may be filled with love."

Charity hesitated a second, then crossed and bent her head, so her father could place the golden chain around her neck. Hope saw that Charity's eyes brimmed with tears as she leaned over to kiss their mother on the cheek, then turned and hugged their father.

Hope slid her arm around Faith as a tear slid down her father's cheek.

"Well, now," their father said, releasing Charity and smiling through his tears. "This is a happy day. Your mother and I are going to go now. We'll see you in church."

The three girls planned to escort each other down the aisle, which was just wide enough for them and their bell-shaped skirts.

"Thank you, Mom, Dad," Faith said. "For all of us. We'll see you soon."

Charity was still holding her heart, staring at it, when they heard the processional begin.

"I guess this is it," Hope said. "No turning back now."

"Do you suppose our grooms have been having the same sort of second thoughts?" Charity asked.

Faith shook her head. "They love us. And they're lucky to get us. And they know it."

Hope and Charity laughed, and a moment later Faith joined them.

"Shall we go?" Hope said, extending her left hand to Charity.

Charity took a deep breath and let it out. "I'm ready." She turned to Faith. "How about you?"

"I've been ready for an hour—and waiting on the two of you," Faith said with a grin.

Hope grabbed Faith's left hand—or rather the hook that substituted for it. "No sense postponing this any longer."

They didn't carry flowers, just held one another's hands. The congregation gasped when they appeared, and stood in awe as they marched slowly down the aisle to their respective grooms.

Jake and Hope stood in the center, with Randy and Faith on the left and Kane and Charity on the right.

"Dearly beloved," the minister began.

Hope wondered if her sisters were experiencing the same difficulty swallowing that she was having herself. Wondered if their hands were also trembling. Wondered if their hearts were beating so hard. She felt Jake's hand tighten around hers comfortingly. Felt his fingertip lift her chin so she was looking into his eyes as the minister began the vows that would bind them together.

Hope had dreamed about this moment constantly for the past three years and despaired of it ever coming to pass. Now that it was here, she damned the blur of tears that kept her from seeing Jake's face clearly.

"Blink," he whispered.

"What?" she whispered back.

"Blink. Again. Again."

And there he was, his blue eyes so filled with tenderness, and with love, that she felt her heart swell with feeling.

"I promise to love, honor and cherish you," Jake was saying.

She wasn't listening to the words, she was looking into his eyes, seeing the promise there of a future filled with love. And with children. They'd spent the past week deciding how many they wanted. At least four. Maybe five. Or six, if Jake wasn't too old by then. He'd laughed when she'd said it, then sobered. Because they'd put off being together for three years, and might already have started their family if he hadn't been so stubborn.

"I, Hope, take you, Jake," Hope repeated after the minister.

She was no longer aware of her sisters, no longer

aware of the congregation. Her eyes stayed on the man whom she loved, whom she would always love, and who had pledged his troth to her. She was surprised to feel his hands tremble as she began her vows, and she tightened her hand in his, reassuring him, as he'd reassured her.

We belong together. This is forever. We will love long and love well.

"I now pronounce you husbands and wives," the minister said. "You may kiss your brides."

Hope heard the plural announcement that made it clear she wasn't alone with Jake in front of the altar. But she might as well have been, because she didn't see or hear anyone or anything, except Jake's quiet, "I love you, Hope," and then the taste of him, as his mouth captured hers, and the feel of his arms circling her, surrounding her with love.

It was the joyful laughter and applause of the congregation that brought Hope back to herself. She looked up at Jake, still stunned that he was her husband, glanced first at Faith, then at Charity, and then grinned at Jake.

"Hello, husband," she said softly.

"Hello, wife," he replied.

Faith and Randy were first back down the aisle, followed by Hope and Jake, then Charity and Kane. In the vestibule the brides hugged each other, as the grooms shook hands. Then the grooms kissed the other brides, and the brides kissed their sisters' grooms.

"I suppose we'll be in a race now to see who can produce the first baby," Jake said to Hope as he led her from the church.

"Faith's already won that prize," Hope said. "But I have high hopes we'll come in second!"

"I'll give it my full attention," Jake promised with a grin.

The reception was held in the church hall, with a single cake from which the three brides fed their husbands.

Jake stuffed a piece of cake into Hope's mouth as she pushed a too-large piece of cake into his.

"And this is symbolic of what?" Jake said through a mouthful of cake.

"That we'll take care of each other," Hope said back in an equally muffled voice.

Jake swallowed and said, "I will, Hope. Always."

"And I'll be there for you, Jake. I promise. Always."

Jake looked around at the crowd and said, "How soon can we get out of here?"

"Where did you have in mind to go?"

"Home."

"No honeymoon?" Hope said with a fake pout.

"Rabb and Amanda are taking the honeymoon I had planned."

"Who'd have thought they'd elope to Mexico? I suppose it was lucky you'd planned a honeymoon in Cancun."

"I envy them right now," Jake said. "Alone together. Somewhere on the beach."

"Knowing how practical Miss Carter is, they're not making love on the sand," Hope said.

"Why not?"

"It itches," Hope replied.

"How would you know that?"

"I think I read it somewhere."

"No firsthand experience?"

Hope shook her head. "The only experience I've had

is with you. Just that one breathtaking afternoon alone, naked in bed—"

"That's enough," Jake said. "Keep that up and my tux trousers won't fit."

Hope glanced down and said, "My, my. Looks like they fit just fine to me."

Jake laughed. "Cut that out, Hope."

"Take me out of here, Jake. Take me home."

"We can't leave yet, Hope. There are still—"

She hooked her hand around his nape and pulled his head down to kiss him, thrusting her tongue into his mouth deep and hard.

He groaned, then grasped her hips and pulled her close.

"Hey, you two, stop that!" a laughing voice said.

Jake broke the kiss, then leaned down and picked up his wife. "We're out of here," he said.

"Great idea," Kane said, picking up Charity.

"Way ahead of you," Randy said, heading for the door with Faith in his arms.

The gathered friends and family laughed, cheered and cleared a path as the three men escaped with their wives.

Once they were outside, Hope stopped Jake and said, "I want to say good-bye to my sisters."

"You're all going to be living right here in town," Jake pointed out.

"I know, but…we're all going to be living separately from now on."

"All right," Jake said.

"You can put me down," Hope said.

"Not on your life. You can say your good-byes just as easily from where you are."

Hope laughed. "You're being silly."

Jake lifted a brow and Hope realized it was a gesture she was likely to see often over the years to come. "All right, Jake," she said. "Faith, Charity," she called.

The other two men turned with their wives in their arms.

"I told Randy I wanted to say good-bye," Faith said.

"And I said the same thing to Kane," Charity said.

The three men converged, allowing the women to say, "I'll see you—"

"In a week," the three men said simultaneously.

Hope turned to Jake and said, "What's going on?"

Jake grinned and said, "Shall we tell them?"

"I suppose this is as close to a surprise as we're going to get," Randy said.

"What surprise?" Hope asked.

"We realized you three probably wouldn't want to be separated so soon after finding one another," Randy said.

"So we arranged a honeymoon for all of us in the same spot," Kane said.

"Where is that?" Charity asked.

"We're all going to Mexico," Jake said. "Actually, we've rented a villa in Playa del Carmen."

"A villa? Where we can see each other every day?" Hope said, eyeing Faith and Charity. "That's wonderful!"

"We thought you might like it," Jake said.

"When do we leave?" Hope asked.

"Tomorrow morning," Jake replied. "Which leaves all of us one night—"

"At home," Hope said, smiling at Jake.

She turned to Faith and Charity and said, "See you tomorrow morning. My husband and I are going home."

"That sounds wonderful. I think we'll do the same thing," Faith said.

"We'll be at Kane's home, if you're looking for us," Charity said.

There was no limousine with tissue roses and shaving cream. No boots and beer cans tied to Jake's truck. They were both too grown-up for that.

But Jake was adamant about carrying Hope over the threshold. "It's for luck," he said.

Hope grasped him around the neck and planted a kiss on his jaw. "For luck," she said as they crossed the threshold to the home they would share.

Jake stopped just inside the door. "I love you, Hope."

"I love you, too, Jake. Let's go make a baby."

Jake laughed. "All right, love. You're the boss."

Hope smiled at him. "I'm glad to see I'm going to get my way when it comes to making babies."

Jake sobered and said, "As many as you want. That's how many we'll have."

Hope grinned. "All right," she said. "You asked for it."

Jake lifted a brow. "How many *do* you want?"

"Lots," she said. "Lots and lots."

EPILOGUE

FAITH, HOPE & CHARITY

JAKE WATCHED AS HIS WIFE NURSED THEIR newborn son, Russell James Whitelaw. He brushed a hand over her smooth breast above where the child suckled. Hope glanced up at him and grinned.

"He's one hungry son-of-a-gun," she said.

Jake sat gingerly on the bed beside Hope and brushed Russ's tiny fingernails. His son's hand opened and closed on his finger, refusing to let go. Jake was amazed at the strength of the baby's grasp. "He's so strong for someone so tiny."

Hope snorted. "For your information, Jake Whitelaw, eight pounds seven ounces is *not* tiny. Your son is twenty-three inches long, for heaven's sake."

Your son. The words still had the power to make Jake's chest ache with pride and with joy. "I suppose he'll end up as tall as I am."

"Even taller, maybe," Hope said. "He's certainly chowing down like a champ. Ouch!"

"Are you all right?" Jake asked, his eyes anxious as he searched Hope's face.

"I'm fine, Jake. Just a little sore from all this nursing.

It'll get better." She reached out a hand and touched his stubbled jaw. He hadn't been home in the past twenty-four hours to shave. "I'm sorry I scared you like that during the delivery."

Everything had not gone exactly as planned. After Hope had delivered Russ, she'd started bleeding. Her blood pressure had dropped and the doctor had threatened he might have to do a hysterectomy if she didn't respond soon to the treatment he'd given her.

Jake was beside himself, uninterested in even seeing the son he'd wanted so badly, too worried that he might lose the wife he'd come to love more than his own life. "Do whatever you have to do," he'd said. They could always adopt more children. But life without Hope wouldn't be worth living.

"I'm fine, Jake," she said, caressing his cheek. "Really."

"I don't ever want to go through that again."

"The doctor says I'll be fine. What happened during the delivery shouldn't keep me from delivering other healthy children."

"We can adopt," Jake said.

Hope laughed at him. "If you insist, we can," she said. "But I'm hoping we'll have a few more of our own to join the brood."

The door to Hope's hospital room swung open and Faith walked in, a babe in arms, Randy by her side. "How's the new arrival?" Faith asked.

"Russ is fine. How's Cindy?"

Faith patted the fussing baby that rested against her shoulder and said, "Growing like a weed."

Late in her pregnancy, Faith had become obsessed

with the idea that her child wouldn't be born perfect, that whatever had gone wrong with her would go wrong with the baby she carried. Hope had convinced Faith to have a sonogram, a picture of the baby in utero, which had reassured her that Cindy was perfect even before she arrived.

"Have you seen Charity?" Hope asked.

"I think she's on her way here," Faith said. "It takes her and Kane a little longer to get organized these days."

"I'm here," Charity said as she and Kane stepped into the room. Each had a baby over one shoulder.

"How are Kevin and Kacey?" Faith asked.

"Noisy," Kane answered. At that moment, one of the little boys howled, causing the other one to cry, as well.

"They do everything together," Charity said with a wry smile. "I'm enjoying them a lot. It makes me think of what it must have been like for you and Faith," she said to Hope.

"It was fun being twins," Hope said. "It would have been better if you'd been there, too."

Over the past year, the three pregnant sisters had spent a great deal of time together learning about babies and preparing their nests for the new chicks. Faith had delivered first, and her two sisters had been there the instant she left the delivery room, to assure themselves she was all right. They'd marveled over their perfect niece and listened avidly as Faith told them what labor was like when you delivered without anesthesia.

"It hurts," she told them. "But it was worth it to be wide awake and able to walk around right after the delivery."

Charity had known early in her pregnancy that she

was expecting twins, and she'd been apprehensive, because she had so little experience with children. Faith had volunteered to let her practice diapering with Cindy, and she was a pro long before her own two boys arrived.

Hope had taken the longest to get pregnant, even though she and Jake had been diligent in their attempts to make a baby. She'd confided to Faith that she wanted desperately to give Jake a child, and she was afraid that because she wanted it so much, it might never happen.

"You got Jake, didn't you?" Faith reminded her. "I have all the confidence in the world that the two of you will make a baby together."

And they had. It had taken nearly six months before Hope missed a period. She hadn't told Jake right away, worried that something might go wrong. But by the second month her breasts were tender, and Jake noticed how she flinched, and questioned her and the truth came out.

Hope wished she had a photograph of Jake's face when he realized he was going to be a father at last. Oh, the joy! And the awe. And the pride. The grin on his face had stretched from ear to ear and hadn't gone away for the rest of her pregnancy. Whenever he saw her, it appeared.

Hope realized Russ had fallen asleep. She buttoned her nightgown under the concealing blanket, then turned to Jake and said, "Would you like to hold your son?"

Jake hadn't taken Russ when the nurse had first offered him, because he was too worried about Hope. He'd practiced with his in-laws' babies, so he knew how to support the baby's head, and how fragile his son was likely to be.

And yet, Jake held his breath as Hope laid Russ in his arms. He felt the baby's slight weight settle in his arms, and cupped his hand around his son's tiny head. "Oh, God, Hope. He's…" He didn't want to call his son beautiful. Boys were handsome. But he could think of no other word to describe the perfect child in his arms.

"Mom and Dad are waiting to come in here," Faith said. "And so are Jake's parents. I suppose we need to get out of here so they can come in."

"Tell them to give us a minute alone," Jake said as the other two couples took their leave.

Hope looked at him speculatively. "What is it, Jake? Is everything all right?"

He rose and laid the baby in the crib beside Hope's bed. "I wanted time alone to thank you for my son," he said.

"It was my pleasure," she said.

He sat down beside her and lifted her into his lap, holding her close. "I'm glad you were persistent, Hope. I'm glad you didn't give up on me. You've made my life so rich. So complete. Thank you for my son, Hope. I love you…so much."

She hugged him tight, and he heard her sniffle. "I love you too, Jake," she said in a raspy voice. "Did you mean what you said about adopting a few kids?"

Jake put enough space between them to look into Hope's eyes. "What did you have in mind?"

"Well, if you wait for me to have babies one at a time, you could be an old man before we have a big family."

Jake smiled wryly. "I suppose that's true."

"We could start right away and find a couple of kids who need a family. Russ could use some brothers and sisters."

"How many kids did you have in mind?" Jake asked.

"I was thinking at least eight—including the ones we produce ourselves," she said with a grin.

"Eight." Jake felt his heart take an extra beat. "Eight," he repeated. "That's quite a family."

"It's not too many, is it?" Hope asked. "Your mom and dad managed to raise eight. We could do it, too, don't you think?"

"Eight sounds fine," Jake said, hugging her tight. "Eight sounds just fine."

REQUEST YOUR FREE BOOKS!

2 FREE NOVELS
FROM THE ROMANCE/SUSPENSE
COLLECTION PLUS 2 FREE GIFTS!

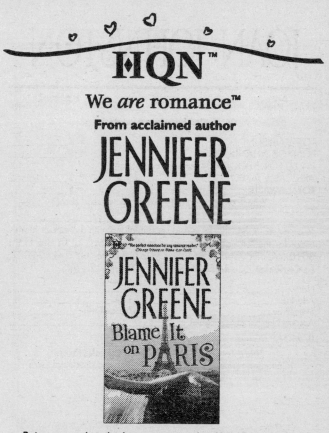

JOAN JOHNSTON

77277 HAWK'S WAY: FARON & GARTH ___ $6.50 U.S. ___ $7.99 CAN.

(limited quantities available)

TOTAL AMOUNT	$ _____
POSTAGE & HANDLING	$ _____
($1.00 FOR 1 BOOK, 50¢ for each additional)	
APPLICABLE TAXES*	$ _____
TOTAL PAYABLE	$ _____

(check or money order—please do not send cash)

To order, complete this form and send it, along with a check or money order for the total above, payable to HQN Books, to: **In the U.S.:** 3010 Walden Avenue, P.O. Box 9077, Buffalo, NY 14269-9077; **In Canada:** P.O. Box 636, Fort Erie, Ontario, L2A 5X3.

Name: _____
Address: _____ City: _____
State/Prov.: _____ Zip/Postal Code: _____
Account Number (if applicable): _____

075 CSAS

*New York residents remit applicable sales taxes.
*Canadian residents remit applicable GST and provincial taxes.

HQN™
We *are* romance™

www.HQNBooks.com

PHJJ0408BL